Critical praise for *8 Se* the 2018 IAN Book Outstanding Thriller/Suspense:

Paul F. Johnson for Readers' Favorite: If you're a reader of thrillers and appreciate stories with everything that goes with them—intrigue, murder, planned destruction and terrorists—then you can't go wrong with *8 Seconds to Midnight*. John Leifer grabs the reader from the first pages and doesn't let go. The author has created an exceptional story filled with everything that makes a thriller a thriller. The cast of characters—the good guys and the bad—is superbly developed and the plot is filled with action and suspense all the way to a satisfying ending. The story moves along at break-neck pace, leaving the reader expectantly waiting to turn to the next page. Very good story, very entertaining. I highly recommend this book.

Catherine Langrehr for IndieReader: This is a great book if what you want is a vigorous, action-packed thriller with lots of suspense, dramatic last-minute acts of courage, and a clearly-defined right and wrong side, with no serious moral qualms or questions to distract. Verdict: *8 Seconds To Midnight* is a thriller packed with energy, action, and suspense, which consistently delivers on the promises of the genre.

Publisher's Weekly/BookLife Review: Well-developed main characters and plausible technical details help make a familiar plot fresh in Leifer's thriller. Fans of Tom Clancy and the TV series *24* will be riveted.

BookLife Prize—2018 Semi-Finalist, score: 10/10. Leifer's novel stands out among others that address terrorist attempts to launch nuclear and biological attack weapons on the U.S. Intelligent discourse, verisimilitude, and a full humanization of characters provide the novel exceptional depth and dimension.

Critical praise for *Terminal*:

Amanda Rofe, Readers' Favorite: I was completely captivated with the story line from the very first chapter. John Leifer writes effortlessly and eloquently. *Terminal* contains all the components of a blockbuster movie. This is a well-researched book which held my attention throughout. I highly recommend it.

4.6 Stars from IndieReader: *Terminal*, John Leifer's page-turning prequel to his book "*8 Seconds to Midnight*" in the Commander John Hart series, proves that more than anything else, it's the power of the story, the plot line, that propels any decent military or government thriller. This one is supercharged and will grab readers by the throat, exhibiting the barely closeted global paranoia of modern times. There is no paranormal or horror story component, but this tale is unequivocally terrifying.

Booklife Review: Leifer (*The Myths of Modern Medicine*) makes his fiction debut with this suspenseful and alarming kickoff to a trilogy.

Sinfully Wicked Book Reviews: *Terminal*, by John Leifer, is a pulse pounding, edge of your seat terroristic thriller set against the backdrop of America and the Middle East. Leifer's writing is so rich you will get lost between the pages, hoping for the story to never end. I was completely drawn in from the first page, and I can truly say this is an outstanding and thought-provoking story. I have a feeling each new book in the series will be all five-star reads for me. Yes, it is that good!

THOU SHALL
N̶O̶T KILL

JOHN LEIFER

Anybody who recognizes Israel will burn in the fire of the Islamic nation's fury.

—Mahmoud Ahmadinejad

The Iranian acquisition of nuclear weapons would be infinitely more costly than any scenario you can imagine to stop it.

—Benjamin Netanyahu

The LORD also shall roar out of Zion, and utter his voice from Jerusalem; and the heavens and the earth shall shake: but the LORD will be the hope of his people, and the strength of the children of Israel.

—Joel 3:16

CONTENTS

LIST OF MAJOR CHARACTERS

Bashar Al-Assad: Syrian president

Asma al-Assad: Wife of Bashar Al-Assad

General Mohammad Ali Jafari: Chief of the Islamic Revolutionary Guard (IRGC)

Hossein Taeb: Iranian Shia cleric and Head of Intelligence, IRGC

Major General Qasem Soleimani: Leader of IRGC's Quds Force

President Hassan Rouhani: Iranian President

Ayatollah Ali Khamenei: Supreme Leader of Iran

Valery Vasilyevich Gerasimov: Chief of the General Staff of Armed Forces of Russia

General Alexander Zhuravlev: Deputy Chief of General Staff and Commander of Russian Forces in Syria

Marwan Issa: Head of Hamas' military wing

David Chaikin: Director of Mossad

Moshe Simon: Chief of General Staff of the Israel Defense Forces

Aaron Lerner: Israeli Ambassador to the United States

Yisrael Katz: Israeli Intelligence Minister

Lt. General Ali Abdulla Ayoub: Syrian Minister of Defense

Jonathan Conner: U.S. President

Brigadier General Gideon Mizrahi: Commander of the IDF's West Bank Division

Andrew Thomas: U.S. Secretary of State

Adam Herrington: U.S. National Security Advisor

Mark Oliver: U.S. Secretary of Defense

Joe Sanford: Chairman of the Joint Chiefs of Staff

General Chuck Rotel: CENTCOM Commander

Katherine Wolf: Director, U.S. Central Intelligence Agency

Marvin Kahn: Deputy Director, U.S. Central Intelligence Agency

Major General Amikam Norkin: Commander of the Israeli Air Force (IAF)

Colonel Levat: Commander of the Ramat David Air Base

Henry Sokolski: Director of Nonproliferation Policy Education Center

Eli Sharvit: Commander in Chief of the Israeli Navy

Maj. Gen. Tamir Heiman: Head of IDF Military Intelligence Directorate

Major General Nitzan Elon: Commander of the Golani Brigade

Captain Levi Arnot: Helicopter Pilot

Colonel Nobi Geller: Commander of Operation Delilah

Colonel Frank Holliday: Cardiothoracic Surgeon

INTRODUCTION

A Prodrome to War

AFTER MORE THAN EIGHT YEARS of crippling civil war, the insurgency that had threatened the rule of Syrian President Bashar Al-Assad was finally quelled. The tide had turned in favor of the ruling Alawite autocracy, thanks to the intervention of a united front of Russian, Iranian, and Hezbollah forces known as the *Syrian Coalition*.

The Coalition crushed all remaining pockets of resistance with impunity. The cost in human lives was staggering: 500,000 Syrians were dead, 100,000 children orphaned, and more than 11 million civilians displaced. Major cities, such as Aleppo, lay in ruins. Billions of dollars would be required to restore even a modicum of civility to the devastated land. But rather than lay down their weapons and begin the arduous task of reconstruction, the Syrian Coalition turned its sights on Israel.

Impelled by a pernicious mix of anti-Semitism and anti-Zionism, the Coalition was committed to the total and complete destruction of the Jewish state. It was a horrific ambition, yet it would be only a stepping stone in the grand realignment of power across the Middle East.

With Iran leading the assault, the Coalition would not stop its march until Jordan, Saudi Arabia, and the Gulf States were under Shia rule.

If it was successful in achieving its vision, the Coalition would drive the United States out and supplant the Great Satan with Russia. Putin's geopolitical power would soar in direct proportion to his control over oil. U.S.-Russian doctrine would no longer rely on Mutually Assured Destruction to maintain the balance of power . . . not when the world's energy spigot was firmly in Russian hands. Now, Russian influence across the globe would be bought by the barrel.

The stage was set for catastrophic global conflict. All that was needed was a match to ignite the conflagration . . . a match the Iranians were hours away from striking.

CHAPTER ONE

East of Tehran

Cloaked in the darkness of a moonless night, the phantom-like G550 Gulfstream sat at the far end of Al-Dumayr Military Airport's single runway, forty kilometers northeast of Damascus, awaiting clearance from the tower.

The radio crackled as the tower communicated take-off instructions, which the pilot summarily acknowledged before throttling-up the twin Rolls Royce engines—each capable of producing more than 15,000 pounds of thrust. As he popped his foot off the brake, the plane lunged forward, pressing its lone passenger, Bashar al-Assad, hard against his seat. In less than a minute, the Syrian president was airborne and headed east.

Sixty seconds after departure, two MiG-29s from the 698 Squadron at Sayqal appeared off the Gulfstream's wingtips. The pride of the Syrian Air Force, their job was to ensure the president's safe passage to Tehran. Comforted by the presence of his formidable escort, Assad leaned back in the spacious black leather chair and closed his eyes. His mind turned to the meeting ahead and its immeasurable importance to the stability of his regime.

He whispered a prayer under his breath—a prayer for a unifying vision that would forever cement the Coalition. It was not merely his life that he sought to protect, but that of his wife, Asma, and their three children. He had no prayers, however, for the people of Syria who had turned against his regime—only contempt.

Bashar al-Assad's life was a far cry from what he had once envisioned. Though he grew up under the watchful eye of his dictatorial father, Hafez, Bashar never planned to follow in his footsteps. The soft-spoken and reserved second son was grateful that succession had been delegated to his older brother, Bassel.

The charismatic and athletic Bassel was well-suited for the task. He was impetuous and hot-tempered, having been compared to Sonny in *The Godfather* by the head of the CIA. It was these characteristics that helped Hafaz's older son rise quickly through the ranks of the Syrian Arab National Guard and become a unit Commander of its 12th Armored Battalion.

Meanwhile, relieved not to be burdened with such awesome responsibility, Bashar pursued a career in healing. He graduated from medical school at Damascus University in 1988 and then spent four years working as an army doctor before returning to London's Western Eye Institute for post-graduate work in ophthalmology. While he was in London, he met his future wife.

For Bashar al-Assad, life could not have been better in the early 1990s. There appeared to be a clear and predictable trajectory to his life . . . something in which he took great comfort . . . until a foggy day in 1994 changed everything in an instant.

In the early morning of January 21, 1994, Bassel was running late to catch a flight to Germany. Relegating his chauffeur to the backseat, he commandeered the Mercedes, then sped off towards Damascus International Airport. A heavy fog permeated the route, and despite the protestations of his chauffeur, Bassel refused to slow down.

A few miles shy of the airport, hidden in the mist, was a concrete roundabout. By the time Bassel saw it, it was too late to course correct. He plowed directly into the structure and died instantly. His chauffeur, protected by a seatbelt, walked away from the crash unscathed.

That singular event irreparably altered the course of Bashar's life.

Overwhelmed with grief and with no heir apparent, Hafez summoned his younger son back to Damascus. Within a few months, Bashar was named the new successor to the throne. He would spend the next six years preparing to assume the reins of power under his father's tutelage.

When his father died in 2000, Bashar was anointed president. Shortly thereafter, he married Asma.

The new Syrian leader would prove worthy of his family's adopted name—*Al Assad*, "the lion," but he would also embody the spirit of his family's original name—*Wahsh*, "savage." Many years after earning his medical degree, his professors and colleagues would marvel at how Bashar al-Assad could have taken an oath to do no harm and then commit untold atrocities.

Over time, Asma would be seen to embody a similar contradiction. The daughter of a London cardiologist and a working mother who had served as the former First Secretary of London's Syrian Embassy, Asma was welcomed with open arms and became known as the "Rose in the Desert."

That moniker proved short-lived as Asma became increasingly viewed as complicit in her husband's atrocities. While barrel bombs spewed chlorine and other toxic gases designed to choke the life out of innocent women and children, an impeccably dressed Asma smiled at the crowds while walking her children to Montessori school. The "Desert Rose" soon became known as the "First Lady of Hell."

The cockpit door swung open with a creak, summoning Bashar al-Assad back to the moment. An hour and fifty-two minutes had elapsed since take-off.

"Mr. President, we are on final approach to Doshan-Tappeh Air Base. We will have you on the ground in ten minutes, Sir," the captain informed him.

Assad bobbed his head in acknowledgment. The captain saluted—a vestige of his military training—then returned to his post. Soon the outskirts of Iran's most populous city appeared on the horizon.

Located just east of central Tehran, Doshan-Tappeh had long served as headquarters for the Iranian Air Force, an atrophied branch of the military that had been in a continual state of decline since the overthrow of the Shah in 1979. Yet the base retained its vitality due to one simple fact: it served as the headquarters of the Islamic Revolutionary Guards Corps known as the IRGC. As such, it housed the IRGC's Joint Chiefs of Staff, Directorate of Operations, and Directorate of Intelligence.

The IRGC was created by Ayatollah Khomeini following the Islamic Revolution of 1979 and had been given the charge of "protecting the revolution and its achievements." It was designed to serve the theocracy much as the medieval crusades served the Catholic Church. It reported directly to the Ayatollah, if it reported to anyone at all.

As he stepped onto the tarmac, Assad was greeted by General Mohammad Ali Jafari, chief of the IRGC. Based upon his graying beard and hair, Assad judged him to be in his late fifties, though his body did little to betray his age. The General appeared taut and formidable under his perfectly pressed uniform.

Jafari had commanded the IRGC for more than a decade. He was committed not only to the Ayatollah's grand vision of Shia domination, but also to the destruction of Israel and its principal ally, the United States. Unafraid of condemnation, he had been a vociferous opponent of the nuclear negotiations with then Secretary of State, John Kerry. In fact, he'd gone so far as to share his dream of directly engaging America in war.

"Welcome to Iran, Mr. President," Jafari saluted his ally. "We've been looking forward to your arrival."

"Thank you, General. I have looked forward to this day for many months."

The two men climbed into the back of a black Mercedes limo and were shuttled to a building several blocks away. As he climbed out of the car, Assad saw what appeared to be more of a bunker than a building. Two sentries armed with Uzis stood guard.

"I see your men carry Uzis."

"Our hatred of the Jews does not render our judgment blind. Few weapons have the reliability and killing power of an Uzi. Would you rather they carry AKs?" This elicited a hearty laugh from both men.

After entering the building, they descended four steep stairways in succession, which ultimately deposited them in the heart of a massive underground complex.

"I'm sorry there's no elevator, Mr. President. If we were attacked, that's the last place you'd want to be. Our conference room is located beneath forty feet of reinforced concrete, making it impervious to the bombs and missiles of our adversaries," Jafari explained.

"You're sure of that?" Al-Assad questioned.

"We've learned not to under-estimate the Israelis. Their ground-penetrating warheads can't reach this deep . . . not unless they carry a nuclear payload. You couldn't be safer anywhere, President Assad."

Assad paused, putting his hand on the general's shoulder. "Considering the roster of guests you've assembled, I don't think any level of precaution should be considered superfluous."

When they reached the conference room, the general gave a perfunctory knock before opening the massive wooden door and allowing President Assad to precede him. Assad quickly sized up the members of the Syrian Coalition, who were intently awaiting his arrival.

One side of the table was dominated by the Iranians, who were seated in order of ascending power. The first in line was Hossein Taeb, an Iranian Shia cleric and head of

Intelligence for the IRGC. Next to him was Major General Qasem Soleimani, leader of the IRGC's Quds Force, a position he had held since 1998.

Soleimani needed no introduction. His ascendancy to power had begun with the pivotal role he played in the slaughter of American troops in Iraq. According to the late U.S. Senator, John McCain, Soleimani was responsible for a dramatic increase in the number of American injuries and fatalities. Under his direction, Iran had armed America's enemies with a new and vastly improved IED, causing the then head of U.S. forces in Iraq, General David Petraeus, to describe his nemesis as "truly evil."

Soleimani was smart, strategic, and ruthless. He was recognized by many as the single most powerful operative in the Middle East. During his tenure, Soleimani had fostered the growth of relationships with pivotal terrorist groups—most importantly, Hezbollah. These proxies enabled him to stage a slow war of attrition against Israel without directly committing Iranian lives.

The meeting was to be Soleimani's show, but first, decorum demanded that appropriate homage be paid to the two leaders of Iran.

President Hassan Rouhani greeted Assad with a smile and firm handshake, followed by the true Iranian commander, the Supreme Leader, Ayatollah Ali Khamenei.

Since the Islamic Revolution of 1979, the power structure of Iran had been turned upside down. Whereas the Shah had attempted to maintain the illusion of a democratic state, there was no such pretense under the absolute rule of the Ayatollah. He controlled the military and all things political, as well as social norms. Though

Iran boasted of a president who was second in power, in reality the presidency was in name only with little actual authority.

However, even the theocracy understood the need for checks and balances, which is why they established the Assembly of Experts for the Leadership—a constitutional body of eighty-six scholars of Islamic law who were empowered to appoint or dismiss the Supreme Leader. Though they were vested with such authority, it had never been exercised, as demonstrated by the fact that only two Supreme Leaders had ruled Iran since the revolution.

Seated directly across from the Ayatollah was the Russian delegation, including General Valery Vasilyevich Gerasimov, Chief of the General Staff of the Armed Forces of Russia, and General Alexander Zhuravlev, Deputy Chief of General Staff and commander of Russian forces in Syria.

Gerasimov had begun his military service in 1976, much of which consisted of serving in and leading various mechanized units within the former Soviet Union. He had developed a reputation as a superb strategist capable of integrating a multitude of disciplines under a unitary plan for the destruction of his enemies.

By contrast, Alexander Zhuravlev was more comfortable executing strategy on the battlefield than developing it at headquarters. Zhuravlev was the recipient of the Hero of the Russian Federation—an award bestowed by President Putin.

Sensing the group's eagerness to get down to business, Assad quickly greeted all of the attendees by name before taking his seat.

The Ayatollah opened the meeting with a prayer in which he asked for God's hand in helping to vanquish the unholy scourge of Israel. When he was finished with his invective, Ayatollah Khamenei relinquished control to General Soleimani.

"Gentlemen, since the earliest days of the revolution, our hearts have been centered on the destruction of Israel. We have bided our time and waited for a moment free from distractions to execute a lethal blow to the Zionist regime. The time to strike has finally arrived." He paused to maximize the effect of his words.

"Hostilities across Syria have all but ceased, due in no small measure to the intervention of our Russian collaborators. The once formidable ISIS has been routed from its last remaining positions, and the United States has withdrawn in defeat. We are no longer relegated to playing defense. We can now mount a major offensive—striking without fear of reprisal, thanks to both the forces that we have amassed along Israel's borders, as well as the massive arsenal of missiles now targeted at the Jews.

"I have spent many hours speaking with each of you as I sought to construct a plan that would engender your unanimous support. We are assembled today to review that plan." Soleimani picked up a three-ring binder and opened it to the title page:

The Twelfth Imam

It was a reference to Muhammad al-Hasan al-Askari, a figure recognized by most Shia as the presumed Mahdi or Messiah of Islam. According to religious texts, he would return from occultation (a place of hiding) to restore peace and justice in the days preceding the final judgment.

"The plan is contained in your briefing books. Once I walk through its most salient elements, I am confident you will agree that it is the fastest path to eliminating the scourge of Israel."

CHAPTER TWO

Hallah, Haifa Oranges, and a Cup of Bitter Coffee

RACHEL RABINOVICH WAS MORE THAN A MATCH for her strong-willed husband. Spirited, smart, and outspoken, she kept Avi on his toes. The couple had been married for more than twenty-five years. Rachel had met Abraham while she was working in an investment banking firm in Jerusalem.

"Where's my coffee?" the sluggish prime minister growled as he emerged from the bedroom in his heavy, brown robe and shuffled towards the breakfast table. His unkempt hair caused Rachel to chuckle.

"It's in the pot," she replied, "and while you're at it, you can pour me a cup."

Rabinovich grunted something inaudible before doing precisely as his wife instructed. Outside of their home, he was the formidable head of the Likud Party and prime minister of Israel. But within the confines of their adobe walls, Rachel ruled.

It had taken three marriages for Avi to finally get the rules straight, though he still veered into dangerous territory at times—including a very public affair with a member of his staff. Rachel had managed to forgive him, despite the humiliation and profound sense of betrayal she had felt at the time.

"I've toasted some hallah, and there's a bowl of oranges and grapes on the table. I've got an appointment with Dr. Eiseman in twenty minutes. Not all of us enjoy a life of leisure."

"It's going to be a slow day at the office," Avi said as he sipped on the steaming cup of dark, bitter coffee. "I don't have any appointments until ten o'clock. Why rush?"

"You never know what awaits you, my dear."

"Don't tempt fate, Rachel! Poo, poo, poo," he uttered quickly. It was an old Yiddish expression used to ward off evil spirits. "I'm learning to enjoy the calmer moments of existence."

"You know they are temporary, Avi . . . the proverbial calm before the storm."

"Who's to say we can't have enduring peace?" he responded.

"Mr. Prime Minister, how many countries are bent on our destruction?"

"I've lost count . . . but fortunately, only a handful possess the capacity to make good on the threat. My job is to ensure that it never happens."

"Then maybe you should get to work!"

She kissed the top of his head, grabbed her coffee cup, and headed for the door. "I'll see you this evening . . . we're having the Davidsons over for dinner . . . you did remember?"

"Who are the Davidsons?" he said to raise her ire.

"You really are something, Mr. Prime Minister. Harry Davidson is among your top five American donors. He's been loyal to you for many years. His wife, Robin, is delightful and beautiful . . . and don't tell me you haven't noticed."

"I haven't! And Rachel, I can recite Harry's complete bio, if it would make you happy."

"No need . . . I'm leaving." She smiled, turned, and walked to the door.

"Why are you going to see Eiseman?" Avi asked before Rachel crossed the threshold.

"I found a small lump in my breast last night while I was in the shower."

"What do you mean by 'a small lump?'"

"Nothing to worry about," she said, more to reassure herself than her husband.

The door closed before Avi could utter another word. Surely it was nothing, he told himself, anxious at the thought of losing what was most precious in his life.

Despite his superlative intelligence, it had taken nearly fifty years of hard living for Rabinovich to grasp what it meant to love someone. Though he had early on developed a keen appreciation for lust and personal gratification, the notions of selflessness, loyalty, and sacrifice had evaded his consciousness until he met Rachel, and he wasn't about to lose her.

CHAPTER THREE

Lessons Written in the Sand

"THE METHOD FOR DEFEATING THE JEWISH STATE is written in its history," Soleimani began his address to the assembled leaders of the Coalition. "The Israel Defense Forces has proven its ability to respond astutely to conventional attacks, but it is less dexterous at managing asymmetrical threats."

"What renders a force as formidable as the IDF impotent in the face of an insurrection?" the Ayatollah asked.

"Two things: First, they fear being branded as brutal in their suppression of 'terrorist threats' emanating from within Gaza, the West Bank, and southern Lebanon. And with good reason—we've succeeded in painting the Israelis as heartless war criminals who respond to bricks with bullets and Molotov cocktails with mortars.

"Second, though they possess an extensive arsenal of weapons of mass destruction, they are fearful of ever unleashing such devastation. If they were truly strong, the IDF would crush its enemies with little concern over so-called collateral damage. But the Jewish ethos won't let them. And that will be a critical element in their defeat."

"Are you suggesting that insurgencies can topple the State of Israel?" the Ayatollah asked incredulously.

"No, but they will play a critical role in Israel's destruction. As you know, the Jews have won battles when they have been attacked on a single front by a single adversary. It has happened time and time again. However, with the notable exception of the Six-Day War, Israel has failed to demonstrate an ability to survive simultaneous attacks using a combination of conventional and asymmetrical attacks against geographically diverse targets."

"Do you agree with this assessment, General Gerasimov?" the Ayatollah asked.

"Completely." Gerasimov responded without hesitation, his words overlaid with a thick Slavic accent.

With an upward flick of his wrist, the Ayatollah gestured for Soleimani to continue.

"Our success will be contingent upon overwhelming the IDF. That means we must move with sufficient speed to negate their ability to deploy reserve forces in time to stop our incursion."

Assad was quick to jump in. "That sounds good in theory, General Soleimani, but should it fail, there are many miles that separate your land from that of the Jews. My country shares a border with them. Damascus is mere minutes from Israeli airbases. In a single day, they can cripple our nation and destroy whatever gains we made fighting a protracted civil war."

"No war is without great risk, President Assad. But I would think that the prospect of eradicating such a reviled adversary would overcome your trepidation."

"My trepidation can only be overcome with logic, General. So tell me the details of your plan, and I will tell you whether I think it can succeed."

"Our plan begins with a diversion. We turn up the heat in Gaza."

"You presume that Hamas will align with your strategy," Assad countered.

"I presume nothing, President Assad. I have spoken with Marwan Issa, who has agreed to a two-fold plan beginning with the Izz ad-Din al-Qassam Brigade infiltrating the Israeli border using their tunnel network."

Qassam, the colloquial name for the brigade, was the military branch of Palestinian Hamas. Marwan Issa was the most recent successor to a long string of commanders, most of whom had succumbed to Israeli assassination. The organization, which was named for a rabid anti-Zionist, was created in 1991 and served as a constant thorn in the side of Israel.

"How do you plan to infiltrate tunnels that were destroyed by Israel in 2014?" Assad asked derisively.

"The IDF destroyed thirty-two operating tunnels in 2014. By 2018, thanks to more than a thousand laborers, there were forty new tunnels running under the border. May I continue?"

Assad nodded grudgingly.

"Hamas will send more than a dozen suicide bombers to neighboring towns, including Sderot, Ashdod, Ashkelon, and Beersheba. Shortly before nine a.m. on May 15, they will travel from their safe houses to key strategic locations. The targets have been selected based upon their population density, and hence the ability to maximize casualties.

"At nine o'clock, the Shaheed—the martyrs—will detonate their explosive vests."

The significance of the date was not lost on anyone in the room. May 15, known as *Nakba*, followed on the heels of Israeli Independence Day and marked the date when Palestinians were exiled from their homes in 1948.

"Hamas will wait ten minutes for the Israeli Home Front Command to deploy emergency workers before launching the first fusillade of Grad Katyusha rockets targeted at these towns. We are confident that the ensuing terror and chaos will be sufficient to captivate the attention of the IDF and Home Front Defense for some time."

"That will put the Gaza squarely in the cross-hairs of the IDF and IAF," Assad protested with impatience.

"That is precisely our intent, Mr. President. Because your ground forces, working hand in hand with our military leaders, will begin an artillery assault on the Golan Heights in synchrony with the Gaza attack. If things go as planned, we will capture the Golan within twenty-four to thirty-six hours."

The Golan Heights was a 690-square-mile swath of land bordered on the south by the Yarmouk River and on the north by Mount Hermon. Part of the land seized from Syria by Israel following the 1967 war, the Golan held significant strategic importance. From its elevated positions, the Coalition could shell vast portions of Israel, endangering the lives of civilian and military personnel.

"We've attempted to repatriate the Golan before unsuccessfully!" Assad referred to a 1973 attack on entrenched Israeli forces that resulted in significant deaths on both sides.

"This time we will be the overwhelming force, President Assad. There are approximately 10,000 Quds forces awaiting deployment. Hezbollah troops in Syria add another 5,000.

If we assume that Syria will contribute upwards of 10,000 troops, then we have an invading force of 25,000. That's surely enough to overwhelm the IDF—if we strike rapidly, before reserve troops can reach the Golan."

But Assad wasn't convinced. "The Israelis are entrenched in highly defensible positions. Plus, despite your claims to the contrary, General, there are still pockets of resistance—mainly ISIS—that remain on our side of the Golan. Sheer numbers will not be the sole determinant of such a battle. The Coalition stands to lose thousands of warriors."

"That's why the attack will begin with an artillery bombardment," Soleimani said in acknowledgement. "We will pound their positions relentlessly to pre-condition the area for a ground assault."

"And what about the IAF, and their ability to knock out our artillery with little effort?" Assad demanded. His forces had endured significant losses at the hands of the Israeli Air Force in numerous skirmishes throughout the civil war.

"Why do you think we provided you with the S400, President Assad?" Gerasimov interjected, clearly tiring of the president's whining.

The S400 was the pinnacle in Russian air defense systems. It was able to engage a full range of airborne threats—from drones to aircraft to incoming missiles—at a range of up to 400 kilometers. It was fast, accurate, and deadly.

"Tell me, General, how effective will the S400 be in engaging Israel's new stealth F35I? Or perhaps you think we should not be concerned about a plane that can fly at Mach 1.6, pull 9 Gs, and carry 4,000 pounds of smart weapons?"

"Israel has taken delivery of only a handful of the fancy new fighter jets. And, yes, President Assad, they may penetrate your air defenses. But the workhorse of IAF, the F16, will be blown out of the sky. As soon as four or five of their planes are shot down, the counter-attack will be called off and the planes will be ordered back to base until a new strategy can be developed."

"You are willing to wager a great deal based upon your beliefs about the S400's capabilities, but you are gambling with our assets," Assad said pointedly at Gerasimov.

"Have faith, President Assad. Our system will perform exactly as promised."

"The S400 did not stop the Americans and their NATO allies from destroying our chemical research facility!" an angry Assad shouted.

"That is because we turned it off before their jets and cruise missiles arrived," Gerasimov responded.

"You what?" Assad bellowed incredulously as he leapt to his feet.

"Sit down, Mr. Assad," the Ayatollah intoned harshly.

"You heard me correctly, President Assad. We allowed them through in a brokered arrangement to de-escalate tensions with the Americans. Had we not, your treasured palace was next on their list of targets," Gerasimov explained.

"May I continue?" Soleimani asked the group. The Ayatollah gestured to move on.

"After twelve continuous hours of artillery strikes, the bombardment will cease and rapid troop deployment will begin. The first troops to assault the Golan will be Iranian Special Forces, who, like their Hamas brethren in Gaza, will utilize a vast network of tunnels to approach Israeli defensive positions. Behind them will be the wave of 25,000 men. We will rout the Israelis in hours, driving them back to the Jordan River."

The Ayatollah closed his eyes and nodded his head in support, as if witnessing the annihilation of his foe.

The general continued, "But our objective is far greater than the repatriation of a strip of land. Our goal is to bring Israel to its knees, which is why we have an additional 10,000 Hezbollah troops manning missile batteries in southern Lebanon and awaiting our orders. As you know, despite Israel's interception of numerous weapons convoys from Damascus to Lebanon, many still reached their intended targets. There is not a single hectare of land within Israel that is beyond the reach of Hezbollah's missiles."

Sensing a need to stroke Assad's fragile ego, Soleimani continued. "Thanks to our joint efforts with President Assad, we've expanded Hezbollah's cache of missiles quantitatively and qualitatively. There are now more than 120,000 missiles under our control in Lebanon, including approximately 400 SCUD-D missiles. Though its numbers are small when compared to the thousands of short and medium range missiles ready for deployment, the SCUD-D brings a new level of threat to Israel. Thanks to a 700-kilometer range, we can target Haifa, Tel Aviv, and Jerusalem with unparalleled precision and deliver a payload in excess of 500 kilograms."

"The Israelis have dealt with missile barrages for years, Alexander Zhuravlev instructed Soleimani. "Other than being able to more accurately target, tell us why this attack will be different."

"At the outset this will appear to be yet another skirmish in the long war of attrition."

"What do you mean by *at the outset*?" Assad asked.

"In the beginning phase of the assault, the missiles will be loaded with conventional warheads—everything from short range Katyushas and Fajr-5s to long-range Zelzal-2s will be deployed. Our primary goal is not to kill thousands of Israelis, though that would be a welcome result, but rather to engage Israeli missile defense batteries so that they expend many of their surface-to-air missiles. If sufficiently depleted, any system, including their three missile defense systems—The Iron Dome, David's Sling, and Arrow—will be rendered ineffective in their ability to stop incoming threats. That's when we fire our final volley of SCUD-Ds."

"And what is so special about this final round of missiles?" Assad pressed.

"There are twelve SCUD-D missiles, four each for Tel Aviv, Jerusalem, and Haifa. We will use Tel Aviv as a 'demonstration site'—a preview of the destruction that will follow if the IDF fails to lay down its weapons."

Soleimani continued, "The missiles targeted at Tel Aviv are armed with chemical munitions. The warheads contain a nose-mounted, high-explosive charge designed to split open the warhead and aerosolize its contents—a Novichok agent. As you know, not only is this an extraordinarily lethal chemical, but a persistent one."

"I also know that it carries the unmistakable signature of Russia. General Gerasimov, I'm surprised at your country's willingness to be so openly complicit in the use of weapons of mass destruction," Assad remarked.

"How is it any different than the Americans turning a blind eye to Israel's nuclear ambiguity? Is that not facilitating the eventual use of weapons of mass destruction?

Besides, it is a moot point. Although it will be immediately apparent that a nerve agent has been deployed, it will take several days for forensic confirmation that it was a Novichok agent versus VX or Sarin. By then, the war will be over."

Zhuravlev continued, "I would be less concerned about the identity of the supplier of death than I would Israel's ability to defend itself. The Israelis have anticipated such attacks for years. Their Homeland Defense has dramatically increased the number of shelters, ensured that all residents have gas masks, and proven they can shield eighty percent of the population in key cities in less than seven minutes."

Soleimani countered, "We agree that the number of fatalities may be limited, but there will be no limit to the terror inflicted. There are risks, however, beginning with a pre-emptive strike on SCUD locations in Lebanon."

"Are they not hidden?" the Ayatollah asked.

"Because of the SCUD's length, we have limited ability to camouflage the missiles. Israel probably has satellite surveillance of their positions. It takes forty-five minutes to fuel a SCUD prior to launch. If the IDF views such activities, they may pre-emptively strike. Since the missiles are geographically dispersed, that would require multiple sorties or precisely guided munitions. We assume they will be too distracted by our attacks on other fronts to carry out such missions."

Zhuravlelev turned to his superior for permission to speak frankly, which Gerasimov granted with an almost imperceptible nod of the head.

"Our intelligence estimates indicate that Israel has between 150 and 400 nuclear weapons ready for deployment.

'Jewish ethos' aside, they will not sit idly by while the country faces an existential threat. They will reach a tipping point, at which time the Israeli government will sanction the limited use of their nuclear arsenal. As you know, Israel's foreign minister, Avigdor Lieberman, went on record stating that the use of chemical weapons by Hezbollah would be a 'casus belli,' ensuring that Israel would respond without hesitation or restraint."

Soleimani confidently refuted Zhuravlelev's comment. "That decision will not be reached lightly. It will take the Israelis time to argue the appropriateness of nuclear reprisal. That is why we plan an abrupt cessation in our aggression following the capture of the Golan, the chemical attack on Tel Aviv, and the uprising in Gaza. We will pause long enough to issue an ultimatum in which we demand the capitulation of the Israeli government, while ensuring the safety of its people. The Israelis will have forty-eight hours or face annihilation."

"What makes you so arrogant as to believe the Israelis will surrender?" Gerasimov snapped at Soleimani. "I think you have seriously under-estimated the resolve of our shared foe. The Jews have a 2,000-year history of oppression. An attack on the Golan, a few thousand lives lost in Tel Aviv pale by comparison to wandering for forty years in the wilderness or being nearly extinguished in the ovens of Nazi concentration camps."

"They will have no choice with a nuclear Sword of Damocles dangling above their heads," Soleimani responded.

CHAPTER FOUR

Cabin Conversations

THERE ARE CERTAIN JOBS that are best relegated to chronic pessimists, including the job of prime minister of Israel. What had started out as a beautiful spring day for Avi Rabinovich was turning ugly fast.

Six hours after the Syrian Coalition concluded its proceedings at Doshan-Tappeh, Rabinovich convened an emergency meeting of the Israeli Security Cabinet at the Bor, a massive subterranean complex located beneath the Defense Ministry in the Hakirya district of Tel Aviv. The facility was designed to protect its occupants against chemical, biological, and nuclear attacks. Access required first passing through massive steel doors that hermetically sealed, then descending fifty feet to the Chief of Staff's conference room.

The conference room was stark and modernistic, containing an oval beveled-edge wooden table that seated twenty and a vast array of flat-panel monitors of varying sizes. The only décor in the room was two large Israeli flags flanking the entrance.

Summoned at a moment's notice, only the most critical members of the Security Cabinet were physically present, including David Chaikin, Director of Mossad, and Moshe Simon, Chief of General Staff of the Israel Defense Forces. Aaron Lerner, Israel's Ambassador to the United States, and Intelligence Minister Yisrael Katz, participated via secure videoconference.

"It appears that our *friends*, the so-called 'Syrian Coalition,' may be preparing to embark on a more ambitious mission than quelling Syria's insurgency," Rabinovich began.

With the press of a button, video screens across the expansive conference room came to life, each with the razor-sharp image that only a drone could have captured.

"These images are from Doshan-Tappeh airbase near Tehran. As you can see from the time and date stamp, the most recent ones are from this morning," Rabinovich explained.

Bashar al-Assad could be easily identified as he descended the stairs of his private jet, as could the man greeting him—General Jafari. The show continued with images of General Soleimani, followed by Iranian president Rouhani and Supreme Leader Ayatollah Khamenei, all entering the same bunker-like building.

Rabinovich paused, although he had not reached the end of his photo album. Staring into the eyes of his most trusted advisors, he called up the remaining two images. There was a collective groan as photographs of Gerasimov and Zhuralev appeared.

"They must have had a hell of a party," Rabinovich's words were laced with his trademark sarcasm.

"As you can see, the surveillance photos show a virtually who's who of anti-Zionists meeting outside of Tehran."

Moshe shrugged his shoulders at the revelation. "There have been numerous meetings between the Syrians, Iranians, and Russians since the formation of the Syrian Coalition. What about this one has you so concerned, Avi?"

"What has me so concerned? What has me so concerned?" he repeated the question, his voice raising a full octave. "Are you serious, Moshe? Have we ever witnessed such a cast of characters assembled in one place?"

Pausing momentarily, he added, "Don't you think that's a hell of a risk for them to take? They must have had a damn good reason for it."

"I'll grant you, Avi, it is an unusual collection of individuals, but it may have nothing to do with Israel. For all we know, it is a summit to discuss the post-civil war plan for governing Syria—including how Iran and Russia will be repaid for ensuring the survival of the Assad regime," Moshe Simon speculated.

Simon was a seasoned warrior. The son of a copper miner from Tiberias, Simon enlisted in the Golani Brigade, one of Israel's most decorated infantry units, in 1978. An unintended lifer in the army, he spent thirty-three years ascending the ranks before eventually being promoted to head Israel's defense forces.

Though level-headed and even-handed, the general was not without controversy. Simon was credited with authoring the *Dahiya Doctrine*—whereby Israel would use disproportionate force, as necessary, to dislodge embedded terrorists, irrespective of whether they were surrounded by civilian towns or encamped at military installations.

"Moshe, based upon the evidence presented thus far, I understand a modicum of skepticism. But listen to what David has to say. Only then, form your final judgment."

Rabinovich turned to the head of Mossad. "Enlighten us, David."

"Gentlemen, as you know, one of our most valuable assets serves as President Assad's personal flight attendant. She was aboard the flight that ferried Mr. Assad to the meeting at Doshan-Tappeh, as well as the return trip to Damascus. I had a chance to debrief her less than an hour ago by sat phone."

"Don't keep us in suspense, David," Rabinovich chided him. "Share with us what you learned."

"She indicated that the president appeared contemplative prior to the meeting. Afterwards, however, his mood was buoyant."

Speaking via teleconference, Yisrael Katz asked his direct report, "So we presume he got something he wanted . . . is that what you are implying, Ari?"

"Yes, Sir. We know that he made two calls en route to Damascus. Our operative believes that the first call was to Lt. General Ali Abdulla Ayoub, the Syrian Minister of Defense. The second call was to his wife, Asma al-Assad."

"And?" Yisrael asked impatiently.

"According to our operative, he told General Ayoub that he was confident that the destruction of Israel was finally at hand."

"And did she overhear his comments to his wife?" Yisrael persisted.

"Yes . . . he said, 'It's almost over.'"

A collective sigh, not of relief but anxiety, was shared by the participants. Rabinovich leaned forward, resting his elbows on the table.

"I don't believe there's much room for interpretation. We knew this day would likely arrive; we just didn't know how soon. The warning claxon has sounded, but the question remains as to how we should respond."

"Respond to what?" Simon posited. "We have no idea what they are planning. It's hard to develop a plan of attack or counter-attack when you don't know who, what, where, or when. We can surmise why."

"So we wait for an overwhelming force to attack our country? Is that what you are suggesting?" Rabinovich responded.

"If I may, Sir?" The voice coming through a speaker belonged to Aaron Lerner.

"Of course. Talk to us, Mr. Ambassador."

Lerner had grown up in Miami, Florida. He had attended the Wharton School as an undergraduate before completing his Ph.D. at Oxford. Aaron Lerner rarely sounded the alarm, although, as Israeli's ambassador to the United States, he was often embroiled in threatening situations.

"I believe we should request an emergency briefing with President Conner. We need an immediate and potent counter-balance to the Russians, which requires U.S. involvement. The U.S. can work behind the scenes to galvanize sentiment among the Saudis, Jordanians, and other countries with a vested interest in stopping any further incursion into the region by the Syrian Coalition."

Rabinovich sat silently for a moment before responding. He looked around the table and to the videoconferencing monitors for agreement. All heads nodded.

"You have an excellent relationship with President Conner. Request the meeting on my behalf," Rabinovich advised him. "Good luck." Rabinovich terminated the video uplink.

Simon wasn't finished. "Despite my prior comments, I suggest we not wait for the Americans before making preparations. When we await their permission, bad things seem to happen. At the very least, we should notify Home Front Command immediately. With the Council's approval, I will speak to Brigadier General Gideon Mizrahi regarding raising our state of alert."

"Permission granted, but surely there is more that we can do than wait for bombs or missiles to rain down on our countrymen. Why else did we spend time modeling every conceivable scenario for an attack on our homeland if not to respond?" Rabinovich demanded.

The statement was rhetorical, but not the question. "Tell me, General, what do you believe is most likely to occur?"

"As you indicated, Mr. Prime Minister, there are many scenarios . . . "

"Put yourself in their shoes, Moshe. If you were commanding a combined force of Iranian, Syrian, and Russian assets, where would you hit us first?"

"Bassar Al-Assad has witnessed our resolve in battle and may be leery about risking further depletion of his military after losing so many soldiers in the civil war. His Air Force would be no match for the IAF . . . which is vastly superior in its technology and training. The Iranians, in tandem with the Russians, are the likely architects of the battle plan. They have been building up their missile stockpiles, while greatly improving the accuracy and payload of these weapons. They can hit us anywhere with conventional or unconventional weapons, all without risking any troop loss."

"So that's where you would place your money?"

"I would hedge my bet, Mr. Prime Minister. There's an alternate scenario that could be equally if not more devastating. They could attack our north from southern Lebanon using Hezbollah forces, strike the Golan Heights to our northeast, and then foment additional chaos by having Hamas rise up in the Gaza. As a coalition, they have the troops and the embedded missile and artillery positions to do a tremendous amount of damage in a short time."

"How do we stop them?" Rabinovich asked.

"In the first scenario, we rely on our integrated missile defense, while preparing for an air assault on critical Iranian and Syrian targets. We would face numerous challenges—beginning with the Russian S400 air defense in Syria. In Iran, we face a different challenge. We can overcome their air defense, but many of our targets are hidden amidst subterranean bunkers spread across thousands of square miles. In short, it will be hell trying to stop them. And I haven't even gotten to Hezbollah, who has an estimated 120,000 missiles aimed at us right now.

"There are, of course, limitations to the effectiveness of those weapon. Most of them can be defeated with our missile defenses, but some will still get through. As for the Golan—it's vulnerable. We can shore up our positions, particularly if we see troop movement in Syria. With appropriate IAF support, our position should hold."

"What about the Gaza?"

"We can crush any insurrection, but it will be impossible to contain collateral damage. The civilian casualties will be high, and the world's attention will be focused on us."

"You haven't mentioned the West Bank, which provides unimpeded access to our coastal plane and the majority of our population, not to mention its vital role in our economy."

"I don't see it as a threat. Despite recent condemnations from Fatah leader Mahmoud Abbas, the Palestinian National Authority remains convinced that a peaceful solution is the only sustainable course of action. There may be pockets of Hamas insurgents lodged within the West Bank, but their numbers remain small. Furthermore, there's no threat of an invasion from the east—as long as our peace with Jordan holds. That's why I don't consider the West Bank to be a viable launching pad for an assault on Israel, Mr. Prime Minister."

"David, you've not spoken a word about our response to your intelligence."

"Sometimes it is better to listen, Mr. Prime Minister. I do, however, have an opinion. I believe that the combined Iranian, Hezbollah, Hamas, Syrian, and Russian forces represent a level of threat that may overwhelm our ability to defend our nation. Before that can happen, we must be willing to consider the deployment of unconventional assets."

"I should have allowed you to remain mute," Rabinovich mused, not ready to consider the use of *unconventional assets*—Israel's nuclear option.

The prime minister realized that the discussion was only going to escalate in intensity and called for a break. They would reassemble in twenty minutes. He walked briskly out of the conference room towards his office. Rachel's earlier comments about her health were weighing heavily on his mind. The minute he was alone, he called her.

"I'm sorry I was so difficult this morning, Rachel."

"Why should today be different than any other day, Avi? You were just being you."

"Well, I'm sorry I'm not a better me . . . particularly when I now know that something was troubling you. Tell me what Dr. Eiseman said."

"He said I appear to have a 2-centimeter lesion in my right breast. He won't know what it is until they biopsy it, but he's concerned it may be cancer. I should have had surgery the minute I learned I was BRCA positive."

"We discussed the matter at length, and you opted to take a chance. Don't second guess the wisdom of your decision—that's a sure way to make yourself feel miserable. When is the biopsy scheduled for?"

"Three days from now . . . that's the soonest they could work me in."

"I'll see about that!"

"No, Avi. Don't pull strings. I can wait a few days . . . my condition won't change. Regardless of what they find, I want to reconsider surgery. I don't want to play the waiting game any longer."

"Of course, you have my complete support."

"We can talk more about it tonight."

"I'm sorry, I know the timing is terrible, but I won't be coming home for dinner. In fact, I'm not sure when I'll be home. Things are heating up once again, and my colleagues at the Bor are greatly concerned. Forgive me, Rachel."

She laughed, "If I can forgive you for your surly attitude, surely I can forgive you for doing your duty. Check in on me when you can?"

"Without fail, Darling."

As he hung up the phone, Rabinovich felt as if a tectonic shift was occurring in the very bedrock of his life. Rachel, his one love, and Israel, his other, were suddenly facing potent foes. The stakes had never been higher.

CHAPTER FIVE

A Pledge of Allegiance

Ensconced in a secure facility, Aaron Lerner picked up the encrypted phone that provided direct access to U.S. Secretary of State Andrew Thomas. Once Thomas was on the line, Lerner began to recount just enough details from the earlier briefing to convey the urgency of the matter. He requested an emergency meeting between U.S. and Israeli officials.

"You know, Aaron, there are other viable explanations," Thomas advised the ambassador, who had become a close friend through the years.

"We considered that possibility . . . but only briefly. The threat assessment, predicated upon our intelligence, portends a major event. We need to be prepared for whatever comes down the pike, Andy. With Iran at the helm and Russia at the stern, we could use your help."

"Why don't we start with something informal—a brief call between the president and the prime minister?"

"If we had the leisure of time, a low-key approach would make perfect sense. But we believe an attack may be imminent. If I may suggest, let's err on the side of inclusion in this first meeting."

"That's not going to be easy, Aaron. Our people are not sitting idly on the sidelines waiting to be summoned."

"Nor ours. If your president orders it, I trust his subordinates will be present. Our leaders will be available at President Conner's convenience."

"I'll get back to you." Thomas disconnected, paused momentarily to reflect on what he had just heard, and then placed a call to Jonathan Conner.

"Thank you for taking my call, Mr. President. I'm afraid I have a matter of extreme urgency," Thomas advised.

"What isn't urgent these days?" an unruffled Conner replied.

Since assuming office, his administration had faced unprecedented threats to national security, including a biological attack that killed tens of thousands of Americans. It was followed a year later by the detonation of a nuclear device in New York. It was a war-time administration, though the threats were not carried out on conventional battlefields, but in solitary acts of terror.

Before the secretary could respond, Conner continued. "If this is about the Israelis' concern that the Iranians are stepping up their nuclear program, it's not the time to discuss it . . . not until we are ready to respond."

"Sir, the concern involves the Israelis but does not focus on the Iranian weapons program. I just spoke with Ambassador Lerner. It appears that the Israelis believe an attack on their homeland may be imminent."

"By whom?" Conner questioned.

"The Syrian Coalition, Mr. President."

"Based upon what? I assume that Coalition has their hands full cleaning up in the aftermath of eight years of civil war. I'm sure they're more interested in determining their respective roles going forward than in destroying their neighbor."

"Sir, Ambassador Lerner suggested that there is credible intelligence to support their assertion—intelligence they wish to share with us in a video-teleconference at your earliest convenience."

"What are they asking for, Andy, beyond the teleconference?"

"I assume they will be asking for our full support as a counter-balance against the Russians."

"That's all we need—just as we are finally beginning to heal as a nation."

"I understand your concern, Sir, but I don't see that we have much choice. To abrogate our responsibility to Israel's security would damage our reputation beyond repair."

"I know that, God damn it! But that doesn't mean I have to like it. Get it set up as soon as possible," Conner ordered.

"Yes, Sir." Thomas reached to hang up the phone, but stopped at the sound of Conner's voice.

"One more thing—I want Commander Hart in the meeting. Understood?"

"Yes, Sir."

Conner disconnected the call.

Commander John Hart was Conner's go-to person in emergencies. Hart had been instrumental in pulling the country back from the abyss during both the biological and the nuclear attacks.

At 6'4" and 250 pounds, the former Navy SEAL was a unique physical specimen. His body formed an inverted pyramid with a small waist giving rise to massive shoulders.

Hart's neck measured more than twenty inches in circumference and led to a strong, handsome face with intense brown eyes.

But as tough as he looked, it was not his physical condition that was most intimidating. It was Hart's formidable intellect.

Hart graduated from Carnegie-Mellon University with a degree in nuclear engineering, then joined the Navy, where he was assigned to an Ohio-class submarine. Following three years of submersion in the world's oceans, Hart was ready to be top-side. He applied to the Navy's Sea, Air, and Land Forces, where he not only passed the SEAL's rigorous physical screening test, but set a record in the 500-meter swim.

Six years of running black ops in the world's sewers followed before the Navy decided there were better ways to harness Hart's gifts. He was sent back to graduate school to pursue a Master's in molecular biology. The commander graduated from Georgetown with high honors, after which he matriculated to Johns Hopkins, where he earned his medical degree. He completed Fellowship training at the United States Army Research Institute of Infectious Diseases. Hart did a stint at the Defense Advanced Research Projects Agency, before settling into his permanent home at CIA.

In short, he was the nation's premier badass—and a man who had survived a close encounter with a 15-kiloton nuclear bomb. Had it not been for Hart, much of New York City would be a radioactive wasteland. And, had it not been for Hart, millions would have perished from a man-made epidemic of hemorrhagic smallpox.

Thomas waited five minutes before calling Conner's chief of staff, Jim Lutz, to schedule the teleconference.

"I plan to clear the president's schedule from 2:00 to 3:00 p.m.," Lutz informed Thomas. "The President will want all attendees, with the exception of Ambassador Lerner, assembled for a short briefing fifteen minutes prior to uplink with the Israelis. The ambassador may join us as soon as that briefing terminates."

Thomas had a green light to begin recruiting additional attendees. He started with Hart, and in short order had arranged for the nation's key advisors to be present, including National Security Advisor Adam Herrington, Secretary of Defense Mark Oliver, Chairman of the Joint Chiefs Joe Sanford, CENTCOM Commander General Chuck Rotel, as well as CIA Director Katherine Wolf and Deputy Director Marvin Kahn. His final call was to the Israeli ambassador.

"Aaron, you've got your meeting. It is set for two p.m. Eastern in the Situation Room. The president has requested that you attend in person. You know the procedure—be sure to allow twenty minutes to park and clear security. And one more request: The president has asked that you provide a list of Israeli attendees ASAP."

"Of course. I will have it to you in the next few minutes. Thank you, Andy."

"The best thanks you can give me, Aaron, is to demonstrate that Avi is not crying wolf. President Conner is going to want proof of the urgency of the situation."

"I'd rather prove almost anything else, my friend, but your point is taken. We will make it clear as to why we have sounded a warning siren."

Commander John Hart was the first to arrive at the Situation Room. Hart had been a virtual fixture at the White House through the recent crises that had threatened the very soul of America. Through both his insights and actions, Hart had earned Conner's trust. But their bond was built upon more than trust . . . there was tremendous mutual respect for the shared values that impelled this warrior and his leader forward.

It had been several months since Conner last saw the commander. At the time, Hart was still recovering from burns suffered in the aftermath of the nuclear explosion in New York.

"Great to see you back to a hundred percent, Commander," Conner said as he clasped Hart's hand with both of his.

"It's good to be back, Sir."

Hart's wounds had indeed healed, but his physicians at Walter Reed had cautioned Hart that he was not out of the woods. There might be long-term sequelae resulting from the high dose of radiation he had received. Not one to worry about risks he could not mitigate, Hart had dismissed the doctors' concerns with a polite but succinct, "Thank you."

Conner continued, "I have a feeling we are going to need your talents on this one."

"Ready to Lead, Ready to Follow, Never Quit, Sir!" Hart repeated a SEAL mantra.

"That's what I wanted to hear, Commander. Have a seat; I'm going to call us to order."

All of the attendees had filed in during the brief time that Conner and Hart chatted. The president took his seat at the head of the long table and waited for the din of conversation to fade before beginning his address.

"Ladies and gentlemen, in a few minutes, we will be connected with Prime Minister Rabinovich, as well as General Simon and Mr. Chaikin. Ambassador Lerner, who will be joining us momentarily, conveyed an urgent message earlier today from the prime minister. Mr. Rabinovich believes that Israel may be facing a grave threat. As you will soon hear, it relates to a recent meeting of the Syrian Coalition, coupled with intelligence that appears to portend the imminence of an attack on Israel."

A brief stir among the attendees caused Conner to raise his hands, then push in a downward motion as if to put a lid on the volume.

"We only have a few minutes . . . if I may continue." The room grew silent. "I am going to ask that you remain in your seats after we terminate the call so that we may debrief. Depending upon what we hear, I may elect to include the ambassador in that discussion. If so, I ask that you speak openly in our ally's presence."

At precisely two p.m., Lerner was shown into the room just as Prime Minister Rabinovich's face appeared on camera. His normal smile was replaced by the look of a deeply troubled man, but his opening words were spoken with genuine warmth.

"Good morning, Mr. President. My colleagues and I extend our well wishes to you and your colleagues, and we thank you for honoring our urgent request."

"I'm pleased we could comply, Prime Minister. You have our rapt attention."

"I believe everyone knows David Chaikin," Rabinovich said, though he knew that Israel's chief spook needed no introduction. "I'm going to ask Mr. Chaikin to brief you on a recent meeting that took place at Doshan-Tappeh airbase near Tehran and its potential implications to Israel."

Chaikin's brilliance was evident the moment he opened his mouth, though he often tried to mute his intellectual prowess so as not to be misperceived as arrogant. He began with a roll-call of the attendees who had been present at Doshan-Tappeh, punctuated at the end by a single observation. "These, ladies and gentlemen, are the executioners assembled to bring death to the state of Israel."

"With all due respect, Mr. Chaikin, that's a bold assertion without substantiation," Conner said.

"Allow me to provide some substantiation—including intelligence gleaned in the last few hours." Chaikin then shared Assad's mid-air conversations with his most senior general and his wife.

"Again, Mr. Chaikin, it could simply be hyperbole."

"President Conner, would such words appear to be hyperbole if spoken by sworn adversaries of the United States? I mean no disrespect, Sir, just a perspective. There is more evidence, however. We've detected troop movement, accompanied by artillery, in western Syria. It appears that Syrian Army, IRGC, and Hezbollah are consolidating close to the Golan."

Rabinovich motioned for Chaikin to be seated, then stood as he prepared to address the group.

"We are a tough country, President Conner, but not tough enough to battle a united front of Syria, Iran,

Hezbollah, and Russia. The Syrian Coalition could represent an existential threat to Israel."

Existential threat was code for justifying Israel's use of nuclear weapons—a fact that was not lost on a single attendee.

"Whatever the threat, it needs to be contained rapidly," Conner stated.

"And how do you propose to do that, Mr. President?"

"By pledging the full military support of the United States in the protection of our ally, Israel. That's something Mr. Putin will understand."

"And will you have the support of your public and Congress for such a pledge? Your country tires of war, and there are ongoing calls for full withdrawal of all U.S. troops from the Middle East."

"Congress understands the strategic significance of Israel, but more importantly, they appreciate the moral responsibility of the United States to defend it. We won't have an issue, Mr. Prime Minister."

"I appreciate your optimism, President Conner. Despite our resolve, remember that Israel is a small country threatened by giants."

"Your people have already proven that a mere sling is sufficient to bring down giants," Conner remarked. "Let's hope that we can contain whatever conflict emerges, and there is no need for further discussion of escalation to unconventional weapons."

"I pray you are right, my friend."

"In addition to CENTCOM's current integration with IDF, I would like a personal emissary on-site at the Bor . . . someone who will be privy to all operational issues as they emerge in real time. I assume that's not too much to ask, Mr. Rabinovich, in exchange for our pledge of support?"

"Who do you have in mind, Mr. President?"

Conner gestured to his right. "Commander Hart. He can be on-site no later than tomorrow morning."

Hart needed no introduction. Rabinovich was acutely aware of the role the commander had played in stopping the biological and nuclear attacks on the U.S.

"We welcome you, Commander. Let us know as soon as your flight plan has been filed and we will arrange transportation from Ben Gurion Airport to the Kiryat."

The Kiryat was the government complex housing key elements of Israel's defense infrastructure.

"There you will meet with the Security Council, as well as those on today's video uplink."

"I will look forward to that, Sir."

When the satellite link was severed, the room seemed to take a deep breath.

"Mr. Lerner, I'm going to ask that you remain while we debrief."

The ambassador nodded in agreement, appreciative of Conner's efforts at transparency.

Joe Sanford, the recently appointed Chairman of the Joint Chiefs of Staff, was first to speak. "I think we may be reading too much into Assad's comments. Though it may be the aspirations of the Coalition to annex Israel, they've just finished one bloody war with tremendous attrition . . . I doubt they are in the mood for another."

"I'm not sure I agree with you, Joe," said Katherine Wolf, the Director of Central Intelligence. "Since the Islamic Revolution in '79, Iran has been counting down the days until the destruction of Israel. If we look beyond the issue of battle-fatigued troops, the timing is quite good for an attack. Coalition troops are poised within striking distance of Israel's borders, and an armed Hezbollah and Hamas are chomping at the bit to strike Israeli cities with their missiles. I think the threat is quite real."

"What are you hearing from your counterparts in Israel?" Conner asked Wolf.

"They're nervous. You saw Amos Yadlin's comments in the spring of 2018. The former head of Israeli military intelligence believes that the coming months could be the most perilous time that Israel has faced in decades. The timing of his prediction may have been too aggressive, but I think his sentiment was right on point."

"Commander Hart, I want impeccable coordination between CENTCOM and IDF, and I want to be kept abreast, by the minute if necessary, of any substantive changes in the situation. Let's get out ahead of this one . . . not have to clean up afterwards. Is that understood, Commander?"

"Yes, Sir!"

Addressing the room, Conner added, "The region is like a pine forest during a drought. It won't take much to set it ablaze. If ignited, the resulting conflagration could easily spread beyond regional borders and evolve into a world war. Russia doesn't want that, but the Iranian theocracy is less predictable. Be prepared to meet at a moment's notice. Thank you—you are dismissed."

Before Hart could leave, Conner cornered him. "John, you are the one I rely on when things go to hell. You've never let me down, and I know you won't this time."

"No, Sir, I won't."

"I've asked Mr. Kahn to have a Gulfstream fueled and ready to go at 1800 hours. That'll give you a few hours to go home, pack, and talk to Liz. You may be gone for a while, Commander."

"Liz will understand, Sir."

"Good luck, Commander!"

"Thank you, Sir."

CHAPTER SIX

Hart Prepares to Leave

HART'S MIND WAS IN OVERDRIVE as he climbed into the form-fitting, black leather seat of his aging 850ci BMW. He fired up the 12-cylinder engine and tapped the gas, raising the car's baritone wail by an octave, then waited for the RPMs to fall before dropping it into gear. It was his one material indulgence—an exquisitely tuned machine that fed his need for speed. His destination was Georgetown, where he shared a two-bedroom condo with his wife, Dr. Elizabeth Wilkins.

As the blocks ticked by, Hart wondered what awaited him in Israel. He hoped that the anticipated threat of an attack by the Syrian Coalition proved to be much ado about nothing. But something in his gut told him otherwise. Israel had long been at a tipping point, and Hart sensed that the fine line separating peace and world war was about to be crossed.

He mused about his fate: How long would he be there? Would he return? How would Liz handle it if he was killed in action? These were new thoughts to the battle-hardened warrior—thoughts he had never before permitted to enter his mind.

"I guess this is what happens when you get married," he said to himself as if surprised. He'd never before questioned whether he would emerge from a mission intact, nor if anyone would shed a tear if he failed to survive.

Hart and Wilkins were newlyweds, married for less than a year. It had been a tumultuous courtship bookended by the two terrorist attacks on their country. The couple vowed that, if they could survive those calamities, they could survive marriage.

They were wed in a small ceremony at Trinity United Methodist Church in McLean, Virginia. Two people officiated over the private ceremony—Pastor Scott Hamilton and President Jonathan Conner. At the time of their marriage, the commander was still on the mend, while his wife was commuting weekly to her job at the CDC in Atlanta.

Liz had always viewed her work at the CDC as far more of a calling than a career. Her responsibilities in the BioLevel-IV laboratory involved studying some of the most deadly viruses and bacteria known to man—so-called "Category A" pathogens.

Each time she entered the lab, Liz donned an impenetrable space suit tethered to long hoses that kept her bathed in clean air. When she left, a strict process for decontamination was required. Yet, even with its unusual demands, it never felt like work to Liz . . . she was fascinated at the efficiency with which such organisms killed, and it became her personal mission to discover ways to defeat them.

Yet, despite her insatiable appetite for learning and her commitment to the CDC, the strain of living apart five days a week had taken a toll. Having twice looked death in the face, she had a new-found appreciation for the fleetingness of life. Now, more than anything, she yearned for a simple life with the man she loved. After discussing it with John, she had tendered her resignation three months earlier.

When President Conner learned of her decision, he implored Liz to remain in government. She had proven invaluable during the bioterrorism attack, and Conner didn't want to lose her. With the president's encouragement, Liz accepted a position as the CIA's senior counter-terrorism analyst over biological threats on the day her resignation from CDC took effect. She now shared both home and work with the Commander.

Without taking his eyes off the road, Hart pressed the speed-dial button on his phone. Liz answered on the second ring.

"Hello, Cowboy, to what do I owe the pleasure?" she cooed playfully. It was her pet name for her lover—one that not only captured his persona, but also alluded to his years spent growing up on a Montana ranch.

Hart's tone was not so playful. "Darling . . . I am glad I caught you. I'm headed back to the condo to pick up my things before catching a flight out of town. What are the chances of you taking off early today and meeting me there . . . say, in thirty minutes?"

"I'm putting on my coat as we speak. I'll see you shortly." Liz could read between the lines. John would never cavalierly request that she play hookey in the middle of the day unless something was up.

Traffic was still light at three p.m., and it took little time for Hart to traverse the twenty blocks to the condo. Liz was not far behind.

Hart had already begun to pack when he heard Liz turning the lock on the front door.

A moment later, she was standing at the door of the bedroom. She greeted him with a kiss before eyeing the large suitcase atop the bed.

"That's no overnight bag, Commander. It looks like you're planning to be gone for a while."

"I don't know. We'll see."

"Can you be less cryptic, Cowboy?"

Since the earliest days of their relationship, there had been a tug-of-war over what Hart could reveal about his missions. Much of that schism had been mended when President Conner intervened, and with her new position, raised the level of Liz's security clearance to that of the commander's. Yet some tension still remained.

With one hand, he raised his finger to his lips to quell the conversation, and with the other he pointed towards their second bedroom, which served as Hart's office. It had been rendered secure from electronic eavesdropping by the Agency.

"You and your secrecy," Liz chided him. "I'm sure that Mrs. Tupper next door is listening with bated breath to our every word." Still, she retreated to the safety of the office.

Hart closed the door before speaking. "I'm leaving for Israel in a few hours. The president has asked me to be his liaison to the Israeli Security Cabinet until otherwise ordered."

"What does that mean? Why is he sending you there?"

"Things appear to be heating up."

"What do you meaning, 'heating up'? How much hotter can they get?"

"I can't get into the details. Suffice it to say there are credible threats against the security of Israel, and the president wants someone on the ground apprising him of any material developments in real time."

"When will you be back?"

"Come on, Darling, how many times have we been through this? I may be home in a few days . . . or a few weeks . . . at the outside, a few months. It's out of my control."

He could see the disappointment in her face. He took her hand in his and guided it gently towards his lips. Kissing it softly, he looked directly into Liz's eyes. "I won't keep you in the dark. I promise."

"You damn well better not, Cowboy!" Liz said with a smile that broke the tension. "Are we done?" she asked.

"Yes, but what's the rush?"

"I thought you had a plane to catch. Come on. I'll help you finish packing."

The Gulfstream comfortably seated twelve, but Hart was its only passenger. The flight from Washington National to Ben Gurion International would take approximately nine hours—landing at eleven o'clock the following morning. Hart knew there would be little chance for sleep once he hit the ground, so he'd better rest now.

He closed his eyes and thought about Liz. Then he turned his attention towards God. Prayer was something new to the commander. Though he had been brought up in a conservative Christian family, Hart's relationship with God had been virtually severed when his youngest brother, Matthew, died while under his watch.

His mother had asked him to keep an eye on the boy for an hour, and promised a fresh-baked cherry pie in return. She didn't need to ask twice—they bolted out the door like a rocket and made a beeline towards the pond. As they approached the muddy bank, John cautioned his younger brother.

"I'm going to teach you how to skip rocks, then I'm going to leave you for just a few minutes to practice while I go hunting for a prairie dog." He pointed to his .22 caliber rifle and nodded confidently. "You know Dad says their holes can cause our cows to break a leg. We wouldn't want that, would we?"

Matthew shook his head *no*.

"I don't want you getting any closer to the water. And do not climb up on the dock. It's not safe. Do you understand me, Matt?"

Matthew nodded his head, *yes*.

Before embarking on his safari, John armed Matthew with a dozen flat skipping stones, and provided him with a modicum of instruction. He reiterated his message to stay away from the water and the dock . . . then left the boy alone.

Less than ten minutes elapsed before John returned from a successful hunt holding one very dead prairie dog in his left hand and his rifle in his right. As he cleared a ridge, the lake came into sharp focus. Matthew was nowhere to be found. John dropped the animal carcass and rifle, and began running full-bore towards the pond.

As he drew closer, he could see beyond the end of the dock—to a body floating faced down in the water. Screaming for help, he dragged Matthew's lifeless body out of the water, but it was too late. He was gone.

That moment in time forever changed the trajectory of John Hart's life. When his second brother was killed in the Twin Towers, any lingering belief in God died with him.

Had it not been for his survival against impossible odds during two terrorist attacks, the commander's heart might have remained forever closed. But those experiences, coupled with his ever-deepening love for Liz, brought grace . . . and with it, the rekindling of his faith. Finishing his prayers, Hart whispered *Amen* before drifting off to sleep.

He remained asleep until the vibrations of his phone brought him back to the moment. He glanced at it to see who was calling. It was CIA Deputy Director Kahn on the line.

"Yes, Sir," Hart answered.

"It's begun, Commander. Gaza has erupted in violence."

CHAPTER SEVEN

Trouble in Gaza

THE ANCIENT TOWN OF BEIT HANOUN was located proximate to the northeastern tip of the Gaza strip . . . within striking distance of Israel. Control of the town had traded hands innumerable times since the rule of Philistine King Hanoun in the eighth century BCE. Today, it was governed by Hamas and served as the launching point for reconnaissance missions into the Jewish state.

But it was not an intelligence gathering operation that caused two men to huddle in the still of a spring night. One of the men would give his life in service to Allah while claiming the lives of countless infidels. The other would remain behind, but with an equal measure of blood upon his hands.

It was four a.m. on May 15. Kamal Hussein had waited patiently for this day . . . a day when the existential pain and hopelessness that permeated the Gaza and defined his life would be replaced with the raptures of heaven. It was a prize to be won through martyrdom, and his life seemed a meager bargaining chip in exchange for such ecstasy.

The 23-year-old Palestinian laborer stood perfectly straight and motionless as Yousef Mustapha cinched the straps securing the suicide vest until it fit tightly against his chest. It was heavier than Kamal remembered from training, weighing nearly twenty kilos. The device contained an explosive core of PETN (pentaerythritol tetranitrate) embedded within a lattice of nails, screws, and ball bearings. One for each Jew, he told himself.

Kamal raised his arms above his head and pulled a soiled t-shirt over the vest before putting on his jacket. Yousef helped him carefully thread the detonator switch down the right sleeve until it was flush with his wrist. He secured it in position with duct tape.

He felt no remorse . . . not a tinge of anxiety as Yousef lifted the trapdoor, revealing a meticulously constructed tunnel. It ran under the Israeli border, terminating in a safe house where he would be met by his handler.

"It's time, Kamal," Yousef instructed. Dawn would break in two hours, and with it, Kamal would lose the protective cover of darkness. He embraced his friend, knowing that it was the last time he would see him alive. "I will see you in Paradise, my brother."

Kamal reached up and turned on the small headlamp strapped to his forehead before descending the ten-foot ladder. Seconds later, his feet hit the cool, dry earth. He lowered his head, bent his knees, and began a stooped march towards his ultimate emancipation.

He was not alone in his mission. That night, Hamas deployed twelve suicide bombers to bring carnage to the Jewish state. It was May 15—the day following Israeli Independence Day, and the date that Palestinians had been exiled from their homes. There was no better time for a blood-bath.

After an hour, Kamal's back ached and his legs felt like rubber, but he trudged on. God demanded that Israel be punished for its aggression against the Palestinian people and he, Kamal Hussein, was God's avenger.

Thirty minutes later, the guide wire that ran the length of the tunnel came to abrupt end. Ahead was a solid wall of earth, but to his right was a ladder. He summoned the strength to pull himself up the rungs, then slowly pressed against the wooden door. As it opened, straw fell through the opening, suggesting he might be in a barn. Like a rat wearily emerging from a sewer pipe, Kamal crawled out of his hole, grateful to be safely behind enemy lines. As he rotated his head, the lamp's beam sliced through the darkness and revealed a man sitting on a stool.

"You are one step closer to Paradise, my friend. Here, let me help you up," the man said as he extended his hand to Kamal. "You can call me, Ali. Make yourself comfortable. We are going to be here for a while. Would you like a cup of coffee?"

"Yes, thank you," said Kamal as he accepted the steaming cup. "Will you tell me my target, Ali?"

"You do not know?"

"They only told me that I would claim the lives of countless Jews."

"If Allah wills it, you will be so blessed. Your target is Sderot." He paused before continuing. "See that book satchel in the corner?"

"Yes."

"You will carry it slung over your shoulder as you approach the quadrangle of Sapir Academic College . . . it's the largest public college in Israel. You will appear to be just another student on his way between classes, until you press the detonator."

"And when will that be?" Kamal's voice revealed his eagerness.

"Patience, Kamal, your time is close at hand. You will strike between 9 and 9:10 a.m. when the quad is filled with students shuttling between their first and second hour classes."

Kamal nodded in acknowledgement. He reached out his hand to accept the steaming cup of coffee from his handler. "Thank you," he smiled, seemingly untouched by the fate that awaited him.

"When will my parents be paid?" he asked. A hefty stipend was given to the family of suicide bombers.

"Immediately following your funeral. Don't worry, my friend, they will be well taken care of, and although their loss will be great, they will take great pride in your sacrifice."

"I hope they understand that I do this in the name of all of Palestine."

"They will understand. Who knows better the bitter fruit of occupation than those who have long suffered, like your parents? Their son will be the deliverer of retribution. You will inflict untold carnage upon the Jews. They will no longer walk the streets without being wary, nor sleep soundly in their beds, fearing the next concussive sound of a bomber claiming his victims. Rest. We leave in a few hours."

Kamal closed his eyes and disappeared into a fog of memory until he was shaken by Ali.

"It's time," Ali told the young man as he prepared to escort him to the campus. "I'll accompany you as far as the outer perimeter of Highway 232. From there, it's a short walk to the school."

"God will guide me," Kamal said without hesitation.

It was a beautiful morning graced by crystal blue skies and no humidity. Kamal could hear the excited buzz of hundreds of students as he cleared the Academy Gate and headed northwest towards the Student Complex across from the library. He no longer strained under the weight of the vest, but felt a buoyancy unlike anything he'd experienced before.

He merged seamlessly into the flow of bodies traversing the campus. It was precisely 9:05 a.m. when he began to recite his prayers.

Two minutes later, he stopped mid-stride. He stared at the heavens then shouted, "Allah Akbar!" before depressing the switch.

In a millisecond, scorching hot metal ripped through the flesh of anyone within Kamal's line of sight. Students dropped to the ground mid-stride. Dismembered bodies soon lined the sidewalks, and blood soaked the grass until it was stained red. Kamal's headless torso lay amid the dead and dying.

At 9:17, Rabinovich's eyes were riveted on a television screen in the Bor's conference room. He'd received the news moments earlier, but he was now witnessing firsthand the destructive aftermath of a suicide bombing. CNN International had interrupted regularly scheduled

programming with a live broadcast from Sderot. A tightly framed shot of the reporter obscured much of the carnage, but Rabinovich sensed intuitively that dozens had died.

"At approximately 9:10 a.m., a powerful explosion rocked this peaceful campus located a mere two kilometers from the border with Gaza. Witnesses described a horrific scene in which the bodies of countless young people lay eviscerated by shrapnel . . . those not dead were crying out in pain."

She paused while the cameraman widened out the shot to reveal a still sanitized version of the mayhem.

"No one knows for certain what the final death count will be, but preliminary estimates from Home Front Security forces put the number killed and wounded in excess of a hundred." She signed off. "Tavia Hadeth, reporting from Sderot."

Members of the Israeli Security Cabinet began pouring into the conference room. It would be their job to formulate a response. Rabinovich rose to his feet as he prepared to address the group, but before he could speak, an aide burst through the door.

"It had better be important," Rabinovich growled.

"Sir, it appears that the attacks are not over."

Within minutes of the first attack, another historic town fell victim to suicide bombers. Founded 4,000 years before the birth of Christ, Beersheba played an important biblical role. It was here that Abraham, the father of the Jewish people, entered into a compact with the Philistine King Abimelech.

The city's fortunes waxed and waned through the ensuing millennia, but by modern times it had grown into a substantial metropolitan area with a population exceeding

250,000. Though the metroplex sprawled across a vast stretch of the Negev desert, there were only a handful of sites where people congregated in mass—one of which was Anzac Memorial Center. Built to honor Aussie and Kiwi troops who had given their lives to defeat the Turks in Palestine during World War I, the memorial had become Beersheba's premier tourist attraction.

A few minutes before the memorial was scheduled to open at nine a.m., a long line had snaked behind ropes leading to the ticket booth. Situated in the middle of the crowd, awaiting entry, was Noor Talal—an attractive young woman wearing a brightly colored headscarf. She chatted nonchalantly with the people next to her in line, smiling broadly as they shared their excitement at seeing the memorial. When the door to the Anzac Memorial opened, Noor closed the firing switch on her suicide vest. No one would recall whether she shouted "Allah Akbar."

Noor Talal was not the only one to rain down terror on Beersheba that morning. Seconds later, a second bomber detonated his vest at Chaikin's Well, also a well-known tourist attraction located on the west side of Old Town.

Ashkelon was next . . . and then Ashdod.

The sounds of cascading explosions reverberated off buildings. Windows burst, forming thousands of jagged projectiles that careened through the air before impaling soft flesh. In all, 223 people died in the attacks, and an additional 417 were injured. Body parts blanketed the sidewalks: heads, arms, and legs torn from their torsos.

The wounded wandered about in a daze. Sirens wailed as paramedics raced to victims, but for many it would be too late.

"My God, my God, what have they done!" Rabinovich said, head held low, before the panicked tone of CNN's Tavia Hadeth summoned his attention once again. The piercing sound of air-raid sirens could be heard above the din of ambulances.

Holding a hand over her earpiece and straining to hear, Hadeth reported, "We don't know what is happening, but the air-raid sirens just sounded."

Her voice was laced with fear as she and her cameraman ran for shelter . . . the televised image from their camera jumping crazily with every stride. Before they could reach safe cover, there was a flash, and the image vanished.

The talking head of the CNN anchor reappeared, "We seemed to have lost our connection with Tavia Hadeth in Sderot. We will bring you an update as soon as we have reestablished a feed from the area."

Rabinovich slammed his fist against the table, "Those sons of bitches. They waited for our first responders to tend to the dying before unfurling their missiles. There can be no mercy for such animals!" he shouted.

Shortly before his plane was scheduled to touch down, Commander Hart opened his laptop and selected the CNN app from the browser. His home page faded, yielding to the image of a reporter surrounded by smoking rubble and what appeared to be bodies. He plugged in his headphones just as the journalist was finishing her broadcast.

"No one knows if the simultaneous attacks that rocked the Israeli-Gaza border are over. What we do know is that hundreds of innocent civilians have been killed or seriously injured in the suicide bombings and missile attacks." She paused, struggling to compose herself as she delivered the final line. "Among the casualties was CNN's Tavia Hadeth. Keira Alon reporting from Beersheba."

The captain opened the cockpit door, waited while Hart removed his earphones, then informed him that they would be arriving shortly.

Hart said nothing but simply nodded in acknowledgment. As he closed his laptop and returned it to his carry-on bag, he wondered how fast things would escalate. Rabinovich would call for a massive retaliatory strike . . . that was almost guaranteed. But were the border bombings just the first step in a more systematic attack on Israel? Only time would tell.

His mind turned to the innumerable war games he had participated in through the years. Many scenarios began with an attack on Israel, which ultimately escalated into World War III. Surely not, he said under his breath, but he knew it was an ever-present possibility.

The wheels screeched as the jet's tires slapped against the tarmac. The pilot reversed thrust on the twin Rolls Royce BR710 engines, reducing the plane to taxiing speed as he navigated towards an IAF installation.

Hart quickly thanked the crew before walking briskly down the stairs and onto the tarmac, where Moshe Simon awaited him.

"General, I wasn't expecting you," Hart said, surprised to see Israel's highest ranking officer at the airport.

"And I'm glad to see you, too," an unfazed Simon said as he gave his old friend a bear hug.

"Are you aware of what transpired this morning?"

"I just saw it on CNN. Has your government responded?"

Simon looked down at his watch. "It is beginning as we speak. The IAF will be flying a dozen sorties. Their assignment is to neutralize any imminent threat of further Hamas attacks without consideration of collateral damage."

"You know you will be fodder for the world's press," Hart cautioned.

"Yes, the press that doesn't give a rat's ass about Jews . . . hundreds of whom were massacred this morning. We are responding to a threat that can no longer be tolerated. Let them label us as mass murderers. All I care about is preventing a repeat of the carnage we witnessed earlier today.

"And, by the way, welcome to Israel, Commander."

CHAPTER EIGHT

A Brazen Attack on the Eastern Flank

RABINOVICH WALKED BRISKLY, his right hand extended like a spear, as he greeted his American guest.

"Commander, I'm sorry to be welcoming you under such difficult circumstances," Rabinovich said as Hart entered the Bor's conference room. "We didn't expect Hamas to hit us so hard and so fast."

"I understand, Sir, and I am sorry for your losses."

Rabinovich nodded.

"I am here, Mr. Prime Minister, to aid you in any way that I can. Those were President Conner's explicit orders."

"Do you know what a *brocheh* is, Commander?" Rabinovich asked, his hand resting on Hart's shoulder.

"I believe it is a blessing, Sir."

"That's right, Commander, and we know you will be a brocheh to Israel. Have a seat. The show is about to begin."

Across the monitors, Hart could see images of planes closing in on their targets. Lasers illuminated buildings seconds before smart bombs and missiles rained down with a fury.

Thousands of Palestinians were decimated, and though Hart understood the rationale for striking structures with resounding force, it sickened him to think about the women and children being torn apart without warning, just as it sickened him to think about Sderot, Beersheba, Ashkelon, and Ashdod. Maybe he was getting too old for the job, he mused.

The relentless pounding of Gaza went on for several hours, after which the smoke from countless fires obliterated the sky and obscured the view of surveillance satellites. Hart's phone rang. Kahn was on the line.

"Will you excuse me, Sir? It's the DDO . . . I assume he's wanting an update."

"Of course. Colonel Marks will show you to the SCIF, where you will have complete privacy."

Once ensconced in the sensitive compartmented information facility, Hart took the call.

"He's waiting to speak to you, Commander." The voice belonged to Dottie, the Deputy Director's long-time admin at CIA Headquarters.

"What the hell is going on over there?" Kahn said by way of a greeting. "We can't see a damn thing through all the smoke, except for the infrared images. It looks like the Gaza has been turned into a God damned inferno."

"I can't blame the Israelis for retaliating, Sir. I'm sure you've seen the images from the border towns."

"Yes. Hamas are animals! I can't comprehend what their leadership thought would be accomplished through such provocation. They had to know that the Israelis would counter-strike with overwhelming force."

"*Animals* is the same word Prime Minister Rabinovich used to describe the attackers. He ordered multiple sorties by the IAF using precision-guided munitions without regard to collateral damage. The casualties will likely be in the thousands." Hart's tone was sorrowful, not resolute.

"Would you have responded differently?" Kahn asked, picking up on the tenor of Hart's voice.

"No, Sir. But I can still feel grief for the civilians who have died unnecessarily . . . on both sides."

"Blame the fucking rigidity of Hamas and their insistence on the destruction of Israel, Commander. Those people don't deserve your pity. Remember, you are not there to be a philosopher or a politician. You are there to ensure that Israel survives and thrives, by whatever means are necessary."

"Yes, Sir."

"Any reports yet on the success of their strikes?"

"It's my understanding, Sir, that they've hit ninety percent of their targets."

"I wish we could achieve those kinds of numbers," Kahn mused before snapping back to a more strident tone. "I'll expect to hear from you the moment anything else of consequence transpires. Is that clear, Commander?"

"Crystal clear, Sir."

It was a classic interchange between a warrior and his master. Hart submitted to Kahn's questioning with appropriate deference, though both men knew Hart retained a fierce sense of independence. That streak of self-reliance, at times, made Kahn crazy. But he knew that Hart was the most gifted agent ever deployed by the Agency.

After hanging up, Hart reflected on his comments, wondering if his empathy for the unfolding tragedy communicated a lack of strength. He had stopped cataclysm after cataclysm, and yet now he was being cautioned not to be weak. What had happened to his resolve—the grit that helped him survive the unimaginable? He shook his head, hoping to clear the emotional fog affecting his thinking, as he walked slowly back to the conference room.

Liz was making her final edits to a report when someone knocked on the half-open door to her office.

"I didn't mean to interrupt you, Dr. Wilkins." The voice belonged to DDO Marvin Kahn.

"I was just finishing up a report," she said with a smile. "I don't see you on this floor very often, Mr. Kahn. What brings you?"

"May I ask what your report is about?"

"Of course. It's on the potential dangers inherent in a series of new gene-editing software programs that I'm concerned will facilitate the creation of novel pathogens."

"Like the one that nearly caused a global pandemic?" he asked, referring to the genetically-modified, hemmorhagic smallpox unleashed on the nation's airports. Had it not been for Wilkins' and Hart's intervention, a global pandemic would have ensued.

"You aren't here to talk to me about bugs . . . so why are you here, Sir?"

"I just spoke with Commander Hart, and I wanted to bring you up to speed."

"He's okay, right?" Liz felt her heart racing.

"He's quite secure and will remain that way, but Israel is under attack. There have been a rash of suicide bombings over the past few hours in towns along their southern border. In response, they've unleased holy hell on the Gaza, please pardon my language, Doctor."

Liz turned away to collect her thoughts. John wouldn't be coming home any time soon.

"I didn't want you to hear it on the news without hearing from me, first." Kahn told her.

"Thank you. That was kind of you, Sir."

CHAPTER NINE

Escalation

BODY COUNTS WERE STILL FLOODING INTO THE BOR from that morning's bombings when the first barrage of artillery shells began to strike the Golan Heights. Israeli soldiers ran for cover as the high-pitched whistle of incoming 120 mm high explosive rounds, fired from fortified positions within Syria, cut through the air, portending death and destruction. Seconds later, dirt and debris were flung high as the rounds carved gaping holes in the terrain.

Colonel Yitzhak Hammer scrambled for the safety of the command bunker but failed to reach it in time. A shell exploded feet from where he stood. Spotting the fallen officer, a medic rushed to his aid, but it was too late. His intestines spilled out from a gaping abdominal wound, and blood spurted from a severed femoral artery. Death came quickly as Hammer bled out.

He was neither the first nor last man, however, to die defending the Golan.

This strategically significant strip of land had remained under Syrian control for nearly twenty years following the formation of Israel. Rising to a height of 1,700 feet, the

Golan provided Israel's enemy with an elevated position from which to shoot down upon their Jewish neighbors. During the Six Day War, the Syrians' sporadic sniping escalated into a full-scale artillery bombardment of the eastern Galilee.

On June 9, 1967, Israel launched an all-out counter-offensive to capture the Golan. Within twenty-four hours, the mission was accomplished, and the Golan was secured. But Israel's hold over the region remained tenuous. During the Yom Kippur War in 1973, the Syrians momentarily regained the Golan Heights before being driven out by the IDF.

Israel was not about to let that happen again. In 1981, the Knesset annexed the Golan Heights, sending an indisputable message to the Syrian government regarding the land's sovereignty. Though sporadic provocations had continued through the years, nothing remotely approached what the Israelis were witnessing on this day.

The shelling was relentless—round after round striking without reprieve. While most of the projectiles did little more than pock-mark the landscape, others scored direct hits, destroying fortified positions and killing or maiming IDF forces. There was nowhere to run and nowhere to hide. The Israeli soldiers were trapped amidst the shower of incoming shells.

Then, as suddenly as it had begun, the shelling ended.

After ten minutes of uninterrupted silence, soldiers cautiously emerged from their burrows, wondering if this was the proverbial calm before the storm. That question was answered in minutes as glinting specks of silver were spotted streaking across the azure blue sky. Spotters identified the outlines of Su-24s preparing to cross Israeli airspace and quickly sounded the warning. Round two of the storm was sweeping in, and IDF troops scrambled to move underground.

Based out of the T4 Airbase near Tyas, the Sukhoi-24 was a high-speed penetration bomber developed by the former Soviet Union in the 1980s. Though its technology was thirty years old, it remained deadly—having been upgraded by the Russians with sophisticated heads-up displays, targeting computers, and navigation systems. Its pilots, members of the 827 Squadron, were Syria's best.

The bombers struck in a thunderous wave, unleashing a combination of thermobaric and cluster bombs. The devastation was immediate and massive. Hundreds of soldiers perished in the assault despite being dug-in.

An aide burst through the door of the Bor's conference room. "Forgive my interruption, Prime Minister, but Major Tovah is on the comm with an urgent call for General Simon."

"Why are you standing there? Put him through!" Rabinovich bellowed as he looked across the table to his general. "Moshe, I'm afraid your major won't be bringing us good tidings."

Tovah's voice broke through the still of the conference room. The rumble of explosions was clearly audible in the background. "Sir, we're under heavy attack with a high level of casualties. Our position is tenuous."

Simon blinked in disbelief. "How could that happen, Major? Where is Colonel Hammer?"

Simon knew Hammer well. He had hand-picked the colonel to command forces on the Golan Heights—a prestigious appointment based upon the strategic significance of the Golan to Israel's defense.

"The colonel was among the first killed, Sir."

Simon lowered his gaze. "Go on," he said, trying to suppress the sadness and panic welling up in his gut. There would be a time for mourning, and it was not now.

"It began with an onslaught of 120 mm rounds pounding our positions. When that finally abated, we thought we might be in the clear. Then our spotters picked up a formation of Su-24s. The aerial bombing began a few minutes later. They hit us with thermobarics and cluster bombs. Thank God they missed the command bunker."

He paused, overwhelmed by the enormity of what he had witnessed, then continued. "We don't know what they're going to throw at us next, Sir, but I'm concerned that the men may not be able to hold their positions if the Syrians strike us in numbers."

"Hold your position, Major. That's an order!" There was a steely coldness to Simon's voice.

"Yes, Sir!"

Simon disconnected the comm line before turning towards Rabinovich. "It's what I feared, and if I'm right, the next attack will originate in southern Lebanon."

"Let's pray you are wrong, Moshe," Rabinovich responded.

CHAPTER TEN

Israel Hits Back

EIGHTEEN MINUTES AFTER MOSHE SIMON ENDED the call with Major Tovah, the first Israeli Air Force F-16s and F-15s were crossing Syrian airspace en route to Homs and Damascus. Their orders were three-fold: Level the T-4 airbase that served as the launching pad for the aerial assault on the Golan; inflict maximum damage on the presidential palace and key governmental buildings in the heart of the Syrian capital; and search out and destroy any remaining enemy planes over the Golan.

Images from the squadron leader's aircraft were being beamed directly into the conference room, providing the pilot's view of the attack. Rabinovich leaned forward and rested his clenched fists against the table.

Within minutes of crossing the Syrian border, a cascade of red lights began to flash within the planes' cockpits, indicating the presence of incoming surface-to-air missiles. Urgent, escalating voice alerts instructed the pilots to take immediate evasive action.

The pilots, among the best trained in the world, had been schooled on the S400 Russian air defense system. But it was one thing to be lectured on its technical capabilities and quite another to experience it.

Without hesitation, they commenced swift, evasive maneuvers, deploying magnesium flares, chaff, and other counter-measures designed to foil the attack. Most of the missiles veered off course and eventually plummeted to the desert below; but four planes took direct hits. Two exploded in mid-air, while two crashed before their crew could eject. It was the first time since the Six-Day War that Israel had lost multiple aircraft to enemy forces.

"Bring 'em back, now, Moshe," Rabinovich ordered. "We need to regroup."

The General was already a step ahead of him . . . and praying that the remaining planes would reach Israeli airspace intact.

The Su-24s were returning to base after having dumped their bombs on the Golan. On the ground, spotters checked the sky to ensure that no enemy aircraft remained before sounding the all-clear. IDF troops took up positions on the eastern edge of the Golan, closest to Syria—not realizing that, though the threat from the air was over, another shit-storm was about to hit.

No sound foreshadowed the killing that followed. Four soldiers were felled where they stood, blood trickling out of bullet holes in their heads. Two had taken rounds to the forehead, another was shot through the right eye, and the final victim was hit in the mouth. All had been killed by Iranian snipers.

The sniper fire continued for an hour, with bullets whizzing precariously close to the helmets of Israeli infantry, sometimes missing by mere inches. There was little the IDF soldiers could do but hunker down and wait it out, since it might be hours before they had air or artillery support.

When the incoming rounds stopped, heavily armed men appeared, seemingly out of nowhere. As they emerged from their underground lairs within meters of IDF forces, they looked like ants scurrying from a disturbed nest. They opened up with automatic rifle fire. Everything up until that point had been a precursor to the brazen ground assault now being led by Quds Special Forces with the support of the Syrian Army and Hamas.

Their numbers were overwhelming. When one wave of invaders had been repelled, another took its place. In total, 25,000 enemy troops were engaged in the assault on the Golan.

Major Tovah called Simon to report in, though he knew the General's order to hold fast would remain despite its suicidal nature.

"I thought my orders were clear, Major?" a clearly irritated Simon barked.

"They are clear, Sir, but I need to apprise you of a new development. We are under siege by ground forces."

"Surely the Israeli Army can hold back beleaguered Syrian forces, Major!"

"Sir, it's not just the Syrians. It appears to be a combined army with Iranian Qud forces in the lead supported by Syrian Army regulars and Hezbollah."

"What are you estimating their troop strength to be, Major?"

"At a minimum, 15,000 . . . maybe as high as 25,000."

There was a long pause as Simon tried to process what he had just heard. Unless his intent was to sacrifice his men in an unwinnable battle, his prior order to hold their position was untenable.

"Pull back, now, Major . . . to the Jordan River if necessary. We'll get reinforcements to you as quickly as possible."

Tovah hung up the phone and sent the order up and down the lines. The troop withdrawal began immediately.

With the IDF in retreat, the Syrian Coalition swarmed over the full expanse of the Golan Heights. Cheers of victory reverberated from the mountain top. An Iranian sniper stood apart from the group, staring westward. He squinted until the faint outline of a human being came into focus, then picked up his rifle and adjusted the scope for elevation and wind. Peering through the eight power monocular sight, he could see that the soldier's uniform was caked with dried blood from what appeared to be a shoulder wound.

Just as he leveled the cross-hairs on the man's back, a Qud officer stepped forward and put his hand on the barrel, gently pushing it downward.

"Let him go, Sergeant. He's no threat to us. Come join your comrades. We have much to celebrate!"

"Do you have a problem with me ridding the world of one more Jew, Sir?" His belligerence was just below the threshold of insubordination.

"I have a problem with you wasting a bullet on such vermin. Come, join your comrades. That's an order."

Knowing that he would have to be alert in the hours and days ahead and exhausted from the incessant pace of developing threats, Abraham Rabinovich took a much needed break. Before leaving the conference room, he instructed Moshe Simon to summon him immediately if there were additional provocations during his absence.

He retired to his makeshift quarters, closed the door, loosened his tie, and sat down on the bed. Without taking his shoes off, he put his head on the pillow, stretched out his legs, and closed his eyes, just for a moment. As he did, an image of Rachel popped into his mind.

She, too, was potentially facing a deadly adversary, and he berated himself for failing to check on her. He pulled out his cell phone and pressed her speed-dial number. She answered on the third ring.

"I was wondering if I was going to hear from you," she said cheerfully. "When are you coming home, Avi?"

"Rachel, have you not see the news?" he asked incredulously.

"No. I've had back-to-back clients followed by a couple of crises."

"The State of Israel is in crisis!"

"What are you talking about?"

"A rash of suicide bombings in the Gaza, the overtaking of the Golan Heights by the Syrian Coalition, and the loss of four IAF planes and their crews. And I have a very sick feeling that there is more to come."

Her sharp inhalation told him he had made the point. "My God, I had no idea. You must be overwhelmed with things to do . . . why did you take time to call me?"

"I wanted to be reminded that there is good in the world," he said, his tone soft. "And I wanted to see if you had any more information from Dr. Eiseman. I know I gave short shrift to the issue of a lump in your breast. I'm sorry."

As strong as she was emotionally, Rachel could not contain the sobs that momentarily overtook her.

"I'm sorry, Avi. I promised myself I wouldn't do that. But I'm scared; scared of losing this precious life that you and I have made. It's perfect despite its imperfections."

"The flaws are mine to own," he smiled, hoping it somehow would be felt through the phone. "And you are not going anywhere. Whatever arises, we will deal with it."

"I think I should be saying that to you, my dear."

"I am and will continue to deal with it . . . to protect Israel and her people. I'm going to say goodbye for now, Rachel, but I promise I will talk with you again soon."

"I love you more than you will ever know."

"And I love you, Darling, and only wish that I did a better job of showing it at times."

He turned off the cell phone and returned it to his pocket. He set the alarm to go off in one hour. A cat nap was better than nothing.

CHAPTER ELEVEN

Missiles from the North

THE AIR IN THE CONFERENCE ROOM HAD GROWN HOT and stale in direct proportion to the number of bodies present. From a handful of men assembled that morning, the ranks had swelled dramatically as members of the National Security Council filed in.

The NSC served as the lead organization responsible for the aggregation and analysis of information—both foreign and domestic—related to Israel's defense. Formed in 1999, it had proven to be invaluable on numerous occasions, and Rabinovich had come to depend on its data-driven, strategic options at times of crisis. Oftentimes it was the only thing with the power to silence acrimonious debate.

"Don't we have any damned air-conditioning?" Rabinovich bellowed. "For God's sake, can we make this place habitable? We're going to be living here for a while."

A young aide picked up the phone and called engineering, relaying the prime minister's request verbatim. Within seconds, the first wave of cool air wafted through the room.

"That's better," he said, nodding to the aide.

"Now that I can concentrate, I'd like to turn our attention to Mr. Meir, whose penetrating voice we can hear above the collective din like a fishwife hawking her wares amidst an unruly crowd. You must be very confident of your position, Gabriel."

"I don't appreciate your sense of levity, Avi . . . certainly not when we are at war. But, yes, I'm quite confident of my position," the head of Security Policy for the NSC responded.

"I didn't realize that we had declared war . . . nor upon whom we made such a declaration," Rabinovich responded.

"Perhaps you think that the overtaking of the Golan Heights is a mere skirmish, or that the wave of suicide bombers was a minor act of terrorism . . . or, even more dangerously, that things won't continue to escalate."

"Quite the contrary . . . I think we are getting our asses kicked, and it's time we kicked back harder."

"Then you support my assertion that we have sufficient grounds for deploying unconventional weapons at this point."

"Excuse me, Mr. Meir," Hart stood and interjected. "You are speaking of nuclear weapons?" his tone one of disbelief.

Having witnessed the near annihilation of New York City following the detonation of a 15-kiloton nuclear bomb, Hart responded viscerally. He could taste the sickly sweet bile rise up in his gut in response to Meir's plea. It was madness to unleash such weapons, but before he could speak again, Rabinovich was on his feet.

"Gabe, you talk casually about unleashing our weapons, as though it would represent a minor escalation on our part. Yet tens, if not hundreds of thousands of people would die in the process. Israel would be a pariah among nations. Even the United States would disavow their relationship with us.

"Are you truly willing to accept that price . . . to incinerate tens of thousands of people in a few milliseconds? And how different would we be then from the Nazis who burned our people in ovens? We would simply be more efficient!" He shouted the last few words, pounding his fists on the table.

"Why do these weapons exist if not to protect the Jewish state? Are they but a bluff . . . a card we will never play? I'd rather go down in history as a protector of our people at horrific costs than stand by impotently as we are invaded!" Meir shouted back.

A red-faced Rabinovich started to respond, but Moshe Simon put his hand gently on the prime minister's shoulder, communicating that he would take the next round.

"I won't argue the moral appropriateness of nuclear weapons, but I will argue the timing from a military perspective. If we deploy them, we need to have absolute clarity regarding our target—which invader represents the greatest threat to our nation. Based upon the information filtering in, it appears that Iran, Syria, Hezbollah, Hamas, and presumably Russia are aligned. But which is the head of the serpent? Whom do we strike? I suggest that we keep our powder dry and respond strategically rather than impulsively, despite our anxiety."

Rabinovich turned towards Hart. "Commander, I don't normally put my guests in the hot seat, but I am ready for you to weigh in on this debate. You speak for President

Conner and as an astute military strategist. Lend us your perspective at this divisive time."

Hart was grateful to have had a few minutes to collect his thoughts. He understood the gravity of what he was about to say, and he chose his words with great care.

"Gentlemen, I can't fathom the existential angst that comes with being a small nation surrounded by powerful enemies intent on my country's destruction, nor the tremendous sense of responsibility each of you feels for protecting the people of Israel. But I have listened carefully to the arguments, and I believe I speak for President Conner when I say that the use of nuclear weapons, at this point in time, would be a grave mistake."

"You say you listened, Commander, but I see little evidence of that based upon your comments," Gabriel Meir snapped.

"Mr. Meir, I did listen, and I believe that General Simon has made a cogent argument. You have no evidence to suggest the imminent destruction of your state, nor a clear target for retribution. It takes only minutes for you to launch a nuclear weapon, but once deployed, it cannot be called back. You will have forever changed history, just as we did in August 1945."

He paused. "So my counsel to you is clear: Respond militarily as you must, but reserve the contemplation of weapons of mass destruction until there is unanimity of opinion that the future of Israel is in peril."

"Moshe, what is our strategy for the Golan?" Rabinovich moved on, hoping to put the argument about nukes to bed.

"We need to address the imbalance in troop strength. We've called up 10,000 reservists, but it will be forty-eight hours before they are ready for deployment. I'll let General Norkin speak to the IAF's response."

Fifty-three-year-old Major General Amikam Norkin had a long history with the IAF. In 1985, he had become the youngest F-15 pilot in the world. Handsome, smart, and a fierce warrior, he commanded tremendous respect from his troops.

"After losing four planes and four pilots, I'm not eager to send additional sorties into Syria at this time . . . " Norkin began.

Rabinovich interrupted, "Why not send in our F-35s? Why did we pay $200 million apiece if not for such an occasion?"

The Lockheed Martin F-35 Lightning II was the most advanced fighter jet in the world, capable of flying at Mach 1.6 and pulling nearly 9Gs. Its stealth design rendered it virtually undetectable by air defense systems, a fact bolstered by Israeli's insistence on incorporating its own electronic warfare equipment to ensure invisibility. The modified plane became known as the F-35I.

"Sir, we can deploy the F-35, and we know that there is an extremely low probability of detection, but allow me to suggest another alternative. Our priority, as I understand it, is to recapture the Golan, and to do so before the Syrian artillery is moved into positions that will enable the bombardment of vital parts of our country. Once the threat from the east is mitigated, there will be ample time for retribution."

"And so what precisely are you recommending, General?" Rabinovich pressed.

"I'm recommending that our F-15s begin saturation bombing of the Golan, while the F-16s provide supportive cover. We won't rout the enemy, but we will inflict heavy casualties and undoubtedly suspend the transport of heavy weapons into the region. The bombing will continue until our reservists are in position to launch a counter-attack."

"And if the Syrian Air Force responds with additional sorties of their Sukhoi-24s?"

"We will blow them out of the sky, Sir, as we have in every previous encounter with the Syrians."

Simon directed the next question to Norkin. "Tell us what has happened in Gaza, General."

"We have destroyed the major repositories for Hamas missiles, as well as their manufacturing facilities. Their command and control structure is no longer viable. We've also hit dozens of locations used to house troops. I would describe it as *utter and complete destruction*, Sir."

"At least that's one flank that no longer represents a threat. Thank you, General. Please have a seat," Rabinovich instructed before continuing. "Once we repulse the enemy in the Golan, much of our stability will be restored."

Heads around the conference room began to nod in consensus, giving Rabinovich the confidence he needed to reassert his aversion to nukes. "I believe that this information simply reaffirms the position shared by General Simon, Commander Hart, and myself regarding nuclear escalation. We will proceed as our military leaders have outlined—unless and until there is an unforeseen event that changes the calculus of this war. I suggest we return to our work and reconvene as needed."

Hart stood to leave, but Rabinovich motioned for him to stay. The prime minister waited until the conference room emptied before shutting the door.

"Sit, Commander. I'm only going to take a moment of your time."

"Yes, Sir."

"And you don't have to call me *Sir*. I'd prefer Avi."

"Yes, Sir."

Rabinovich chuckled for the first time since Hart's arrival. "Okay, Commander, I see that some things are just too ingrained to change. On a serious note, you were just privy to a conversation involving the contemplated use of nuclear weapons. I heard your words . . . highly rational, well-chosen words . . . in response to Mr. Meir, but now I want to hear from your heart. Before you speak, however, know that if another shoe drops, the pressure to utilize our most destructive weapons will escalate in proportion to the threat."

"If I may speak freely, Mr. Prime Minister . . . "

"That's what I'm asking for, John."

"It scares the living hell out of me. If you were to act as Mr. Meir advised, your presumed target of attack would be Damascus."

"And why not the entrenched forces in the Golan?"

"Because you will successfully remove the enemy with conventional forces and IAF bombs. Furthermore, you wouldn't want to render the area uninhabitable. But that won't eliminate an authoritarian regime poised on your border who has tasted blood. A 100-kiloton nuclear bomb mated to a cruise missile targeted at the presidential palace will put a permanent end to the brutal Assad reign."

"Would that be so bad?" Rabinovich asked, playing devil's advocate.

"We all want to see Basheer Al-Assad in a grave, but not accompanied by a quarter million civilians who may not share the same sentiment . . . people who have had little choice but to support the regime during the civil war. But that's not what scares me."

"I didn't realize anything frightened Navy SEALs, Commander."

"When you live through the detonation of a nuclear bomb or the release of a biological weapon, you gain an appreciation for the fragility of life, as well as for the darkest side of human nature. If you nuke the Syrians, or the Iranians for that matter, the Russians may elect to retaliate. And when that happens, America will be quickly drawn into direct confrontation with our most formidable adversary."

"It sounds like you are describing World War III, Commander."

"That is precisely what I am describing, Mr. Prime Minister."

"Let's hope it never comes to that," Rabinovich said in a subdued tone. "I know you must keep President Conner informed. Please give him my regards and tell him that we are doing our best to navigate the difficult road ahead."

"I will, Sir."

Hart excused himself and headed for the SCIF. Within seconds, Jonathan Conner was on the phone.

"What's happening there, Commander? We've been watching the Golan in real time and saw as it was overrun. I never thought I would witness an Israeli retreat." He paused. "We also know that Israel has lost four warplanes over western Syria—presumably to the newly installed S400 SAM batteries."

"That's correct, Sir. For the past hour, there has been an aggressive debate on how to respond . . . including the potential deployment of nuclear weapons."

"Tell me you're kidding, Commander. That would be political suicide. Every nation, including ours, would abandon Israel for the unjustified escalation."

"Yes, Sir, I told them as much. That debate has, for the time being, ended."

"Thank God you are there to lend a sane perspective and support the prime minister. He's got his hands full with the hard-right members of his party—especially Meir. I remember when people thought Avi was extreme. Now he's considered a moderate."

"Yes, Sir. Neither the prime minister or General Simon will respond in haste to a threat, but they will protect their country."

"Then let's pray that the other shoe that Avi alluded to never drops."

CHAPTER TWELVE

The Other Shoe Drops

TWO SHARP RAPS ON THE DOOR of his temporary quarters took Hart's eyes off of the casualty report he'd been studying and onto a statuesque IDF officer standing in the doorway. That was one of things he loved about Israel—women made up the majority of officers in the IDF.

"Can I help you, Ma'am?" he asked with a smile.

"Sir, the prime minister requests your presence in the conference room. He indicated it was urgent, Sir."

"Thank you. I'll be on my way momentarily."

"My orders are to escort you now, Commander," she replied firmly.

Hart tossed the report he was reading on the desk, grabbed his Navy jacket, and walked past the officer.

"I'm all yours, Lieutenant."

There was no playful repartee; the officer was all business, and Hart soon understood why.

Sadness seemed to envelop the conference room like an early morning fog. Rabinovich appeared deeply troubled.

"I'm afraid the situation is deteriorating, Commander. Hezbollah has begun launching rockets into Israel," Rabinovich said.

Hart imagined the second hand on the Doomsday clock moving one second closer to midnight.

Gabriel Meir approached, spewing his vitriol as he closed in. "Tell me, Commander Hart, do you now have sufficient evidence to justify Israel's use of nuclear weapons?"

"That will be enough, Gabe! I don't want to hear another word about nuclear weapons . . . not now," Rabinovich commanded.

"Then when?" Meir demanded.

"Do I need to ask you to leave, Mr. Meir?" Rabinovich's tone was steely.

Meir locked his fingers together and looked down at the table. "No."

Rabinovich turned to his top military advisor. "What do we do now, Moshe?"

"They've launched hundreds of missiles just in the last thirty minutes . . . mostly short-range Katyushas aimed at Zareet, Sasa, and Baram. They are now in the process of upping the ante by deploying more accurate Fajr-5s and Zelzal-2s. We're getting reports of missiles impacting Nahariya, Maalot, and Safed. Next, they will probably target Haifa, Tel Aviv, or Jerusalem."

"How are they getting through our air defenses?"

"It's a game of numbers. Most of the missiles are being intercepted, but the sheer volume fired almost guarantees there will be some penetration regardless of the strength of our missile defense," Simon explained.

Israel's investment in missile defense systems had begun decades ago as their enemies realized that the most effective way to strike the Jewish state was from a distance. Hundreds of millions of dollars had been poured into increasingly sophisticated systems—from the *Iron Dome* to *David's Sling* and then *Arrow*. No system was perfect, but together these defensive batteries were capable of preventing innumerable casualties.

"Have you pinpointed where the missiles are originating?" Hart asked.

"The majority are coming from just south of the Litani River in south-central Lebanon. The Katyushas have come from dozens of locations—thank God they are neither accurate nor very destructive."

Hart continued. "General, why aren't they attacking with their SCUDs?"

SCUDs were the deadliest weapon in Hezbollah's arsenal. The SCUD-D was the latest iteration of a missile whose earliest design was based upon the German V-2. It had undergone continual refinement by the former Soviet Union and its successor state, Russia. In its present iteration, the liquid-fueled rocket was capable of delivering a 500-kiloton warhead to any city in Israel. Thanks to an inertial guidance system with digital scene-mapping, it was accurate to within fifty meters.

"They may be holding the SCUDs in reserve, presumably concealed under camouflage nets, as they plan some kind of dramatic finale. Thank God we have one thing in our favor—it takes so long to fuel the damn things prior to launch!" Simon said.

"What about Dimona? Has it been targeted?" Hart asked, referring to the site of Israel's nuclear reactor. A direct strike could have devastating consequences—scattering deadly radioactive material across a densely populated area. It would be like Fukushima on steroids.

"They did target the reactor, but our air defense battery performed flawlessly."

After listening patiently to the exchange, Rabinovich resumed the helm. "I want a damage and casualty report as soon as possible. And I want to know how quickly the IAF can respond, General Norkin."

Although the vast majority of Hezbollah's missiles were concentrated south of the Litani River in close proximity to Israel, its long-range missiles were concealed further north, near the Nabatieh Heights. Based upon their complexity, these missiles required a different level of infrastructure to maintain, and thus they were under Hezbollah's Beirut Command.

"Remove the nets!" Nabil Salah ordered, as he pointed to the camouflage covering used to obscure a nest of SCUD-D missiles located two kilometers west of Beaufort Castle, a stone structure of unknown origin dating to before the Crusades.

Salah knew they had to work quickly. Once they were exposed, the missiles were vulnerable to an Israeli attack. It wouldn't take long for satellite or drone images of the installation to be picked up by IDF's intelligence services and forwarded to the IAF.

"We have forty minutes in which to fuel the rockets," Salah advised one of his subordinates. "Not a second more," he cautioned.

Fuel trucks emerged from a subterranean facility that had been carved out of the landscape in 2008 with the help of North Korean engineers. Hoses were connected to dual tanks designed to hold an oxidizer and a propellant. Within seconds, the deadly mix began to flow. Suddenly unearthly screams pierced the air.

Salah rapidly rotated his head back and forth, trying to get a fix on where the noise was coming from. Then he jumped into a jeep and sped past startled men, shouting at them, "Don't stop!"

He didn't slow down until he reached the furthest launch site, where a grim scene awaited him. Half a dozen men were writhing on the ground bathed in RFNA—red fuming nitric acid, the oxidizer used in SCUDs. The hose carrying the highly corrosive liquid had not been properly secured to the fuel tank. When it broke loose from its mooring, it unleashed hundreds of gallons of the liquid before a shut-off valve on the truck could be activated.

A ring of men watched in horror as the flesh of their compatriots' bodies dissolved before their eyes. Salah grabbed an AK-47 from the jeep. Choking on the vapors, he took aim and fired one shot into each man's head. He stopped when the screaming stopped.

Staring into the eyes of the remaining troops, he bellowed. "You now have thirty minutes in which to complete fueling," and then sped off in his jeep.

General Norkin stood to address the prime minister. "Sir, the planes are being fueled, flight plans finalized, and we expect them in the air by the end of the hour. Southern Lebanon will be hit hard minutes after they launch."

As he was speaking, his aide entered the room and handed him a note. He read it twice before gazing at Rabinovich.

"My aide just received a communiqué from our Directorate of Military Intelligence. Aman has picked up images of SCUDs being fueled near Nabatieh." He moved towards a computer. "If I may, Mr. Prime Minister . . . " he asked, gesturing to the keyboard.

After he typed in a command, images began to cascade across the monitors in the room—each one an order of magnitude closer to the ground. He stopped when an image of four SCUD missiles with their fuel trucks came into frame.

"Commander Hart, I think we now have the answer to your earlier question," Simon stated.

"How old are the images, General?" Hart asked of Norkin.

Norkin looked at his chronograph before answering. "Twenty-four minutes, Commander."

"That means you have, at most, twenty minutes in which to respond," Hart said after quickly doing the math.

"Can you destroy these missiles in that amount of time, General?" The question came from Rabinovich.

"Maybe."

CHAPTER THIRTEEN

Decoys and Deception

THE BARRAGE OF MISSILES ARCING across Israeli's northern border was unremitting, yet despite the massive number of projectiles fired, property damage and casualties remained light.

"What in the hell are they trying to accomplish? Surely they must tire of having their missiles shot from the sky," Rabinovich observed, not anticipating a response.

"What if that's their objective?" Hart questioned.

"What are you saying, Commander? Why knowingly pursue such futility?"

Simon picked up on Hart's drift. "Sir, if I'm tracking with the commander, their strategy is not one of futility, but one that seeks to exhaust our missile defense capabilities, albeit briefly. Is that what you are suggesting, Commander?"

"Yes. Eventually your missile defense systems will be depleted, at which point they will need to be reloaded with interceptors. I assume that you stagger the deployment of your surface to air batteries so that not all of your systems go down at once . . . but, even so, there will be heightened vulnerability as you restock munitions. The precious few minutes lost will provide Hezbollah with significantly better odds of hitting high-value targets with their SCUDs."

"So everything up until this point has been a distraction?" Rabinovich asked in disbelief.

"You could say that, Sir. It's all the more reason for taking out their SCUDs. As we all know, those missiles are capable of delivering unconventional weapons."

"I'm aware of that, Commander." Rabinovich turned abruptly to face Norkin. Ten minutes had elapsed without any update on the deployment of aircraft.

"Well, General, is it still 'maybe?'" Rabinovich's tone was stern in response. Norton was equivocating about the IAF's ability to take out the SCUDs.

Norkin didn't respond, but rather picked up a secure phone to Ramat David Air Base. It was home to the F-16C—a plane affectionately known as *Barak (Lightning)* to the members of the 117th and 110th squadrons that flew it.

"Put me through to Colonel Levat," he instructed the officer manning the phone.

"I'm sorry, Sir, but Colonel Levat is unavailable. He's in the briefing room. The crews are in the final stages of preparation for their mission. I'll have him call you as soon as he is free."

"Interrupt him," came the staccato response.

Norkin tapped his foot impatiently during the thirty seconds it took to summon the colonel.

"Hyam, you need to get your birds in the air now!" Norkin ordered. "The SCUDs are almost hot, and we're concerned about their payloads."

"We'll be wheels up in ten minutes, General. That's the best I can do, Sir."

The flight time from Ramat to the Nabatieh Heights would be just over six minutes on full after-burners. They were cutting it close, too close for Rabinovich.

"Put the call on speaker," the prime minister commanded Norkin.

"Colonel, we don't have that much time!" Norkin recognized Rabinovich's voice instantly.

"Understood, Sir."

"Then move!" Rabinovich yelled as though the volume of his voice would propel the colonel forward.

Hyam Levat didn't wait for another word. He burst into the briefing room. "We're done in here. I need you airborne in three minutes." A major started to object. "We don't have time, Major, we're under orders."

Helmets in hand, the aviators sprinted past the simulator building and onto the tarmac where their planes awaited them. Within seconds, they were cleared for take-off.

CHAPTER FOURTEEN

Operation Intercept

ALL EYES WERE FIXED ON THE MONITORS carrying live images from the F-16C squadron under Hyam Levat's command.

Norkin provided narration. "You can see a mirror image of the lead pilot's heads-up display in the upper right hand corner of the screen. The aircraft are coming in at a low altitude . . . just under 5,000 feet, at a speed of Mach 1.2. That will put them on-target in less than three minutes."

The sweeping second hand on the large wall clock seemed to slow to a crawl as time ticked by.

With one minute left before engagement, the squadron leader ordered, "Weapons hot, get ready to light 'em, gentlemen."

Thirty seconds later, his voice broke through again, "Oh, my God," as five streaks of light suddenly appeared on the horizon. The SCUDs were accelerating to a speed in excess of 5,000 feet per second. There was no way for the F-16's targeting computers to get a lock on projectiles moving faster than a bullet.

A dispirited Norkin ordered over the comm, "Save your munitions, gentlemen. Return to base."

The timing could not have been better for Israel's adversaries. Just as Hart had feared, key Israeli missile defense batteries were going off-line, creating momentary gaps in the defense shield. They would remain down until new interceptors could be loaded. In all probability, several of the SCUDs would get through.

The heat signatures of the SCUDs were picked up by U.S. and Israeli satellites seconds after launch. As soon as the missiles had reached sufficient altitude, land-based X-band radar began tracking their trajectory. Within seconds, those trajectories were translated into targets. A map depicting the anticipated sites of impact close to Tel Aviv appeared on the monitors, as well as on monitors in the headquarters of Home Front Defense.

"What now, General?" an angry Rabinovich asked his highest ranking officer.

"We hold our breath and pray," Simon responded.

"I need to apprise the president, Mr. Prime Minister," Hart said as he prepared to leave the conference room. "I will return as quickly as I can."

Avi Rabinovich barely nodded.

The call was put through immediately. "I've been expecting your call, Commander. You are on speaker in the Situation Room, where we are tracking the missiles."

"We've got to pray that the Iron Dome will take them out, Sir."

"My God, Israel's got the most advanced missile defense systems in the world. Do we really need to pray, Commander?"

"Sir, the onslaught of shorter-range missiles caused a momentary exhaustion of interceptors on some of their key batteries, leaving gaps in the Iron Dome. So, yes, Mr. President, we are holding our breath and praying that the SCUDs do limited damage."

"I trust you are safe, Commander."

"Yes, Sir."

"Let's pray that those SCUDs are not armed with unconventional warheads. Keep me posted, Commander."

Hanging up the phone, Hart returned to the conference room.

"What's happening?" Hart asked as he walked into a room full of people who seemed to be in shock.

"Our air defense systems managed to take out one of the SCUDs, but three targeted at Tel Aviv got through. Replay it for him," Rabinovich said to Simon, his tone subdued.

Satellite images of missiles on terminal trajectory appeared on the monitors. As the warheads closed in on their targets, surveillance shifted to ground-based cameras located throughout Tel Aviv. The conference room was silent, as if everyone was anticipating the impending explosions.

But they never came. 500 feet above the ground, a small explosive charge blew apart each nose cone, releasing a dense cloud of nerve gas.

CHAPTER FIFTEEN

The Gassing of the Jews

AIR RAID SIRENS BEGAN BLARING a warning six minutes before the SCUD missiles dispersed their deadly payload over Tel Aviv. As the cacophony signaled impending destruction, a fine mist began to enshroud the sun. From it, a beautiful rainbow emerged that stretched from the Performing Arts Center to Frishman Beach. It faded slowly as the liquefied agent drifted gently towards the ground.

People scrambled for the closest shelter—in their homes, offices, schools, and civil defense facilities—leaving the streets of Tel Aviv largely abandoned except for those too old, too infirm, or too disoriented to run. They would succumb to the poison. Gas masks, part and parcel of everyday life in Israel, were donned instinctively as residents shut and sealed windows, turned off fans and air-conditioning units, then braced for an apparent gas attack.

Miriam Shecter picked up the remote and turned on the television. Home Front Defense had interrupted regularly scheduled programming with a dire warning: No one was to leave their home or shelter for any reason.

"Did you hear that, Ellie? Are you listening?" she chided her husband, who was staring out the window of their fourth floor apartment, a dazed look on his face.

"Ellie, what are you looking at? You are frightening me and the children!"

"I'm looking at bodies, Miriam, dozens and dozens of bodies. Some are writhing on the street, others lying still. These are our neighbors, Miriam, our friends." There was no emotion in his voice.

For those who did not make it to a shelter in time, an agonizing death followed within minutes of inhaling the nerve agent, but inhalation wasn't the only way to fall victim to the toxin's effects. A single droplet landing on bare skin was just as lethal.

Once in the bloodstream, the chemical agent hijacked the body's ability to control its voluntary and involuntary muscles. By inhibiting the neurotransmitter acetylcholinesterase, the nerve gas flooded the synapses of muscles with acetylcholine—in effect, paralyzing them.

What started with a runny nose and chest congestion escalated rapidly. Pupils constricted, foam dripped from victims' mouths, and then seizures began. Death occurred when victims drowned from fluid-filled lungs. Those fortunate enough to survive often experience irreparable neurologic damage and psychiatric impairment.

"Close the curtains!" she ordered. "There's no reason to terrify the children. Let us pray that we remain safe in our home." She turned up the volume on the television as a recorded message from a colonel with Home Front Defense played.

"Do not wait to act. Take the following steps immediately." As he spoke, a list of instructions appeared on screen:

- Put on your gas mask and do not remove it until advised by Home Front Security.
- Ensure that all windows are closed and fans are turned off.
- Seal your windows with duct tape, and place a wet towel over the transom of exterior doors.
- Do not leave your premises for any reason. No one is to go outside for any reason!

The message began to loop. "Home Front Security has determined that a chemical agent has been dispersed at multiple sites across Tel Aviv. The specific agent has yet to be identified, but it appears to be a highly lethal nerve gas. Exposure, either through inhalation or direct contact with the agent, can result in death. The agent is likely to be persistent. If so, it will remain on surfaces rather than being degraded by the sun and wind. Steps are being taken to identify and neutralize the agent. You will be advised if and when it is safe to remove your protective gear and emerge from your homes and shelters."

Soon the blare of ambulances careening through the streets overshadowed the air raid sirens. Ellie returned to his perch at the window, parting the curtain with his hand. EMTs outfitted in full chem/bio suits were rushing towards victims. He could see them stooped over bodies, presumably assessing whether a spark of life remained, before moving on to the next victim.

When they found someone still moving, their bodies jerking convulsively from organophosphate poisoning, the EMTs jabbed needles into the thighs of victims. Ellie, a bio-chemist, assumed it was atropine—a possible antidote. He removed his hand and let the drape fall closed. Miriam was right; there was no reason for the children to see such horror.

Reports began to flood into the Bor from different parts of the city. Live video streams of the impact zones showed people dropping mid-step to the ground, parents sprawled on the street cradling dead or dying children.

"What the hell is happening?" Rabinovich demanded.

"Chemical weapons, Mr. Prime Minister," David Chaikin answered. "Home Front Defense reports that the first victims are being evacuated to hospitals as we speak. Remote feeds are being established in the ERs. You should be able to get a preliminary evaluation of what we are dealing with momentarily from the treating physicians."

"I need more information!" Rabinovich ordered frantically.

"It will take time for our chemists to complete a forensic identification of the agent, Mr. Prime Minister," Chaikin responded, to which Rabinovich shook his head.

"I want to know now!" he roared.

Ten minutes later, the head of Ben Gurion Hospital's emergency department, Dr. Martin Perelman, was on the screen. Perelman, an American ex-pat, had settled in Tel Aviv in 2005 after a lengthy career running the University of Maryland's Shock/Trauma Center.

"What are you seeing, Doctor?"

"An onslaught of the dead and dying, Mr. Prime Minister. We've already outstripped the capacity of our morgue."

"Can't you do anything?" Rabinovich responded in exasperation.

"We are doing our best, Mr. Rabinovich. Survival depends on the level of exposure and the elapsed time since inhalation or skin contamination."

"Any idea of what they were exposed to, Doctor?"

"Based on the level of fatalities, coupled with the fact that pralidoxime did nothing to improve patient status, my guess is a Novichok agent—presumably Novichok-5. We are currently administering atropine accompanied by an experimental drug called galantamine. It lets us lower the dose of atropine significantly, thereby reducing the risk of toxicity from the drug."

Rabinovich took a moment to take stock of what he had just heard.

"Dr. Perelman, do you understand the implications of what you are saying?"

"Yes. That there will be hundreds of casualties."

"No, I meant the nature of the attack . . . the agent in question . . . and the fact that only Russia is known to possess quantities of Novichok-5. I understand that it will be some time before a full analysis is done, but I'm taking your comments as an early warning sign that Russia is doing more than merely giving advice to the Syrian Coalition."

Novichok-5 was a poison produced exclusively by Russia. While structurally similar to other nerve agents, it was far more deadly than Sarin or VX.

"It appears that way to me, Prime Minister."

"Back to the drugs you are administering. Are they working?"

"It seems to be stopping the cholinergic crisis for a number of patients. However, if it is a Novichok agent, our treatments will likely not prevent any serious long-term effects from the toxin."

"I'm not a physician, Doctor. Could you please translate what you just said into plain English for me?"

"Of course," Perelman said, then proceeded to explain the debilitating, often fatal effects of nerve gas exposure. "It's ghastly, Mr. Prime Minister. Patients progressively lose control over their bodies—they fall to the ground, foam coming from their mouths, and involuntary urination and defecation follow. Once the acetylcholine builds to a sufficient level, respiration and cardiac function begin to shut down."

Perelman paused. "The only way to prevent death is to either re-establish the presence of acetylcholinesterase through a compound such as galantamine and or to block the effects of acetylcholine on the muscles—which is what atropine does."

"And if you are able to save these people, what type of long-term consequences are you referring to, Doctor?"

"I don't know. There's virtually no literature on Novichok exposure. However, it's probably safe to assume that the after-effects could include an inability to walk, seizure disorders—including epilepsy, blindness, and serious psychiatric problems—to name just a few.

"Please forgive me, Mr. Prime Minister, I have to get back to my patients."

"Of course, Doctor. Godspeed!"

Rabinovich disconnected the line, then turned to Commander Hart.

"It looks as though things are heating up, Commander. I trust that President Conner will want to know about this latest development as soon as possible."

"Yes, Sir," Hart said as he moved towards the door.

CHAPTER SIXTEEN

The Sunni Solution

"You'll have to excuse me," Conner told the army of advisors assembled in the Situation Room, then stood to hasten their departure. In less than a minute, the president was alone.

"Put Commander Hart through," he informed his chief of staff.

"Commander Hart?"

"Mr. President."

"I assume your call pertains to the SCUD missiles launched from southern Lebanon. The fact that you are calling is some reassurance that, at least, they were not laden with weapons of mass destruction."

"I'm afraid that is not correct, Sir. One of the SCUDs was shot out of the sky; the remaining three deposited a lethal load of nerve gas over the skies of Tel Aviv. Preliminary indications suggest it may have been a Novichok agent."

"It's far too soon to draw that conclusion . . . not even the Israelis could have completed a definitive forensic analysis so quickly. So tell me what you are basing your conclusions on, Commander—conclusions that could draw us into a world war."

"The attending physician at Ben Gurion Hospital is an ex-pat named Martin Perelman. I know him from his time at U of M's Shock/Trauma Center. Perelman was part of the team Liz assembled in New York charged with formulating an emergency response to the massive number of casualties resulting from the nuclear event. The man has impeccable credentials."

Hart paused to emphasize his point. "Perelman's belief that a Novichok agent was deployed is based upon the victims' response to various therapeutic interventions, including an experimental treatment. I listened to his argument, and his logic is hard to refute, Sir."

"What is the tone of the Defense Council? And what about Rabinovich?"

"The prime minister is giving Perelman the benefit of the doubt. He's looking at the chess board and assessing his next move. It's not easy when you are outnumbered and attacked on multiple flanks. Plus, in the prime minister's mind, the use of WMD just changed the rules of the game. I believe Mr. Rabinovich will recommend a ferocious response, Sir."

"I'm concerned that the more he feels alone and isolated, the more likely he is to utilize every weapon at his disposal."

"He knows we stand behind him, Sir."

"It's nice rhetoric, Commander, but other than you, what boots do we have on the ground? By the time we get carriers and other critical assets into position, this war could be over."

"I'll do what I can, Sir."

"You are one man, Commander. You may have pulled off the miraculous before, but it almost cost you and Dr. Wilkins your lives. On this tour of duty, you are an advisor, Commander Hart—it is not your battle to fight. Am I clear?"

"Yes, Sir."

"Rabinovich needs allies who are in lock-step with him—ready to do battle."

"What are you suggesting, Mr. President?"

"I'm suggesting that the recent actions that imperil Israel may also create an opportunity."

"An opportunity? How is that, Sir?"

"The speed, intensity, and resolve with which the Syrian Coalition hit Israel has to strike fear into neighboring Sunni nations who realize they could be next.

"They may hate the Jews, but their hatred of the Shia is much more intense. War makes for strange bedfellows, which is why we don't think it would take much encouragement to forge an alliance with the Jordanians, Saudis, Egyptians, and others committed to stopping the Syrian Coalition."

"How do you think Mr. Rabinovich will respond to your suggestion, Sir?"

"Not well, at least not initially. That's where you come in, John. I need your help to convince him that his historic adversaries are about to become his new best friends."

"I will do my best, Sir."

CHAPTER SEVENTEEN

A War of Words

ONLY ONE WORD CAME TO MIND as Abraham Rabinovich struggled to describe what was happening in Israel. It was a word so emotionally charged that he hesitated to use it in his forthcoming address to the nation. But Israel was under siege, and Rabinovich knew that uttering the word *Holocaust* would galvanize his people, as well as Jews throughout the world. Then, and only then, would he have the necessary support to employ any means necessary to protect the Jewish state. Before speaking to the nation at large, he first needed to ensure unity within his inner circle.

The Israeli Security Cabinet had occupied the Chief of Staff's conference room since the conflict began. Rabinovich expanded the audience to include additional representatives from IDF, Mossad, and Aman leadership—the majority of whom joined via video teleconference. Once a quorum had been reached, Rabinovich launched into a vitriolic diatribe.

"Ladies and gentlemen, over the past forty-eight hours, there has been an unprecedented attack upon our nation.

Not since 1967 have multiple enemy forces coalesced with the singular goal of exterminating the Jewish state.

"The bombing of southern Israeli towns by Hamas extremists, as well as the assault on the Golan, now look like minor injuries compared to the gas attack on Tel Aviv. Though we don't yet have casualty figures, it is anticipated that the number of people killed or injured will exceed any prior attack by orders of magnitude.

"These attacks have been fomented by Iran and executed by Syrian, Hamas, Hezbollah and IRGC forces. Other nations, most notably Russia, appear to be involved.

"The carnage will continue unless we respond. We cannot wait for another attack. We must strike now—with a response so overwhelming that the Syrian Coalition dare not strike us again.

"Earlier, I scoffed at Mr. Meir for suggesting the unimaginable—tapping into our nuclear arsenal. With this latest attack on Tel Aviv, I have become increasingly convinced that my colleague was right. But the deployment of such weapons is not my decision to make alone, but rather in concert with this group."

Rabinovich paused long enough to allow the full impact of his words to be absorbed by his audience before continuing.

"Despite being faced with a possible existential threat, we cannot summarily react. First, we must plead our case in the court of public opinion—justifying our right to retribution as well as protection from further attack. Our words must reach beyond the people of Israel . . . they must reach across the globe. We cannot afford for a single ally to turn against us at this pivotal moment in our history."

Glancing up at the clock, Rabinovich concluded the meeting. "In fifteen minutes, I will share my prepared remarks on television. When I am finished, we will pick up this conversation where we have left off. I expect you to provide an answer to my question: How far is Israel willing to go to stop this threat?"

Abraham Rabinovich already knew the answer. The National Security Council would give their unanimous approval to the deployment of nuclear weapons in response to the perceived existential threat facing the nation. The final decision, however, would be his. The magnitude of that responsibility weighed heavily on his soul.

CHAPTER EIGHTEEN

Inside the Emergency Department

WHAT STARTED OUT AS A STEADY STREAM of nerve gas victims escalated into a deluge that flooded Tel Aviv's David Ben Gurion Medical Center. Realizing that the number of admits would soon overwhelm the department, Dr. Martin Perelman ordered a triage team to intercept all incoming emergency transports and redirect them to a parking lot adjacent to the hospital.

As each ambulance rolled to a stop, a medical team outfitted in chemo-bio suits was to rush to the back gantry, open it, and begin a field assessment that would determine the patient's fate. If the patient was unresponsive, had no pupillary reaction to a penlight, and appeared to be in the end stage of respiratory arrest, they would be diverted to a hospice tent. If, however, there was a hope of saving a victim's life, the patient would be rushed across the street to the Emergency Department.

Perelman stood just outside of the sliding glass doors of the ED, performing a secondary assessment on each patient as their gurney approached the department's threshold. An elderly woman had just been wheeled in. She was fighting for breath—on the cusp of death. Her O^2 saturation was at a level incompatible with life. Based upon her age and condition, he was surprised that she had not been relegated to the hospice tent, but it was now his job to save her life.

He began rattling off orders to a nurse, but before he could finish, an EMT approached from behind and grasped Perelman's upper arm, her fingernails pressing into his skin.

He spun around until he was eye to eye with the woman.

"What the hell are you doing?" he asked the paramedic, who immediately released her grip.

"I'm sorry, Doctor, but I need you in the hospice tent now."

"This woman needs me here. The patients in that tent are there for a reason . . . and it isn't for medical heroics."

"I think the triage team made a mistake with one patient—a young boy, maybe ten years old. He still has life left in him. We can't give up on him without a fight."

"Look around," Perelman said with a sweeping gesture of his arm, "Death is all around us."

He turned back and gazed at the woman on the gurney, who seemed to be fading in and out of consciousness. "She will die without prompt care. Is that what you want?"

"Of course not, but this woman is old . . . her life is nearing its end. The boy's life is just beginning. Perhaps your triage team made a mistake. All I'm asking is that you have a look."

"There are not enough doctors to manage the patients in the ER. I can't abandon a patient."

The EMT started to argue, but realized the futility. "Okay," she said as she turned and began walking away, tears streaming down her cheeks.

She was no more than a dozen yards away when Perelman called out to her.

"Wait, I'm coming with you." He took the elderly woman's hand in his and said, "Forgive me. I will look in on you as quickly as I can." Her only response was a slight flutter of her eyelids.

He turned to the nurse beside him. "Sometimes there are no right decisions . . . start the patient on oxygen and get her into decontamination. I'll be back as quickly as I can." He turned abruptly towards the EMT.

"Let's go," Perelman shouted, as he attempted to run in the cumbersome bio-protective suit.

If there was a hell, it must look a lot like the hospice tent, Perelman thought. The air was fetid from the stench of patients soiling themselves as they lost all bowel and bladder control. Many writhed in pain, while others lay rigid, their muscles locked in a death grip. Amidst this sea of human tragedy was a small body curled up in a fetal position on a gurney. The boy was the same age as his grandson and namesake, Marty.

Perelman looked the boy up and down. Blood-tinged foam oozed from his mouth. His chest spasmed, preventing life-sustaining air from flowing into his partially paralyzed lungs. His pupils were fixed pinpoints. He was minutes away from drowning in his own fluids.

"It's too late!" he snarled at the EMT.

"Please, Doctor. There has to be something you can do."

"What do you expect me to do? I'm not God."

Perelman looked back at the boy, then at the EMT. He knew he would be forever haunted by his decision if he didn't try to save the boy.

"Okay . . . you win . . . we need to get him to the ED immediately, but I don't think it's going to help."

The first semblance of a smile touched the EMT's lips as she said, "Thank you, Doctor."

Together, they hurriedly pushed the gurney across the parking lot and through the door of the emergency department.

"Have you administered anything?" Perelman asked en route.

"We gave him 2-PAM and atropine."

"How much atropine?"

"One milligram—we estimated his weight at about 35 kilos."

Perelman hesitated to administer more, knowing that excessive atropine could hasten the boy's death. He was walking a tightrope trying to bring him back from the abyss.

"I need 0.5 mg of atropine plus 100 mg of galantamine, STAT!" he yelled in a voice that could be heard above the fray. Seconds later, a nurse appeared and handed him a syringe. He wasted no time thrusting the needle into the boy's thigh.

Perelman spoke to the boy—calming words in Hebrew—but the child remained unresponsive. He turned to the EMT.

"If he makes it through the acute crisis, there's a chance he will survive. The nurse is going to take him into decontamination. From there, he will be put in the holding area where we can monitor him. There's not a lot more that we can do but wait."

"Can't you intubate him . . . put him on life support until he can breathe on his own?" the EMT pleaded.

"I wish it were that simple."

He walked over to the gurney where the elderly woman lay. A blanket had been pulled up to cover her face.

CHAPTER NINETEEN

Antipathy towards the Jews

LIKE A SPECTER QUIETLY STALKING HER, Marvin Kahn knocked once again on Liz's office door.

Before she could speak, he informed her, "Rabinovich is about to make a televised address. CNN is on in the conference room. Why don't you join me?"

Liz rose from her chair immediately, asking as she pulled on her jacket, "What are you expecting to hear?"

"I will tell you what I am praying not to hear: any threat by Israel to go nuclear."

Rabinovich was in the final stages of preparation before delivering the most important speech of his life—words that would live on long after his death. He sat in front of the camera rehearsing, stopping only to adjust the cadence of the teleprompter. He wanted to ensure that the tempo of his words matched the gravity of the situation.

The director stepped onto the set and cued the prime minister. "Thirty seconds, Mr. Prime Minister."

Avi straightened his tie, folded his hands, closed his eyes, and whispered a portion of the twenty-third psalm.

"The Lord is my shepherd; I shall not want. He maketh me to lie down in green pastures: he leadeth me beside the still waters. He restoreth my soul; he leadeth me in the paths of righteousness for his name's sake . . . Yea, though I walk through the valley of the shadow of death, I will fear no evil; for thou art with me; thy rod and thy staff they comfort me . . . Amen."

He hoped God was listening.

"Three, two, one." The director pointed a finger at Rabinovich, cuing him that the show had begun. Behind the prime minister was a green screen onto which was displayed a normal street scene from the heart of Tel Aviv.

"My fellow countrymen, at ten o'clock this morning, Israel was the target of an unprovoked and horrific attack using a weapon of mass destruction. From a base just north of the Litani River in southern Lebanon, Hezbollah fired missiles into the heart of Tel Aviv. These were no ordinary missiles. They were weapons supplied by Iran and armed with deadly nerve gas. Were it not for impeccable planning and preparation by Home Front Defense, fatalities would have numbered in the thousands."

He looked down briefly, as if recounting a painful memory, before locking his eyes on the camera.

"Seventy-five years have passed since the gassing of Jews in Nazi concentration camps. Hitler's so-called *final solution* called for the extermination of our people. But against all odds, we survived; and we promised ourselves—and the world—'Never again!'"

A stream of images began flowing across the green screen behind him—graphic images of people asphyxiating in the streets of Tel Aviv.

"The use of weapons of mass destruction imperils the very existence of Israel." His tone shifted to one of absolute resolve as he slammed his fist against the desk. "Our retaliation must be swift and devastating. No one will—again—doubt Israel's promise of Never Again!"

Rabinovich held his gaze on the camera until his image had fully faded from the screen—replaced by panels of correspondents eager to speculate on what Israel would do as retaliation.

Thousands of miles away in northern Virginia, Liz Wilkins shook her head in disbelief. "Surely he's not intent on nuclear retaliation," she said, turning slowly towards Kahn.

"I'm afraid that's exactly what he's threatening."

Rabinovich did not return immediately to the conference room. Instead, he sought out a few moments of silent refuge in his private office. He brushed past his executive assistant, indicating with a raised hand and no eye contact that he did not wish to speak or be disturbed. Entering his office, he left the lights off, closed the door, and dropped to his knees in prayer.

"Hear, O Israel, the Lord is our God, the Lord is One. Blessed be the Name of His glorious kingdom forever and ever."

But it was not the expansive kingdom of God that filled his mind, but scenarios of unimaginable destruction as he considered Israel's next steps . . . steps that would forever change the world. Unlike the leaders of ancient Israel, whose biblical sense of justice demanded an eye for an eye, Rabinovich was governed by a more complex set of principles . . . for he fought not with slings and arrows, but with weapons capable of destroying entire countries.

After thirty minutes, he finished his meditation by turning to God one final time and praying for divine guidance in the hours ahead. Then, as silently as he had entered, he walked out and headed for the conference room.

While Rabinovich did not expect to be greeted with applause, he also did not anticipate the gloom that permeated the air.

"What the hell is going on?" he bellowed. "You look as though we've already capitulated!"

Moshe Simon took Avi's arm. "There was an announcement of breaking news following your press conference. We tried to call your office, but we were told that you were not to be disturbed. CNN has been running a feed from Al Jazeera. I'll have it cued up for you."

Seconds later, Rabinovich's attention was riveted on the screen. A banner cried "BREAKING NEWS." Christina Amanpour appeared on camera. "Ladies and gentlemen, we are going live to an Al Jazeera broadcast."

A second later, an image of Iranian president Rouhani filled the screen. Without taking his eyes off the monitor, Rabinovich lowered himself slowly into a chair, dumbstruck at the speed with which the Iranians had responded.

"What you have just heard are lies—a well-staged publicity stunt by Israel's prime minister to engender false sympathy while his country prepares for war. Do not be deceived by Israel's duplicity—these are merely Zionist lies designed to justify the impending slaughter of innocent civilians.

"It is our moral indignation that has been pushed to the limit! Iran has stood by passively for years and allowed Israel to strike with impunity. Today, Israeli tyranny comes to an end. It is not Israel, but the broad and deep Shia community that says, 'Never again!'

"We stand, fist raised, with our brothers in Gaza, Lebanon, Syria, and the West Bank. Israel has felt the brush of our sword against its neck, and tasted the trickle of blood that flowed. That was a warning. Any further act of aggression on the part of the Jewish state will result in the decapitation of Israel. That is our promise."

As the screen went black, Rabinovich turned to his most trusted supporters. "They have turned my words against us. But how . . . how did they respond so quickly?"

David Chaikin answered. "They are following a methodical plan that anticipates our response to each provocation. If we wish to be a step ahead rather than a step behind, we must act in a manner that is uncharacteristic."

"Put all of our forces on high-alert—including nuclear," Rabinovich barked out the order. "Not another drop of Jewish blood will be spilled on my watch!"

Simon responded without hesitation. "Understood, Mr. Prime Minister."

Rouhani remained at the podium, spewing vitriolic rhetoric about the manipulative Jewish state. As he started to raise his arm in a crescendo of hatred, he was interrupted by an aide approaching the podium. Rouhani stepped away from the microphone and listened intently as something was whispered in his ear.

Returning to the podium, the color drained from his face, Rouhani spoke. "I've just been informed that Israel's nuclear forces have been put on high alert. It appears that Mr. Rabinovich is bracing for a fight.

"I suggest you pay heed to what I am about to say, Mr. Prime Minister, for the fate of your country hangs in the balance."

DDO Kahn turned to Liz. "I guess you have your answer," he said.

CHAPTER TWENTY

An Existential Threat

THE FIRE HAD GONE OUT OF ROUHANI'S ORATORY. The words that followed were delivered with a chilling level of detachment . . . the kind of detachment needed to commit mass murder.

"Iran has five ballistic missiles targeted on the Jewish state. Each one carries a boosted nuclear warhead with a yield of 150 kilotons. That is ten times the destructive force of the Hiroshima blast that killed 100,000 people.

"Our ally, Hezbollah, has proven the vulnerability of your missile defense systems. The Iron Dome may succeed in eliminating four out of five missiles, but chances are that at least one will get through. When it strikes Tel Aviv, Jerusalem, or Haifa, the body count will number in the hundreds of thousands. Your shelters will be turned into furnaces as the surface temperature rises to 10,000 degrees.

"Israel cannot afford to gamble with the lives of so many. Therefore your only option is a complete and unconditional surrender. We will allow you time to consider our offer. You have forty-eight hours . . . not a second more!"

The Al Jazeera feed ended abruptly.

"Is he crazy?" Rabinovich bellowed at his colleagues in disbelief.

"Does it matter?" Moshe Simon responded. "If what he says is true, we have precious little time in which to respond."

"How do you respond to the barrel of a gun leveled at your head, General?"

"Very carefully," the words came from David Chaikin.

"How real is the threat?" Avi asked his chief spook.

Before Chaikin could answer, an aide interrupted. "Excuse me, Prime Minister, but President Conner is on a video-teleconferencing line."

"Perhaps we should hear what President Conner has to say before I delve into the threat assessment," Chaikin proffered.

"Put him through," Rabinovich instructed the aide.

"I didn't anticipate that we would be speaking again so quickly, Mr. Prime Minister, but having watched the Iranian broadcast, I felt an obvious urgency to reach out," Conner began.

"I'm glad you did. We need our friends close at hand during such perilous times."

"Your fate and the fate of my country are inextricably bound, Avi. So I ask, what do you propose to do—assuming you believe that the threat is real?"

"I was just asking Mr. Chaikin for his threat assessment when we learned you were on the line. If I may, I will ask David to proceed."

"By all means, Mr. Prime Minister."

Chaikin took the cue. "President Conner, when your country was contemplating withdrawal from the Iran nuclear deal, we worked hand-in-hand with your DNI and others to develop a data-driven justification for the U.S. decision."

"Of course . . . I was privy to many of those conversations, as you know, Mr. Chaikin."

"Then, as I'm sure you recall, we provided evidence as to the advanced state of Iran's nuclear weapon production capabilities. Based upon cross-validated sources, we believed that the Iranians possessed half a dozen nukes at the time they entered into the non-proliferation agreement. We assessed the yield of those weapons to be in the 10- to 15-kiloton range."

"That's a far cry from what they are threatening to unleash upon your cities, Mr. Chaikin," Conner observed.

"We believe that the Iranians subsequently acquired the knowledge necessary to transform their bombs into thermonuclear devices, which would account for greatly enhanced yields."

"Where did they get the nuclear material for these devices, Mr. Chaikin?"

"We assume it came from the Bushehr reactor, Mr. President. As you know, that reactor has been on-line since 2011 . . . plenty of time to amass a sizable amount of plutonium without IAEA detection."

"Beyond your protected sources, do you have any external corroboration of these assertions?"

"What I would deem soft corroboration, Sir. Henry Sokolski, the director of the Nonproliferation Policy Education Center, has commented on the absence of the Bushehr reactor from the JPCOA. He has gone on to speculate that the reactor could generate enough plutonium for dozens of bombs per year."

Conner turned to the director of National Intelligence, who was seated across the table from him in the Situation Room. "What do you think, Carl? Is what Mr. Chaikin said plausible?"

"The Bushehr reactor produces in excess of 250 kilograms of plutonium per year. But it was built by the former Soviet Union with the express agreement that Iran would be prohibited from reprocessing its spent fuel rods. Presumably the Russians have held fast on this pledge."

Rabinovich interjected, "With all due respect to the DNI, I wouldn't be so quick to trust the Russians.

"If the gas used against Tel Aviv proves to be a Novichok agent, as suspected, we will know that Russia is fully complicit in Iran's efforts to eradicate Israel. Furthermore, you have seen the satellite images of the presumed reprocessing plant that was built in the Parchin military complex adjacent to the reactor. Why was it built if not to produce weapons grade plutonium? I see no other reasonable conclusion . . . not now."

"That may explain how Iran could get its hands on a bomb, but not how they would deliver it to a target 1,200 miles away," Conner countered.

Chaikin responded, "Mr. President, allow me to reference February 2008 briefing notes from a meeting of the IAEA. The critical issue under discussion pertained to Iranian documents depicting the design of nuclear warheads, including high tension firing systems, EBW detonators capable of firing in near simultaneity, and other memoranda that could relate only to the development of nuclear armed missiles. The Iranians referred to the collective development of these capabilities as *Projects 110 and 111*."

"What make you believe they've crossed the thermonuclear threshold?" Conner asked.

"Intelligence coming out of Pyongyang." It was a stunning revelation. Chaikin looked to Rabinovich for permission to proceed.

Rabinovich impatiently nodded for Chaikin to continue.

"There is evidence to support the allegation that Kim Jong Un jump-started Iran's thermonuclear arsenal by contributing three nukes to Tehran in the spring of 2017. The devices were purportedly shipped via commercial airliners with stopovers in Russia.

"That fall, on September 3, 2017, North Korea successfully detonated a weapon estimated to be in the 140- to 250-kiloton range. We assume that a technology transfer followed on the heels of this test—with Tehran gaining the vital insights needed to produce boosted weapons."

"This is all based on human intelligence—in other words, speculation," Conner challenged.

"Without wishing to sound arrogant, President Conner, when has Israeli intelligence been wrong?"

Chaikin had a point. Conner sat perplexed, wondering how the Israelis could be out so far ahead of the U.S. in their intelligence assessments. But now was not the time to get mired in such thoughts. He had to hope that there was a chink in Iran's armor.

"What about their missiles—they sure as hell aren't going to reach your cities with their aging fleet of bombers."

"The modified Shahab-3 is fully capable of striking our country," Chaikin asserted. "But my guess is that they turned once again to North Korea. We know that in 2013, missile technicians from Iran's Shahid Hemmat Industrial

Group were invited to Pyongyang. Mossad suggests it wasn't a sight-seeing trip; they were being instructed on the evolving Hwasong-14 and 15 missile platforms.

"Those delivery systems became operational a few years later. If my hunch is right, the Iranians are relying on modified versions of the North Korean missiles to strike any city within our borders."

"Mr. Chaikin, what you are saying, albeit politely, is that the Iranians played us for fools!" Conner said in disbelief. "We accepted their word, and all the while they were building their nuclear capabilities under our nose."

"We tried to warn you, President Conner," Rabinovich gently reminded him.

"Yes, you did, Mr. Prime Minister, and any blood spilled will be on our hands."

"Let's hope it doesn't come to that, Mr. President."

"What are you going to do, Mr. Rabinovich?"

"I don't know. But one thing is for certain. Israel will never surrender!"

CHAPTER TWENTY-ONE

The Response

RABINOVICH'S NEXT STEPS WERE CRYSTAL CLEAR, despite any assurance to the contrary to Conner. He knew Conner would advocate for thoughtful deliberation before Israel took any action, but from Rabinovich's perspective, there was no time to seek out a gentlemanly solution to their looming annihilation. He had to act, and act now.

Turning to Eli Sharvit, Commander in Chief of the Israeli Navy, he immediately began issuing orders.

"Eli, I need our submarines in position to launch on my command. You know what we are up against. So I need your recommendation, and I need it now."

Sharvit didn't hesitate. He had mulled over such scenarios countless times in his mind and knew exactly how he would arrange the chess pieces.

"Sir, first I would order one of our Dolphins through the Strait of Hormuz and into the Persian Gulf—putting much of Iran within range of our cruise missiles. Then I would station a sub proximate to the Gaza in the Mediterranean

Sea. Finally, I would position a Dolphin off the coast of Beirut. From there, we could hit Lebanon or Syria."

"Execute all three orders simultaneously," Rabinovich instructed Sharvit, "and tell me how long it will be before the subs are in position."

"We can have all fronts covered within hours, Sir."

Each Dolphin-class submarine carried nuclear-armed cruise missiles capable of destroying a small city. Flying at sub-sonic speeds 1,500 feet above the ground, the missiles were virtually undetectable by all but the most sophisticated air defense systems.

"Communicate to your commanders that this is no drill. I don't want as much as a blink if they receive launch instructions."

"Understood, Sir."

"Commander Hart, I'm asking you not to speak with President Conner until I sanction it. I know that puts you in a difficult position, but I cannot have the United States dictating war-time policy to Israel."

"Sir, you understand that my obligation is to my president. May I ask why you have not simply excused me from the discussion?"

"Because I value your thinking, Commander, just as your president does. I understand the bind I have put you in, but I promise you that President Conner will not be kept in the dark for long. Furthermore, I believe your orders are to assist me in any manner required. Therefore, I'm afraid you have no choice, Commander."

"Understood, Mr. Prime Minister," Conner affirmed, although he felt a sudden queasiness in his gut.

Rabinovich then asked those assembled for input. David Chaikin was the first to speak, catalyzing what was to become a heated debate.

"Iran has been shouting 'death to Israel' since the birth of their theocracy. In their minds, our destruction represents the fulfillment of biblical prophecy and the return of the true Messiah. As such, they will not be satisfied until Israel is reduced to cinders. Their ultimatum simply legitimizes such action by suggesting that they offered terms for surrender, knowing that surrender is not an option for the Jewish people."

"I wouldn't be so sure of that," Moshe Simon challenged his Mossad colleague. "For every nuclear warhead they purportedly possess, we possess thirty. They are betting on a single missile getting through and doing untold damage to one Israeli city, knowing that we would respond with the complete destruction of their country. We may lose 200,000 of our people. They will lose twenty million. The Ayatollah may indulge in fantasies, but such a trade-off would be true madness."

"This is not a war that will be won by force, General. It is an ideological war with religious fanatics who believe their death puts them one step closer to Paradise. The theocracy won't shed a tear over twenty million martyrs, and that makes our nuclear advantage somewhat of a moot point," Chaikin said with almost religious fervor.

Rabinovich interrupted the debate. "Commander Hart, now I want to hear from you."

"Yes, Sir."

"Well, then?"

"There is wisdom in both General Simon's perspective, as well as that of Mr. Chaikin."

"I'm not looking for a politician, Commander. I need your opinion on an appropriate strategic response to our situation without any concern for being politically correct."

"Sir, while the theocracy may be focused on calling forth the twelfth Messiah, the head of the Quds forces has a much more pragmatic agenda. I believe that General Jafari wants one thing—to see a consolidated Middle East under Iranian rule. That means the end of the Jewish state and the elimination of Sunni governments. And I trust he is willing to sacrifice a great deal to achieve such an aim."

"Twenty million of his people, Commander?"

"Probably, but it's not human lives lost that will stop him. Jafari knows that your bombs will eviscerate Iran's command, control, communications, and intelligence infrastructure needed for such a massive conquest. His war machine would be like a tank with no treads."

"So what are you suggesting, Commander? That we proceed with a strike—retribution, in a measured form, for the damage they have already done . . . or capitulation in the hopes that they will be honorable and merciful in dealing with the Israeli people? As you know, our people have been in bondage before."

"That I must leave it up to you, Sir. I've already said more than I should in this situation."

"You've said what President Conner would expect you to say, Commander . . . nothing more, nothing less."

Rabinovich turned to Simon. "Moshe, I don't believe Iran is bluffing. And we know that surrender is not an option. Therefore, I think we need to send a message . . .

a message that we are prepared to respond biblically . . . an eye for an eye."

"You are suggesting the use of a nuclear weapon?"

"Yes—a single nuclear warhead detonated precisely over the site from which the chemically-laden SCUDs were launched."

"Why not Damascus or Tehran?"

"How would we defend such an attack on the world stage? And would it not guarantee the Iranians' deployment of their missiles? But a response, in kind, to the horrific use of a weapon of mass destruction by Hezbollah . . . that represents a defensible response."

Simon's tone was subdued. "Avi, the destruction won't be limited to the coordinates of the launch site in southern Lebanon. We will kill or maim every living thing within a radius of several miles. Even at a distance of five to ten miles, there will be massive deaths from radiation poisoning."

"Did we start this war? No, we did not! Did we issue an ultimatum calling for the unilateral surrender of our adversary? No, we did not! And are our people dying in the streets due to a weapon of mass destruction? Yes. It is our obligation to respond!"

"May I make a suggestion, Mr. Prime Minister?" Simon took on a more formal tone.

"Of course. Show me a way out of this predicament, Moshe."

"If you are convinced that there must be a nuclear response, then deploy the weapon against the epicenter of Hezbollah's position in southern Lebanon. It's near Jouaiyya, just south of the Litani River. It clearly represents a military target. I believe that such a response would have the greatest air of legitimacy, while also neutralizing future threats from Hezbollah. Bear in mind, Mr. Prime Minister, that the collateral damage to the Lebanese population will be immense."

How far is Jouaiyya from our northern border . . . 10 or 15 kilometers?" Rabinovich asked.

"10 kilometers."

"And the impact of the bomb on towns such as Kiryat Shmona and Nahariyya? We have nearly a hundred thousand people in those towns alone . . . what will happen to them, Moshe, under your scenario?"

"We risk killing many of our own people—not so much from the blast, but from the radiation that follows."

"Moshe, get Major Strik on the line. Tell him he has fifteen minutes in which to move people into shelters, but give him thirty minutes before we actually strike."

"What are you calling for, Mr. Prime Minister?"

"What you recommended—a single nuclear weapon, in the form of a 150-kiloton bomb, set to explode at an altitude of 1,500 feet above the Hezbollah encampment. I suggest you get Colonel Norkin on the phone. He will need my authorization to launch the F-35I."

"And those who cannot be sheltered in time, Mr. Prime Minister? What happens to them?"

"The greatest good for the greatest number, General."

"Do we not live by a higher standard, Mr. Prime Minister?"

"We are a practical people, Moshe, just as we are a principled people. My orders stand."

Hart was crawling out of skin. He jumped to his feet and formally addressed Rabinovich. "Mr. Prime Minister, with all due respect, Sir, you are about to kill a hundred thousand people. The nuclear genie has been kept safely locked in a bottle for more than seventy years. Are you sure you want to be the one to release it?"

Rabinovich gestured to one of the monitors carrying live-feed from the Ben Gurion Emergency Department. "Take another look, Commander, and then ask me if I have any other choice."

"I don't deny the atrocity committed against your country, but I urge greater deliberation before making this leap. At the very least, Sir, I implore you to speak with the president."

"I will speak with President Conner, but not at this moment, Commander. Have a seat. You've done your duty. Now let us do ours."

The next twenty-eight minutes unfolded in virtual silence . . . until the unearthly quiet was finally broken by the voice of Colonel Norkin. "Mr. Prime Minister, our pilot is two minutes out from the target. He is requesting permission to go hot."

"Permission granted, Colonel. The authentication code is being transmitted to your pilot as we speak. Can you patch me directly into the cockpit, Colonel?"

"Patching you through, now, Sir."

"Major, it's Avi Rabinovich."

"Yes, Sir. I recognize your voice, Sir."

"We are asking a great deal of you at this moment. I know you understand the full consequences of your orders, Major."

"Yes, Sir."

"I want to make certain that you also understand that you are the very tip of the sword that will pierce the heart of those who have sought Israel's destruction. Tragedy is inevitable in such situations, but you will help avert an even greater loss of life that might otherwise follow."

"Thank you, Sir.

"The weapon is hot, Sir. Requesting final authorization for the weapon's release."

"So authorized. Godspeed, Major." The comm line went dead.

"Now put me through to President Conner," Rabinovich barked, his eyes focused on Commander Hart.

"What in the hell is happening over there?" Conner demanded. "Commander Hart has not reported in for hours. Tell me you are not doing anything foolish, Avi."

"That is not the Commander's fault, Mr. President. I have forbidden him to leave the conference room until we have resolved how to respond to the current crisis."

"And what did you resolve?" Conner's words came fast, a sign of anxiety over what he might hear next.

"Mr. President, I have given the order for a retaliatory strike against Hezbollah. An F-35 is poised to drop a single 150-kiloton weapon on the epicenter of Hezbollah's position in southern Lebanon."

Rabinovich had barely finished his sentence when Conner jumped in. "Do you have any idea of how many people will die . . . innocent people!" he implored.

There was no response.

"Are you there, Mr. Prime Minister?" a frantic Conner asked.

"A moment, Mr. President."

Rabinovich watched as the second hand on the clock ticked down to the moment of detonation. A video screen carried an image of the target from a camera mounted on the plane's belly. A blinding flash appeared, followed by a roiling ball of flames.

"I'm afraid it's too late, President Conner."

"My God, Avi, what have you done?"

Before he could respond, Rabinovich heard some commotion on Conner's end.

"That was my chief of staff confirming a nuclear detonation in southern Lebanon. The world is going to turn on you, Mr. Prime Minister. "

"When has the world ever sided with the Jews, Mr. President?"

"Have we not supported you, supplied you with the means to defend your nation, Mr. Prime Minister?"

"Of course you have, and it is not my intent to imply anything to the contrary. The United States has been a great friend to Israel—and you and I, Mr. President, have enjoyed a long and trusting relationship. But my first allegiance must always be to my people."

"I need to speak with my staff. I'm sure you can understand that, Mr. Prime Minister. And I need to speak with Commander Hart."

"I will have the Commander contact you immediately."

"Thank you. May God help us all."

CHAPTER TWENTY-TWO

Hiroshima Revisited

THE SKY WAS AN UNBROKEN POWDER BLUE as the F-35I, under the command of Major Mark Levin, flew undetected across the Israeli/Lebanon border. Flying 20,000 feet above the Litani River valley, Levin could see the outline of Tyre to his left and Jazzin ahead at one o'clock. His target, Jouaiyya, would soon be directly below.

Three loud beeps resonated in the tight confines of the cockpit, indicating the arrival of a nuclear authentication code. Each nuke in Israel's arsenal was outfitted with a Permissive Action Link, a safety mechanism designed to prevent inadvertent detonation should the weapon fall into the wrong hands. Levin responded to the beeps by punching in a 13-digit confirmation code that fused and armed the bomb. As he entered the last digit, Avi Rabinovich's voice came through his headphones . . . the last confirmation that hell was about to be unleashed on earth.

"The weapon is hot, Sir. Requesting final authorization for the weapon's release."

"So authorized. Godspeed, Major." The comm line went dead.

The bomb, predicated upon a pilfered design of the U.S. Air Force's W-80, weighed a scant 350 pounds. It measured twelve inches in diameter and thirty inches in length.

Levin struggled to wrap his mind around the level of destructive force contained within the stainless steel cylinder as he adjusted the weapon's yield to 150 kilotons.

He removed a metal gate covering a flashing red button. Without a second thought, he pressed it. He could feel the tug of hydraulic louvers opening in the plane's bomb bay. When the light turned green, Levin pressed the button a second time, releasing the device.

The pilot lowered the blast visor on his helmet, then banked hard to the left, taking the F35 out to sea. A belly-mounted camera tracked the bomb's trajectory, transmitting images of the trailing topography to the Bor and to Levin's heads-up display.

The nuke was fused for an aerial burst at an altitude of 1,500 feet. That would maximize the blast effects while significantly reducing the amount of radioactive fallout generated from vaporized ground debris. That meant IDF troops would be able to occupy the land within a few days, if necessary, without exposure to unsustainable levels of radiation.

It would take about forty-two seconds for the bomb to free-fall nearly 19,000 feet. He watched as a chronograph located in the weapon's control system clicked off each second until detonation. As the last second evaporated, Levin witnessed an unearthly brilliance—evident even through the seemingly impenetrable visor. A fraction of a second later, the initial shock wave smacked the tail of the F35I with a force equal to 3 Gs, tossing it like a paper airplane.

Levin wrestled with the joystick before regaining full command of his craft. It was then that the magnitude of what he had unleashed hit him. Raising the visor, he peered at the images on his heads-up display. A massive fireball was rising on the horizon. With the press of a button, he had become one of the greatest murderers of all time.

"Foxtrot Whiskey Bravo 7 . . . is everything okay, Major?" It was the tower calling at Ramat Airbase.

"Roger, Tower. Just more of a kick than I anticipated. Beginning my turn now on vector 177, headed home." He tried to conceal any feelings of remorse that he feared might be evident in his tone.

"There's a crowd of well-wishers waiting for you, Major."

Levin didn't respond.

Osama Hiram saw something glinting in the sunlight. He shaded his eyes with his hand, hoping to make out the indistinct image.

"Look!" he yelled to the soldiers under his command, but all he received were shrugs as his comrades searched the heavens for the invisible bogey.

It was no bird—far too large and too high—nor was it drone, for it appeared to be free-falling. And then it dawned on him—the horrific realization of what was descending from the heavens.

"Run!" he screamed, "Now . . . get in the shelter!" His voice rose in alarm with each word.

But Hiram's words came too late. Just as he averted his eyes, the weapon detonated high above the Hezbollah encampment. Osama Hiram was vaporized by a flash of energy traveling at the speed of light. All that remained of the officer was his shadow.

150 million calories of energy were released in the form of light and radiation. The surrounding air fueled the formation of a fireball that expanded in seconds from no larger than a basketball to a half a mile in diameter. Temperatures at its core exceeded 200 million degrees.

Steel melted, concrete crumbled, and wood was turned to carbon.

More than a thousand people simply ceased to exist in the seconds following the explosion. Some left shadows on the ground or on walls, as had Osama Hiram. Others left nothing but dust.

That initial pulse of energy—consisting of both thermal and radiation—killed thousands. Exposed skin was charred black within a three-mile radius of the blast. It fell from victims' bodies in sheets—leaving muscle, bone, and sinew exposed to the elements. Anyone sustaining third degree burns over more than 25 percent of their body would likely go into shock and die within hours.

Other victims emerged from partially collapsed structures, many bleeding from severe injuries such as bones jutting through their skin. People screamed in pain and begged for water to soothe their parched throats. Within a mile and half of the blast's epicenter, total body radiation exposure equaled 300 to 500 rads, a dose incompatible with life.

Even at a distance of five miles, there were innumerable casualties with second degree burns. People stumbled and fell due to temporary flash-blindness as their retinas were overwhelmed by the white-hot light.

The once powder blue sky was now dark, transformed by a mushroom cloud that reached 40,000 feet into the heavens and spanned nearly seven miles across at its top.

As the fireball reached its zenith, a dirty rain began to fall. People opened their mouths to capture the droplets, hoping they would bring some small measure of relief. But they quickly spit it out because of its strong metallic taste. The rain was laced with the afterbirth of a nuclear bomb—a dozen by-products of radioactive fission and fusion that included Cesium-137, Strontium-90, and Tritium, a deadly combination, for the few survivors who lived long enough, only to ultimately succumb to the effects of such fallout.

People who had been sheltered from the initial pulse of ionizing radiation were not spared the bomb's devastating effects. The blast wave created tremendous over-pressure that toppled buildings, burst lungs, and shattered eardrums. While an over-pressure of four psi is considered sufficient to destroy homes and small buildings, in the immediate blast area, it exceeded ten psi. Winds in excess of 750 miles an hour ripped across the landscape, leveling everything in their path.

The unimaginable carnage expanded far beyond the immediate target. In Tyre, ten miles to the west, windows had shattered, sending deadly shards of glass flying through the air and resulting in irreparable eye damage to dozens; others wounds were even more severe.

The hands of death reached deep into the countryside and squeezed the life out of thousands of additional civilians, like Issa.

Seven-year-old Issa Najar was on the playground of her school in Maarakeh at the instant the bomb detonated.

She had been facing north, in the direction of Beirut, and the flash was at her back, but that didn't save her. She cried out as her blouse ignited in a flash, leaving its pattern indelibly burned into her skin. She ran screaming towards the school, but only rubble remained. It had been crushed by the explosion, as had the bodies of 160 children and their teachers who had been awaiting their turn for recess. She fell to her knees, wailing in pain for her mother, surrounded by corpses with blood streaming from their ears, mouths agape.

The scene in Ain Baal, a town famous for housing the sarcophagus of King Hiram I, was little different. Though its inhabitants were spared instantaneous death, it was within a ring of land that received 300 rads of radiation. Though the outward effects of the bomb were less apparent, within hours, victims became nauseated and disoriented and suffered from increasingly severe gastro-intestinal cramping.

Zeke Abbar had been standing at the high point of his property, a little hill covered with olive trees, when he was overwhelmed by the unearthly flash of light. He dropped his basket, spilling hundreds of ripe olives as he fell to the ground. He didn't know how long he had been lying there, hours probably, when a neighbor came to his aid. Ishtar Kama helped the man struggle to his feet, crushing olives beneath his sandals. The two men wove their way down the hill, eventually reaching Abbar's small home.

"Lie down, Zeke, I'll get you some water."

But Abbar waved him off. "Thank you, my friend, but I'll be okay." Forcing a smile, he politely dismissed the man.

When Ishtar returned that night to check on Zeke, he found his neighbor acutely ill, dry retching and writhing in pain.

"Tell me how to help you, my friend. I don't know what to do!" Ishtar cried out in exasperation.

Abbar shook his head, sensing that there was nothing to be done. There were no medical facilities within miles of Ain Baal. Though his wounds were far less severe, large blisters covered Ishtar's hands, arms, and face. Still, his focus was on his friend.

Ishtar emptied the pot into which Abbar had vomited, refilled a bottle with water, and promised to return in the morning.

When he returned, Abbar was fading in and out of consciousness. He had begged for God to take him—to end the suffering, but God did not appear to be listening. It would take seven days for Zeke Abbar to succumb to acute radiation sickness. Enough time for the lining of his intestines to slough off, his skin to slowly disintegrate, and his nervous system to shut down.

All in all, there would be few survivors within three miles of the epicenter. Even at five miles, the survival rate would be only fifty percent.

Hezbollah had been embedded in southern Lebanon. The terrorist group had surrounded itself with civilian shields—believing that the Israelis would not risk the collateral damage of killing innocent women and children.

But Hezbollah was wrong . . . dead wrong. They had miscalculated the level of provocation created by their first use of a weapon of mass destruction against Tel Aviv. In return, Israel had released a force of biblical proportions . . .

a force that was indiscriminate in doling out death to all within its reach.

If there was good news to be found amidst such tragedy, it was that the prevailing winds—from the south and east—carried much of the radioactivity out to sea rather than over northern Israel.

Even so, a heavy price had been paid in Kiryat Shmona, Nahariyya, and other Israeli border towns. Though only given a brief warning, Homeland Front had successfully sheltered eighty percent of the population. Of those who remained on the streets or in the homes, there were massive casualties.

Rabinovich watched every moment of the drama unfold following his order to release the bomb. As the mushroom cloud roiled, he tried to imagine the devastation wrought on his command. The bravado he had exhibited earlier with President Conner had evaporated in the brilliant flash of nuclear devastation.

A data-feed from Israeli Military Intelligence provided an initial assessment of the number of fatalities and injuries. The death toll was expected to climb to just under 20,000, with an additional 45,000 injured.

Almost falling to his knees, Rabinovich steadied himself enough to land in a chair. He covered his eyes with his hands and rocked slowly back and forth.

"My God, my God, what have I done," those closest to the prime minister heard him whisper. After a moment, he withdrew his hands from his face and turned to Simon.

"General, we are now fighting for our very existence. I need to collect my thoughts. If you would take the helm for a moment, I would be grateful."

"Yes, Sir."

All eyes were trained on an electronic map of Iran on which icons in the shape of missiles indicated key launch sites. If a missile was deployed, it would be picked up by satellite-based infra-red sensors and depicted on the map with a red circle. Ground-based radar would then track the missile's trajectory. Once the targets had been extrapolated, they would appear on a map depicting the estimated time to impact.

People sat on the edge of their seats awaiting signs of the impending retaliation. But nothing appeared on the screen. Fifteen minutes passed before a shaken Rabinovich stood to address those assembled.

"What I have done is unconscionable, just as was the chemical attack launched against our nation. Right now, we don't have time for recrimination. The Iranians may already be preparing to launch their missiles rather than wait for the forty-eight-hour deadline to lapse. It is vitally important that we not lose another second as we determine our next step . . . a step that must result in the elimination of the Sword of Damocles that Iran has hung over our nation."

The Iranians were apoplectic as they watched reports of the bombing stream in. The Ayatollah, President Rouhani, and a host of other Iranian leaders had been whisked off to the fortified bunker at Doshan-Tappeh. Ayatollah Khamenei looked around the table before picking up the phone connected to Moscow.

"General Gerasimov, I am giving you the courtesy of an advance warning as I prepare to order deployment of our missiles against the Jews," the Ayatollah began, only to be summarily cut off by the Russian.

"You will do nothing of the kind!" Gerasimov seethed. "You've gotten but a small taste of the destructive force the Israelis can unleash on their enemies. Strike them now, and I can assure you that your country will be incinerated in a battle with the Jews!"

"General, our countries enjoy a powerful alliance that is about to reshape the political landscape of the Middle East. Russia will gain dominance over the region, displacing the Americans, and Iran will have eliminated a scourge that stains this land. Why do you wish to stop us at this critical moment?"

"Because I want us to succeed . . . not become martyrs in some holy war designed to invoke the return of your twelfth Messiah."

"Your words are laden with contempt, General. That's something I would expect from our enemies, not our friends."

"Russia is neither your enemy nor your friend, but an ally in a fragile alliance that can be shattered through impulsive decisions that put the entire Coalition at risk."

Gerasimov paused, contemplating the wisdom of what he was about to say before proceeding. "General Soleimani, whom I know is with you at this moment, possesses a particularly vitriolic hatred of the Jews."

"And for that, I offer no apologies!" Soleimani shouted before being silenced by the Ayatollah.

"Battles are not won by mad dogs, but by calm minds, gentlemen. Under no circumstances will you release your weapons without my explicit orders. Is that understood?"

"I understand what you have said, General Gerasimov, but my orders do not come from you or from any other mortal. Do you understand that?"

"If you release your missiles prior to the expiration of the deadline, you will have two nuclear armed adversaries with whom to deal!' Gerasimov slammed down the receiver of the phone.

The Ayatollah appeared calm despite the threat. "I will pray, and then we will determine how to respond."

CHAPTER TWENTY-THREE

Conner and Hart Speak

"My God, Commander . . . I sent you there to be an advisor, not a passive observer of Armageddon! Couldn't you stop him?" It was an obligatory question by Conner, for which he already knew the answer.

"I am sorry, Mr. President. I tried to weigh in, but my comments were dismissed by the prime minister. Mr. Rabinovich and his Security Council are convinced that Israel faces an existential threat. Being here on the ground, it is hard to argue with their conclusion."

"How far is the prime minister willing to go?"

"I believe there is no limit to what Mr. Rabinovich and his supporters are willing to do to protect the Jewish state."

"That's what I was afraid of."

"What would you have them do, Mr. President?"

"That's the problem, Commander Hart; I would do the same damn thing! But Israel may suffer the consequences of their actions. The nuke they dropped in southern Lebanon will likely be sufficient provocation needed for Iran to unfurl its missiles. That's why I'm pulling you out of there. There's a plane waiting for you at Ben Gurion airport. I want you on it in thirty minutes."

"Permission to speak openly, Sir?"

"Granted."

"You know I don't run from a fight, Sir. You sent me here for a reason . . . to support a vitally important ally under peril. From my perspective, that job is just beginning."

"What are you suggesting, Commander?"

"If the Iranians were going to strike, I believe their missiles would be in the air. Something is holding them back—maybe the Russians. So the chess game continues, albeit on a greatly accelerated timetable."

"And what would you recommend as a next move, Commander?"

"A two-pronged strategy, Mr. President. The first part would be a diplomatic effort to coalesce the Saudi-led Sunni coalition you suggested earlier. It would need to happen with resounding speed."

"Things have changed, Commander. What makes you believe they would rally behind Israel after witnessing the carnage created in southern Lebanon?"

"Because they understand that the prime minister's actions were essential to Israel's survival, and they respect his show of strength in response to Iran's imperialistic ambitions. This morning, it was Tel Aviv in Iranian gun sights. A day, a week, a month from now it could be Jeddah, Riyadh, or Cairo under siege. Such a threat requires an immediate response."

"And Israel's response to such an initiative? We would be asking them to welcome historic enemies into their tent. Are we going out on limb, Commander?"

"No more than Roosevelt did when aligning with Stalin to defeat Hitler. The Israelis will support it."

"And once we have a coalition . . . what then? Is it a fighting force in name only?"

"We plan the immediate invasion of Iran, not with a massive troop movement that would force their hand, but with tremendous stealth. You're familiar with Operation Delilah, Sir."

"Yes, Commander, and its risks."

"We would need the Sunni Coalition to open up their airspace to the Israeli Air Force, giving it access to a deployment area near the Iranian border. They would also need to provide some degree of air support."

"Can it be done?

"It will take some time to work out the details, Mr. President."

"Then I suggest you get on it, Commander. I am extending your tour of duty until the expiration of the Iranian ultimatum. I'll do my part to accelerate the discussions with our Sunni friends.

"Are you in front of a monitor, Commander?" Conner continued.

"No, Sir."

"Well, you need to be."

CHAPTER TWENTY-FOUR

"Israel Will Never Capitulate!"

SEATED BEHIND A SMALL DESK, Rabinovich began his second televised address in little more than three hours. "My people, I wish that I brought you good news," the prime minister began. "But the death toll from the heinous attack launched earlier this morning against Tel Aviv continues to climb. Although Home Front Defense has done everything in their power to respond to the catastrophe, men, women, and children lie dying in our hospitals."

He paused while images from Ben Gurion Hospital appeared on a split screen.

"There has never been any doubt as to the perpetrator—Hezbollah. However, the sophistication of the weapons used in the attack suggests that Iran and other members of the Syrian Coalition were complicit. We cannot allow the brazen use of a Weapon of Mass Destruction to go unchallenged.

"That is why, at 9:57 a.m., we responded by deploying a single nuclear device targeted at the epicenter of Hezbollah's missile complex near Jouaiyya in southern Lebanon. The destruction was not limited to military targets, and some of the effects of the blast impacted our own people in northern Israel.

"Realizing that this might be the outcome, the decision was made only after lengthy deliberation by the National Security Council and others branches of government. But I have no interest in placing responsibility on a faceless bureaucracy. The full burden of this painful decision rests squarely on my shoulders. Now I know what President Truman meant when he said, 'The buck stops here.'

"Justice has always been a defining principle of the Jewish people, as has mercy. But when our people are slaughtered in the streets, we must respond with our fists, not merely our words. The Jewish people came close to annihilation during the Holocaust, and when we finally achieved a homeland through the birth of this great nation, we pledged: *Never Again.*

"Although the bomb neutralized the menace of further major attacks by Hezbollah, another threat looms. Israel remains under the shadow of an Iranian ultimatum . . . one that demands our complete surrender. President Rouhani, acting on behalf of the Ayatollah, has given us forty-eight hours in which to capitulate or face the possibility of Iranian nuclear missiles striking our cities."

Rising to his feet, Rabinovich raised his fist and shouted angrily. "We will never capitulate! We will meet force with overwhelming force! Stand down, President Rouhani! Do not escalate this conflict. To do so will result in the utter destruction of your country and the death of millions of Iranians."

He remained standing until the director said, "Cut." But the pre-emptive programming did not stop. In a well-choreographed hand-off, President Jonathan Conner picked up the prime minister's theme as he spoke from the Oval Office.

"You have just heard Prime Minister Rabinovich of Israel describe the potential existential threat facing his nation. While the United States condemns the use of nuclear weapons under any and all circumstances, we respect the right of Israel to preserve its safety and sovereignty.

"The world has moved one step closer to war. I had hoped that this day would never arrive, but now that it has, we must deal with it as a unified nation resolved to stand by our principles—beginning with our commitment to ensure the safety of all Americans, as well as that of our allies.

"If you believe in God, now is the time to pray. Pray that this crisis is averted and a degree of sanity is restored in our world."

With that, Conner signed off.

CHAPTER TWENTY-FIVE

Holding Down the Fort

HER EYES GLUED TO A MONITOR at Langley, an overwhelming sense of dread enshrouded Liz as she listened to Israeli Prime Minister Rabinovich and President Conner deliver back-to-back accounts of the events unfolding in the Middle East. Tel Aviv was on lock-down following a devastating chemical attack, and her husband was right in the thick of it.

As Rabinovich said the words *weapon of mass destruction,* memories of the horrific attacks perpetrated against the United States flooded her mind. The fact that she and John had survived both nuclear and biological events was miraculous. She wasn't interested in testing fate a third time.

The sound of her cell phone startled Liz, instantly dissipating the fog of memories. She quickly muted the TV before answering.

She said, "Hello," but there was no response. She looked at the number—"Private Caller." It had to be John. "Hello!" she shouted into the receiver.

"I'm right here, Darling, no need to shout."

Liz let out a long sigh. "Thank God you're okay!"

"Why wouldn't I be?" Hart answered as if bemused. "I'm so sorry I couldn't call you sooner. I've been captive in a conference room for hours, and the topic du jour is a pretty heavy one. I finally caught a break, and you were top of my mind."

"John, I saw the images of Tel Aviv—the dead and dying lining the sidewalks." Her tone was serious.

"You know where I am, and you know that the facility is protected against such attacks. So, that's one worry you can let go of."

Until Liz entered his life, Hart rarely thought about the risks involved in a mission. You didn't get into this line of work if you wanted to die peacefully in your sleep. You got into it because you were impelled by some force, a demon that put country above safety and subjugated all fear.

But something had changed in Hart. He had a job to do, and he'd do it impeccably. But then he wanted to return safely to the woman he loved.

"What can you share with me?" Liz's anxiety was palpable.

Though she held a Top Secret clearance, everything John was doing was compartmentalized—shared only on a need-to-know basis . . . and emotional distress did not constitute a need to know.

"It's ugly. As you heard on television, Iran has given Israel less than forty-eight hours in which to capitulate. I'm sure you can imagine how that's going over with the Israelis."

"Promise me you're not going to get dragged into the fight, Cowboy . . . not beyond offering guidance to the prime minister, per your orders."

"Darling, I'm not part of the Israeli Defense Force. I'm merely an advisor representing the interests of the United States at the behest of our president. You know that."

"And I know you," she responded without missing a beat. "You have some kind of a complex about saving people. It's one of your most admirable qualities . . . and one of your most maddening ones—at least, for someone who loves you. Don't do it this time. I have a feeling . . . it's strong enough that I'd even call it a premonition."

"Come on, Liz. Don't go getting superstitious on me. Your premonition is just anxiety. Put those thoughts out of your head."

"Don't be patronizing. I'm serious, John."

"So am I, Darling. This event is going to play out over the next few days, and then I'll be home grabbing your ass and anything else I can put my hands on."

For the first time in hours, Liz laughed. "You're incorrigible, Cowboy!"

"That's why you love me. Remember?"

"Yes, I remember. Call me, John. Don't keep me in the dark. My mind goes to bad places."

"Yes, Ma'am. I love you, Darling."

"Love you, too!"

As he disconnected the call, Hart prayed that Armageddon had not begun.

CHAPTER TWENTY-SIX

Mutually Assured Destruction?

HART HAD BARELY HUNG UP THE PHONE when someone knocked on the door of his quarters.

"Mr. Prime Minister . . . I wasn't expecting you, Sir."

"May I?" Rabinovich asked as he walked through the door.

Hart gestured to the couch and pulled up a chair facing the prime minister.

"I wanted a chance to talk with you alone, John. We both heard President Conner's carefully chosen words. And I know you will be equally careful in your response to what I am about to ask you. But I also trust that you will be honest."

"Yes, Sir. And there's something of great importance I must discuss with you."

"So tell me, do we truly have the full support of the United States at this perilous moment in our history?"

"I thought that was explicit in President Conner's remarks, Mr. Prime Minister."

"Is your president willing to risk a direct confrontation with Russia to protect the interests of the Jewish state?"

"Yes, Sir. You have our full support, Mr. Prime Minister. That is not the issue."

"Then what is the issue, Commander?"

"Our support may not be enough."

"What are you saying, Commander Hart?"

"We need additional assistance from the region. President Conner has been in dialogue with the Saudis, Jordanians, and Egyptians since this conflict erupted. He believes, as do I, that the Sunni nations will join forces with Israel to defeat the Shia theocracy. All they need is a little encouragement from the U.S."

"You are asking me to partner with our adversaries? Is that what you are saying, Commander Hart?"

"We are asking the very same thing of your so-called 'adversaries,' Mr. Prime Minister. Pick your poison, Sir, the Sunnis or the Shia . . . one has nuclear-tipped missiles pointed at your country; the other offers possible salvation."

"You are presenting me with a Faustian bargain, Commander."

"No, Sir. We are asking that you keep an open mind at this dire time."

Rabinovich nodded his head slowly . . . acknowledging, perhaps, that he had little choice.

"We have hours, Commander, not weeks, in which to defuse the situation. Surely you and President Conner discussed more immediate interventions."

"Sir, you may recall a joint-response planning exercise convened in spring 2017. The war game involved a hypothetical Iranian missile crisis similar to what we are witnessing today. Based upon the outcome, we formulated a strategic response to an imminent attack on Israel."

"Yes. Delilah!" Rabinovich proclaimed.

"Correct, Sir. The President believes it may be time to shear the hair of the Iranians."

"And you see this as a viable option despite the timetable?"

"Yes, Sir. I see it as our best option."

"I am surprised that President Conner would support the additional use of nuclear weapons—arguably moving us closer to mutually assured destruction."

"Under Delilah, the nukes are not intended to kill, but to disarm. The President asked that I share our recommendation with you at the appropriate time."

"I guess my visit was fortuitously timed."

"I had planned to request a meeting with you, Sir."

"I'm going to ask you to repeat to the NSC exactly what you just shared with me."

Rabinovich stood and moved towards the door. "Come on, Commander—it's show time."

Hart's briefing to the NSC was under two minutes in length, yet it provided the requisite grist for a heady discussion.

Rabinovich turned to David Chaikin and Major General Tamir Heiman, the newly appointed head of the IDF's Military Intelligence Directorate.

"Do we have the necessary intelligence to execute the strategy laid out by Commander Hart?"

Before responding, Heiman typed a series of commands on a keyboard, bringing up a map with icons indicating the locations of Iran's so-called missile cities. They covered a broad geographic area, much of it inhospitable.

"We've identified these subterranean silos, each of which houses hundreds if not thousands of missiles and their mobile launch vehicles. We believe that the silos are constructed of steel-reinforced concrete with sufficient depth to withstand a direct surface strike . . . maybe even our bunker-buster munitions. If that is correct, the only thing that stands a chance of taking them out with certainty is a nuke."

"So we are going to avoid nuclear war by deploying more nuclear weapons . . . is that what you are saying, General?" Rabinovich asked.

"I see no other option, Mr. Prime Minister," Heiman responded.

Sensing Rabinovich's reluctance, David Chaikin spoke.

"I believe we can significantly improve our odds, Mr. Prime Minister."

"And how is that, David?"

"Despite the vast array of silos, we have a high level of confidence that only five currently house Iran's most advanced missiles. All are within striking distance of our special forces—if they are rapidly deployed."

"Go on," Rabinovich prodded.

"We could execute a modified version of Delilah, as Commander Hart alluded to in his remarks. Our teams would be armed with backpack nukes . . . a more sophisticated version of the U.S. B-54. They have an adjustable yield, as well as a relatively low radiation signature. If set to deliver a one- to two-kiloton blast and properly situated, we're confident that the silos would be destroyed with little to no collateral damage."

"If I may interject, Mr. Chaikin," Hart stood to speak. "Unless we destroy all five silos simultaneously, IRGC Missile Command will order a retaliatory strike upon evidence of an Israeli incursion into Iran."

"Are you suggesting that it is too risky, Commander?" Rabinovich questioned.

"No, Sir. Delilah anticipated this threat. To overcome it, we must decapitate their missile command structure by initiating an attack on its nerve center located at the Semnan Missile and Space Center. By severing all forms of communications from Semnan, we force the Iranians to do a work-around to fire their missiles . . . and that will take time, Mr. Prime Minister."

Rabinovich turned to his senior intelligence officer. "You said we had a high probability of success if our forces were deployed rapidly. What constitutes *rapidly*, Mr. Chaikin?" Skepticism was evident in the prime minister's voice.

"Within a twelve-hour window."

"Moshe, do you agree with this assessment, and is it doable?" Rabinovich asked Simon.

"That depends, Sir."

"On what?"

"On whether President Conner can convince our Sunni neighbors to collaborate. Our ability to traverse their air space without threat of retaliation is critically important to these missions. If we can draw a straight line from our airbases across Jordan and Saudi Arabia, then we will dramatically shorten the time required to reach the Iranian border."

All eyes turned towards Hart, awaiting confirmation.

"I know he is working on it as we speak," Hart responded.

"Two hours, Gentlemen, at which point I will expect a detailed briefing describing the operation," Rabinovich ordered before standing to adjourn the meeting.

Rabinovich retired to his quarters, knowing there was one more crisis that he had to address. He picked up the phone and dialed his wife.

"Before you say anything, Rachel, know how sorry I am for not calling sooner."

"My darling Avi, I'm just relieved to hear your voice. What kind of wife would I be if I were mad at you? I know the grievous issues that weigh on your mind."

"Grievous indeed! I don't know how this will all play out, but pray that it does not end with the destruction of our beloved country . . . or with countless deaths."

"You really believe that's a possibility?" she asked, the pitch of her voice rising.

"Yes. But I want to talk with you about something else . . . I want to know what Dr. Eiseman said about the lump in your breast, and what he is recommending."

"He said there's a two-centimeter lesion in my breast, and it's cancer. The good news is that it can be removed and Eiseman doubts that there will be any lymph node involvement."

"Is there bad news?"

"The MRI showed what may be a highly diffuse lobular cancer in the same breast. He did a PET scan, which does not show any overt signs of metastatic disease. Even so, he's recommending contralateral mastectomies based upon my current disease, as well as my BRCA status. In fact, he politely reprimanded me for not prophylactically dealing with the ramifications of being BRCA positive."

"I feel lousy. You've had to shoulder this burden while I've been completely absorbed in my world. That wasn't fair to you."

"The greatest good for the greatest number. Isn't that what you say, Avi?"

"I never meant for those words to apply to you."

"Oh, but they do. They apply to everyone equally . . . that's the beautiful part about utilitarianism. But if it appeases your conscience, know that I've been grateful for the time to think before acting. And now I'm ready to have surgery. Dr. Eiseman has tentatively scheduled it for two weeks from today."

"Are you worried?"

"No. I'm resolute. I want this cancer out of my body . . . and I want to get on with my life . . . our life . . . that is, assuming there's a life to go back to after the conflict ends."

CHAPTER TWENTY-SEVEN

The Battle Plan is Drawn

Two hours seemed to pass in an instant as Rabinovich's key advisors worked feverishly to formulate a detailed battle plan before returning to the conference room. Among the last to file in were Moshe Simon and Commander Hart.

"I thought maybe you had gone out for a bite of lunch, Moshe," the prime minister jabbed at his general, only partly in jest.

Though he feigned a smile, it was clear that something was bothering the general.

Simon wasted no time in getting to the issue. "Avi, something troubles me about Delilah," Simon began. "Overall, it's a good plan, but it may rely on a flawed assumption . . . a potentially fatal flaw, if I may use that phrase."

"And that is?"

"If we succeed in taking out the missile command center at Semnan, we've significantly reduced the Iranians' capacity for launch. But that's not good enough. From my perspective, the possibility of a retaliatory strike must be zero."

"I don't see how that is achievable," Rabinovich said, tilting his head to the side.

"If I may, I would like to walk you through a modified plan from the beginning. I'm going to ask Commander Hart to assist me."

"Do the modifications reflect your thinking, as well, Commander?"

Hart nodded, leaving elaboration up to Simon.

"The commander recommended two important changes, which I will get to in a moment." Simon paused briefly.

"Our plan calls for the deployment of five ten-man Sayaret teams."

Sayaret referred to Israel's elite Special Forces, whose lineage dated to the formation of a unique commando unit in 1953, Unit 101, under the leadership of David Sharon. Since then Sayaret had evolved into a sophisticated fighting force with units dedicated to special missions ranging from field engineering to reconnaissance. Its naval unit, known as Shayetet 13, became widely celebrated for its high-profile missions, including the raid on Entebbe on July 4, 1976.

"Once we have secured permission to cross Jordanian and Saudi airspace, assuming that President Conner is successful in persuading the Sunnis to collaborate, the teams will travel by C-130 to a departure point just south of the Kuwaiti border near Hafar al Batin. They will use it as a staging area, waiting until we have successfully executed two sentinel events designed to create a warm welcome for our troops. Then they will be shuttled by helicopter to their targets."

"What do you mean by *sentinel events*, Moshe?"

"The modifications that Commander Hart and I agreed were needed to bullet-proof the plan."

"Go ahead," Rabinovich said impatiently.

"Seconds before the teams depart, our Dolphin located in the Straits of Hormuz will fire a single Popeye cruise missile aimed at Semnan Missile Control Complex. Its warhead will be set to a micro-yield, just under a kiloton. Thanks to GPS guidance, it will explode within six feet of our intended target. Nothing will remain."

"And the second sentinel event?"

"Once we've taken Iran's missiles temporarily off-line, we will need a more permanent solution. You will order the Dolphin to fire a Jericho III intercontinental ballistic missile armed with a one-megaton nuclear warhead aimed at the geographic center of Iran."

"Have you and Commander Hart lost your minds? Why would we kill millions of innocent civilians when our primary goal is to mitigate a threat?"

"We wouldn't kill anyone with the nuclear blast, at least not directly. Rather than allowing the weapon to descend to earth, it will be detonated 200 miles above the target in the ionosphere. The bomb will cause no immediately visible physical damage. However, the resulting EMP will shut down all but hardened electrical circuits in the country, making communication impossible. It will effectively return Iran to the Stone Age.

"You know how this would work, Avi; you've studied the results of Starfish Prime in the early 1960s. The U.S. blew out electrical circuits 900 miles from the blast site."

"What if the SAM batteries remain operational?"

"I would assume as much," Simon conceded. "The newer batteries undoubtedly employ hardened circuitry. We plan for a squadron of F-15s equipped with electronic warfare devices to criss-cross Iranian air space to ensure that all

SAM batteries have been neutralized. F-16s will provide further cover for our helicopters.

"After that, we own the skies over Iran."

Simon typed a quick command on his computer, causing a map to appear on the monitors.

"Our helicopters will be ready to depart for targets that include Parchin Military Complex west of Semnan on the outskirts of Tehran; the Karaj Missile Development facility also proximate to Tehran; Hamadan Gostaresh Scientific Research Facility, Isfahan Missile Complex in west-central Iran; and Bakhtaran Missile Base near Kerman Shahan in western Iran."

As Simon spoke, flashing red dots appeared on the screens signifying the location of each missile silo. "As you can see, there's a lot of ground to cover.

"The helicopters transporting the Sayaret units will be coming in low, at an altitude just over 200 feet. The birds will be painted to resemble those used by the Iranian Air Force. That should confuse anyone guarding the silos and delay any defensive action."

"Will the silos be undefended?" Rabinovich asked in disbelief.

"At most, we expect our forces to encounter minor opposition at the sites, which will be quickly dispatched with automatic weapons fire and air-to-ground missiles prior to landing."

"I don't understand . . . If I was Rouhani, I would have a small army guarding such weapons," Rabinovich countered.

"They believe in their omnipotence, as well as in the inability of Israel to penetrate their air defenses, Sir. Assuming I am correct, our teams will then have less than ten minutes in which to fuse, arm, and place their weapons in a manner that will inflict maximal damage to the subterranean silos—including the time required to re-board the helicopters and get the hell out of harm's way."

"When will they be in the safe zone?"

"If they are able to place the devices at sufficient depth, the safe distance from ground zero will be significantly reduced, perhaps to as little as a mile. However, in order to minimize any exposure to thermal or ionizing radiation, not to mention a shock wave that could drop a bird from the sky, we're instructing them to be five miles from ground zero at the moment of detonation."

"What are the mission's key points of vulnerability, Commander?"

All eyes turned towards Hart, waiting to see if he would expose the fly in the ointment.

"There are always unanticipated dangers. With that said, I believe our greatest vulnerability is our capacity to mount and execute the strategy, as defined, in the time remaining before the expiration of the ultimatum.

"Frankly, Sir, we don't have a chance in hell without the cooperation of the Saudis and Jordanians."

As if on cue, an aide appeared. "President Conner is on the line, Sir."

"Put him through on speaker," he ordered.

"Mr. Prime Minister, I have some good news for you at this troubled time."

"That would be music to my ears, President Conner. Please, share your good news with all who are assembled here, including Commander Hart."

"You are cleared to utilize Saudi and Jordanian airspace, as well as Hafar al Batin for staging. Both countries have pledged to fly air support missions as needed."

Rabinovich was awestruck. "Would you repeat that, Mr. President?"

"You heard me correctly, Mr. Prime Minister. The Saudis and Jordanians are on board. We expect similar collaboration from the Egyptians shortly. So, Delilah proceeds!"

"With one major modification, Mr. President."

"And what would that be, Mr. Prime Minister?"

Rabinovich outlined the intent to fire an ICBM capable of generating a strong EMP.

"You are running a hell of risk, aren't you? The Russians may feel justified in responding to such a brazen act on behalf of their ally."

"That's why we are counting on you, President Conner, to communicate that such an action would result in American retaliation. We are relying on the principle of MAD."

"I will take that under advisement, Mr. Prime Minister. I know you have your hands full and speed is of the essence. Good luck."

As Conner was disconnected, Rabinovich turned to Moshe. "Good news, and potentially bad news. Are there other obvious threats that we've failed to address?"

"There are two other silos at Mashad and Tabas, on the eastern border of Iran. We do not believe they represent a material threat, based upon intelligence that is several weeks old. Furthermore, we believe that the IRGC would house missiles more proximate to their target—not at the furthest points from Israel."

"I pray you are right, my old friend. I doubt there will be much opportunity to sleep once we put Delilah in motion," Rabinovich stated. "Let's take time now to regroup and, to the best of our ability, get a moment's rest. The mission will commence tomorrow at 0700 hours.

"Commander Hart, you will be leading one of the teams."

CHAPTER TWENTY-EIGHT

Memories of Khrushchev and Kennedy

CONNER KNEW THERE WOULD BE NO WINNER in a shooting match with Russia. The principle of Mutual Assured Destruction had proven instrumental in preventing nuclear war for more than seventy years, despite periods of intense bellicosity. He prayed that sanity would continue to rule as an image of the stoic Russian president seated at a massive walnut desk came into focus.

"Thank you, President Putin, for speaking with me at this precarious moment in history . . . a moment that could inadvertently drag both of our nations into an escalating conflict."

"I'm afraid that I'm not following you, President Conner. What could possibly escalate to the point that Russia and America would find themselves in direct confrontation? That hasn't happened since President Kennedy was in office."

Conner studied the face of his adversary on the monitor. Putin was a practiced liar, his eyes failing to betray any hint of deception.

"We don't have time for denials. There's far too much at stake—in the Middle East, as well as within our borders."

"Are you speaking of the Israeli aggression against Lebanon . . . a horrific escalation involving the use of a nuclear weapon? Do you pretend to justify such actions, President Conner?"

"The United States deplores the use of any weapon of mass destruction, particularly when it represents an existential threat to a sovereign nation. Therefore, we condemn Hezbollah and its Iranian sponsors for unleashing a nerve agent on Tel Aviv."

"You are justifying the death of thousands in Jouaiyya by citing an action that may have killed a few hundred Israelis. Is that the calculus under which you operate, President Conner?"

"There would have been virtually no casualties had the SCUD missiles not been armed with a deadly nerve agent. And although we don't yet have the forensic toxicology to confirm the specific compound, there are strong indications that it was a Novichok agent . . . a weapon unique to your country's arsenal."

Putin chuckled. "So now you are accusing us of supplying terrorists with weapons of mass destruction. The Iranians and Syrians have maintained stockpiles of Sarin and VX for years. I suggest you wait for your chemists' findings before making such reckless accusations, President Conner."

"We don't have time for sparring, President Putin, so let me be crystal clear. The Russian government supplied Iran with weapons of mass destruction, specifically a Novichok-5 agent that was subsequently transferred to Hezbollah in Lebanon via Syria. It is you who helped the

Syrian Coalition draw first blood in Israel. It is you, Mr. Putin, who has Jewish blood on your hands."

Conner wasn't finished. "I thought Russia had stopped its genocide of the Jews following the pogroms."

Putin shifted slightly in his chair, the first visible sign of discomfort.

"It is not Jews who have been the target, but an imperialistic, authoritarian Zionist state that threatens the stability and safety of the region."

"Now you sound more like the Ayatollah than the president of Russia. Do not attempt to morally justify that which is reprehensible, Mr. Putin."

"I find your comments more annoying than provocative, but this conversation is rapidly growing tedious. What are you hoping to accomplish, President Conner? Do you wish to foment a war between Russia and America?"

"I hope not, but that may be the result." He paused to let his words sink in. "My intent, Mr. Putin, is to keep Russia from doing any further damage to Israel—either directly or indirectly."

"That's very admirable, Mr. President, but Russia will comport itself in a manner that it deems necessary to protect our national interests."

"As will the United States." He slowed the cadence of his speech. "Let there be no ambiguity to my words: If Russia takes any type of military action against Israel, there will be an immediate response in kind by the United States of America—including, but not limited, to a nuclear response."

"You are threatening Russia with nuclear war!" Putin yelled in outrage.

"I am glad we have reached an understanding, President Putin."

Conner terminated the call.

Five minutes later, all U.S. nuclear forces were put on high alert.

CHAPTER TWENTY-NINE

Reclaiming the Golan

IT WAS THREE A.M. ON A MOONLESS NIGHT as Syrian Coalition sentries manned their posts, confident that all remaining threats had been dispatched.

300 meters away, concealed along a line parallel to their position, Israeli snipers were making final adjustments to the Leupold Mk4 telescopic sights mounted on their M-24A3 sniper rifles. Accurate up to 1,500 meters, the U.S.-made bolt action rifles fired a .338 Lapua Magnum cartridge. With a muzzle velocity approaching 2,600 feet per second, Syrian Coalition forces would never even hear the shots that felled them.

Once their scopes had been adjusted for altitude, wind speed, and the effect of gravity on the bullet, a signal was sent to Command confirming they were ready.

Encamped 400 meters below the line of snipers, 5,000 members of the Golani Brigade and 10,000 IDF reservists were poised to retake the Golan. The men and women were under the command of Major General Nitzan Elon. Regarded as one of Israel's premier military strategists,

Elon was known for terrorizing his enemy shortly before striking with overwhelming force.

On Elon's order, a single mortar shell was dropped into a firing tube. Loaded with white phosphorus, it emitted a mournful cry as it arced across the night sky before landing in the middle of the enemy encampment. Screams pierced the air. Men, startled from their sleep, stumbled for their guns before rushing to find the source of the attack.

With the sky brilliantly illuminated, the snipers went to work, the echo of their .338-caliber rounds reverberating off the hillside. The results were immediate: Syrian Coalition forces were blown off their feet as rounds impacted torsos and heads.

Lieutenant Abdu Nadar wasn't one to panic. That's what they wanted, he told himself, stopping to light a cigarette before he joined his men.

Darkness returned momentarily as the phosphorus burned out. Then the flares went up—a steady stream of pyrotechnics that turned night into day.

"Our position is unassailable," he reassured the twelve young soldiers under his command. "This battle will be short and decisive. Some day you will tell your children about the slaughter of Israeli soldiers at the hands of the Syrian Coalition. Still, we must be prepared. They will likely come in waves, so conserve your ammunition if possible."

"Where are they, Sir . . . the Israelis?" Panic was evident in the young private's voice.

Nadar stubbed out his cigarette, walked over, and put one hand on the boy's shoulder. With the other hand he pointed at an area several hundred meters below their position. "I'm guessing they are close. Don't worry, they won't get any closer." The boy nodded and prayed that his sergeant was right.

But he wasn't. The bullet arrived without warning . . . neither sound nor muzzle flash betrayed its deadly flight. When it struck Nadar, it ripped a hole the size of a grapefruit in the middle of his neck. His head slumped onto his shoulder, and his body went limp before crumpling to the ground.

Standing over him in horror, the young soldiers were easy targets for the snipers. The next round struck the young private mid-chest, blowing apart his lungs and eviscerating his heart. Three more men went down in quick succession before the remaining seven dove for cover.

Up and down the lines, Syrian Coalition officers watched men drop like flies—all with massive, mortal injuries. The hunting continued unabated for more than an hour with officers being the most prized targets. Watching through a night vision scope, Elon smiled as he saw the terrorized troops frantically scrambling for cover.

When the number of visible targets had diminished to a mere handful, it was time for the second phase of the operation to begin. The 118th mechanized infantry unit of the Golani Brigade was called in. As soon as they were in position, a fusillade of 120 mm shells from cannons mounted atop Merkava IV battle tanks started raining down on the Golan.

Each round pierced the silence with a concussive bang, followed by a whistling sound as the round closed in on its target. Dawn had yet to break, and there was nowhere for the enemy to run or hide. The level of chaos created by the tank fire was overwhelming. Elon's strategy was working.

With less than an hour of darkness remaining, Elon signaled for the troops to move in. More than 500 rounds had been fired by the tanks, decimating large portions of the enemy's position.

A massive wave of humanity emerged from under camouflage netting and began the treacherous ascent up nearly 1,000 vertical feet. Sporadic fire came from the Syrian Coalition forces, but they were literally shooting in the dark. As Israeli forces closed in, the cannons on the tanks were silenced to eliminate any chance of casualties from friendly fire.

The first wave of Israeli combatants suffered heavy casualties at the hands of surviving Coalition troops. But their sacrifices would prove not to be in vain as a second wave of Israeli soldiers swept over the enemy like a tsunami. Syrian Regular Army soldiers, Qud Forces, and Hezbollah surrendered en masse—beseeching Israeli soldiers not to open fire.

When the battle was over, Elon radioed Moshe Simon at the Bor.

"General, it's a good day at the Golan Heights."

It had taken less than six hours to rout the enemy.

"How heavy a toll did we pay for such a good day, Nitzan?"

"Less than anticipated, but more than we would ever wish. Still, control of the Golan has been returned to Israel, and more than 10,000 Coalition forces have laid down their arms. Perhaps we've bought another decade of peace on our eastern border," Elon mused.

"Let's hope Israel survives to celebrate your victory and enjoy a time of enduring peace."

Simon's attention was diverted to a monitor carrying a broadcast of the Ayatollah. He bade Elon goodbye and focused on the Grand Leader's words.

"Only a complete surrender can spare the Jews from the fate that awaits them," the Ayatollah cried, shaking his fist in anger. "Mr. Rabinovich, bask in the short-lived glory of recapturing the Golan Heights, for it will prove to be a hollow victory when we incinerate Israel's largest cities.

"If you wish to prevent massive and unnecessary deaths, I suggest you spend the remaining hours preparing for surrender, not further provoking a nation whose missiles stand at alert—ready to wipe Israel permanently off the map."

CHAPTER THIRTY

An Attack on Iran

"It's time to go, Commander. There's a helicopter waiting for you on the roof," Benjamin Sheraz informed Hart.

"Let's do it," he said, moving quickly towards the door.

"Mr. Rabinovich has asked to speak with you before you depart, Sir."

As they approached the prime minister's war-time office, Sheraz stopped mid-stride. "He will speak to you in private, Commander."

Hart knocked on the door.

"Enter," Rabinovich stood to greet his guest.

"You asked to speak with me, Sir."

"Relax, John. I simply wanted to thank you. This is not your fight, yet you go willingly to defend our nation. May I ask why you would make such a sacrifice?"

"I'm planning on returning, Sir, so I guess the sacrifice isn't so great."

"I appreciate your quick wit, but grace me with a serious answer, Commander."

"As you request, Sir. I am here at the behest of my president, Mr. Prime Minister. I'm acting in accordance with his wishes."

"I understand why President Conner relies on you when things turn to shit and no one else can be relied upon to get the job done. May God be with you, Commander Hart. Come back in one piece, and may you help remove the threat that hovers over our nation like an angel of death."

Hart saluted the prime minister, "Thank you, Sir. I'll do my best."

"I know you will, John."

Hart turned and walked out of the office to rejoin Sheraz. Before ascending to the roof, both men needed to don protective chem-bio suites.

The rotor was turning slowly on the UH-6A Blackhawk as Hart approached the helicopter. The flight chief, dressed in protective gear, opened the rear door for the Commander, saluting him as he boarded the bird. In seconds, they were thousands of feet above Tel Aviv, headed for Amman.

Captain Levi Arnot handed off control of the bird to his co-pilot, then turned towards his solitary passenger.

"Welcome aboard, Commander. We are on heading to King Abdullah Air Base in Amman. The flight computer is showing a flight time of fifty-three minutes. When we arrive, the Blackhawk and all aboard will go through decontamination. After that you will join the rest of the team."

"Who has been assembled thus far, Captain?"

"We're the last ones to the party, Sir. The other Sayaret units are in place."

"If I may, Captain, how are the teams composed?"

"Of course. Each team consists of ten troops—seven from Unit 269, Sayeret Matkal, who will provide armed support, and three from Sayeret Yahalom, who will manage demolitions. They're as good as you get, Sir. The field engineers are Sapper 11—our most experienced officers. I'm sure you are familiar with Sayeret Matkal."

"Yes . . . and I'm glad they'll have our backs."

"Coming from a Navy SEAL, that's quite a compliment. Your team is eager to meet you, Sir. They know of your heroic acts in America."

Hart laughed, patted the pilot on the shoulder, and said. "I hope I can live up to their expectations, Captain. I assume we are boarding a C-130 to ferry us from Amman to Hafar al Batin?"

"That's correct, Commander. It's 647 miles to Qaisumah Airport. It's a civilian facility, but its runway is 9,800 feet—plenty long to handle the Albatross. The Saudis are closing it to all civilian air travel for thirty-six hours . . . no explanation given to the poor bums scheduled on flights. You can do that when you are a monarchy!"

Captain Arnot continued, "From there, you will board Blackhawks, like this one, but more heavily armored. Each Blackhawk will be escorted by an Apache equipped with a Ground Fire Acquisition System. As you know, its sensors and thermographic camera can pick up any muzzle blast within a 120-degree field of vision—then promptly eliminate the threat. Suffice it to say, you will be in good hands."

"What time do the Blackhawks depart Qaisumah?"

"They are staggered, Commander, based upon the flight time to their final targets. Everyone will be on target at precisely the same time."

"What about hostiles en route to Qaisumah? The Russians and Syrians are still flying sorties."

"You'll have F-16 coverage by the Royal Jordanian Air Force from Amman to the Saudi border, at which point four Eurofighter Typhoons from the Royal Saudi Arabia Air Force will take over."

"Thank God they joined us," Hart responded.

"Agreed, Commander, but I've got to tell you that it makes me queasy to have the fate of Israel resting on the cooperation of the Jordanians and Saudis."

"Understood, Captain, but that's who we're taking to the dance."

"Yes, Sir." The Captain smiled, saluted, and returned to his flight duties.

Hart's mind turned to Liz and what he had told her about being an advisor . . . not a combatant . . . a change he could not have foreseen at the time. Even so, he felt as though he had lied to her. Such deception had almost brought an end to their courtship. The last thing he wanted to do was undermine the most important relationship in his life. He would ask for her forgiveness after he returned state-side in one piece.

The Blackhawk began a precipitous drop in altitude as it approached Amman. Within a minute of landing, a truck circled it, then parked adjacent to the copter. Its crew jumped out and began spraying the exterior with a powerful decontaminant. As soon as they were done, Hart was instructed to disembark and be hosed down, after which he was directed to an exterior shower for a final rinse before removing the protective suit. Then he was escorted to the flight briefing room, where the balance of the attack force awaited him.

As he opened the door, soldiers jumped to their feet and remained rigidly at attention. Hart strode to the front of the room, saluted the operation's commanding officer, and introduced himself.

Colonel Nobi Geller returned the salute, "Welcome, Commander. We've been eagerly expecting you. We don't have much time. I trust you were briefed by Captain Arnot on your flight from Tel Aviv."

"Yes, Sir."

"Do you have any questions, Commander, before I introduce you to the group?"

"Are we prepared to disable Iranian Air Defense as outlined by General Simon, Sir?"

"Yes, those plans will be implemented fifteen minutes before our first team departs Qaisumah. Anything else?"

"When do we leave, Sir?"

"Wheels up in one hour."

CHAPTER THIRTY-ONE

En Route to Qaisumah

"Gentlemen, I'm not a religious man, but I'm going to ask that you pray with me," Hart began the short meeting with Team 5 under his command. It was something he'd never done before, and he wasn't sure why he was doing it now.

"May God grace our mission, deliver us home safely, and render our actions the first step towards lasting peace in the region." The team of battle-hardened soldiers responded, "Amen."

"Who is carrying the nuke?" Hart asked.

"I am, Sir." The response came from a major standing close to the commander.

"What do we know about our target, Major?"

"Bakhtaran Missile Base is located near Kerman Shahan in western Iran. Fortunately, Mossad procured the construction schematics for the base shortly after it was completed. The subterranean facility descends nearly ten stories. Its infrastructure utilizes rebar-reinforced concrete tested to thirty psi. In other words, it was meant to remain operational despite taking a beating."

"And the missiles stored there?" Hart asked.

"It has the capacity to store and launch hundreds of missiles, including ICBMs."

"Have you identified the point of maximum structural vulnerability, Major?"

"We've simulated the effect of a one-kiloton explosion placed adjacent to the launching pad forty feet beneath the surface. The result will be a catastrophic structural failure, including a total collapse of the silo."

"What about collateral damage?"

"I wouldn't want to be within a mile of the site at detonation . . . whether on the ground or in a helicopter climbing to altitude. Even though it's a small yield, it's going to pack a hell of a punch."

Hart turned to the two remaining field engineers from Sayeret Yahalom. "You are clear on your responsibilities?"

"Yes, Commander," came the response in unison.

"Who is my field medic?" Hart asked the group.

"I am, Sir," a female officer answered.

"Well, I'm glad you are aboard, but I pray we don't need your services, Lieutenant."

"Yes, Sir. I pray that, too."

Finally he turned to the seven-man unit from Sayeret Matkal. "Gentlemen, you have one job—to get us in and out without injury. We're launching a frontal assault on one of Iran's crown jewels. The Apache will soften up any initial resistance, but it may not eliminate the threat in total. Do not, I repeat, do not underestimate what may await us. Is that understood?"

"Yes, Sir," came the loud response.

"Then let's get on board!"

Hart closed his eyes and tried to clear his mind as the 83,000-pound C-130 lumbered down the runway and began a tedious climb to altitude. Because the plane had no windows, he had to trust that the promised air support was somewhere off its wingtips. If he was going to go down, he didn't want it to happen in a lumbering transport plane.

When he opened his eyes and checked his watch, he was surprised to discover he had been sleeping for more than an hour. That meant they would be well into Saudi airspace.

Colonel Geller, who was seated next to him, said quietly, "I see you've rejoined the living, Commander. I must say, I admire any man who can sleep so soundly shortly before going into battle."

Hart laughed. "An acquired skill, Colonel. You don't get much sleep when on assignment with the SEALs, so you learn to snatch every bit you can. I'm sure the same can be said of the Sayeret."

"Indeed, Commander. You know, we have similar backgrounds, at least in one respect. I spent almost a decade in Shayetet 13."

Hart recognized the unit immediately, for it was modeled on the Navy SEALs, but with a reputation for being even more formidable.

He exclaimed, "I thought I recognized a fellow snake eater!" Both men laughed.

"Tell me, Commander, do you have a family?"

"I have a wife. Actually, I'm a newlywed—Liz and I have only been married for a little less than a year. What about you, Colonel?"

Geller reached into his back pocket and extracted his wallet. Opening it, he flashed a photo of his family—Hannah, his wife of twenty years, and two boys and a girl.

"What a great-looking family. You are a lucky man, Colonel."

Geller smiled, revealing the gap between his two front teeth. "I am lucky, indeed, Commander. And I pray that luck holds.

"We'll be landing soon. Things are going to move fast after that. Good to luck to you and your team."

"And to you, Colonel."

CHAPTER THIRTY-TWO

The Aftermath

Miriam and Ellie Schecter remained captive within their apartment following the dousing of Tel Aviv with a deadly nerve agent. How long they would be holed up was anyone's guess.

"Look on the bright side, Ellie," Miriam counseled her husband. "At least we have ample stores of food, water, and medicine. That's a lot to be grateful for." She knew that Ellie would not last long without access to metformin for his diabetes and warfarin for a serious arrhythmia.

From their vantage point on the seventh floor, the couple watched as dozens of hazmat workers bathed the neighborhood in decontaminant. The identity of the agent had yet to be confirmed, and there was ongoing concern about its persistence.

Across town, the scene at Ben Gurion Hospital's emergency department was less chaotic. The influx of new patients had finally slowed. Overcrowding had been eased by the death of a large percentage of the acutely ill patients who had succumbed to the toxin.

Dr. Martin Perelman was exhausted. He'd been on his feet for hours with scant breaks, and he knew that fatigue was beginning to take a toll on his clinical judgment. When a nurse approached him and suggested it might be a good time to get a few hours of sleep, he didn't push back.

"You're right—I just need a little cat-nap, but not before I check on the boy," he said.

He found the boy lying on a gurney in the hallway adjacent to the ER. His eyes were open and unblinking, and his skin a chalky white. He's dead, Perelman thought at first sight, but as he neared, the boy blinked and turned his head toward the doctor.

"I want to go home," Itzie said in a barely audible voice. "Where's my Mommy?"

A nurse whispered in Perelman's ear. The parents had not survived. Their bodies were lying in the hospital's morgue.

"How about some ice cream? I'll bet that would taste good to you!" Perelman feigned a smile while his soul was weeping.

The boy nodded with what little strength he could muster.

"Will you get him a dish of ice cream?" he asked of the nurse, "And I want to assume full responsibility for this patient going forward. Do you understand?"

"Yes, of course, Dr. Perelman."

"It worked!" Perelman told himself. The galantamine seemed to be the magic ingredient that, when combined with atropine, allowed the boy's body to ride out the storm. He hoped it would spare him the sequelae of nervous system damage that was associated with Novichok exposure.

Reassured by the boy's improving status, Perelman made his way to the staff lounge and sprawled out on a bench. Before closing his eyes, he called his wife who, like Miriam Schechter, was ensconced in their home.

"Are you okay, Marty?" asked his wife of 38 years.

"As okay as I can be after seeing so much death. What about you . . . are you okay?"

"I'm fine; you don't need to worry about me."

Without any segue, he launched into Itzie's story.

"There's a young boy here . . . about the age of our grandson. When he arrived at the hospital, he was as close to death as any patient I have ever treated. He would have died in minutes if a paramedic had not intervened and insisted that I treat him immediately."

"Did he die, Darling? You know you can't save everyone."

"No. Miraculously, he pulled through."

"That's great news!"

"Now he's asking for his parents to take him home."

"And I assume he can't go home because of the contamination?"

"No, he can't go home because his parents died from exposure to the nerve agent. In fact, from what I've been able to piece together with others, his entire family may be casualties of the attack."

"How tragic. And how cowardly," she added.

"Darling, I don't know anything about this boy, other than he has a precious smile. If he truly has been orphaned, I'd like for us to consider giving him a new home. Does that sound like the crazy rantings of an exhausted trauma surgeon?"

"No, it sounds like deeply felt words from the heart of a man I've known and loved for many years. I'll support whatever decision you make, Marty. We've already raised five children. A sixth would be a welcome addition to our home."

They both laughed, and then cried.

CHAPTER THIRTY-THREE

Beneath the Strait of Hormuz

COMMANDER ISAK NACHMAN ORDERED THE ENGINES silenced on the INS Rahav as they drew within range of the entrance to the Strait of Hormuz. Ahead lay a narrow strip of water that connected the Gulf of Oman, the Persian Gulf, and the Arabian Sea.

The Strait served as the primary conduit for oil within the Middle East, with more than twenty million barrels flowing each day to India, Japan, China, and other nations. As such, it represented a dangerous potential choke-point for more than twenty percent of the world's oil supply . . . a fact the Iranians threatened to exploit.

The Rahav, named aptly in Hebrew for Neptune, God of the Sea, was the latest submarine to join Israel's growing fleet of German-manufactured diesel/electrical boats. The 220-foot-long vessel was capable of speeds in excess of twenty-five knots at depth and could remain submerged with its crew of thirty-five for a month thanks to its air-independent propulsion system.

It had slowed to a crawl, its only propulsion coming from the deep ocean current pushing it along at a depth of 190 feet.

Turning to his lead sonar officer, Nachman asked, "What are you hearing, Joseph?"

"Nothing, Commander."

"Let's hope it remains quiet."

As Nachman was speaking, Joseph raised one hand to his earphones and the other in the air, signaling that he was picking up something.

"I am hearing . . . " he paused as if struggling to make out the faint noise. "It sounds like an electric motor, Sir."

Seconds passed before he spoke again. "Yes, Commander, I think it's a Kilo, and I'd place it 1,000 meters off our bow on the starboard side."

The Kilo was an Iranian class of submarines that were easily outmatched by their Israeli counterparts. It lacked the depth, speed, weaponry, and maneuverability of Israel's most important deterrent.

The Rahav was armed with the Popeye Turbo cruise missile, which was capable of delivering a nuclear warhead more than 1,000 miles. That meant Tehran, Qom, Tabriz, and other pivotally important cities were all within range.

"Close in slowly," the commander advised the captain.

"All ahead five knots," he ordered.

Joseph had brought up a sound-signature identification system and received confirmation that it was, indeed, a Kilo. "We have confirmation, Commander."

Turning to his weapons control officer, Nachman barked, "Hit it with a single fish," then quickly maneuvered the Rahav to ensure that the bow-fired torpedoes had the greatest likelihood of striking their target.

The yeoman advised, "In position, Commander."

The weapons officer confirmed, "Tube 1 flooded and ready, Sir."

"Fire!"

It only took a few seconds for the captain of the Iranian sub to realize his inescapable fate. Traveling at more than forty-five knots, the Kaved torpedo hit the Kilo mid-ship seconds after firing.

"Take me to periscope depth," Nachman ordered.

He could already see the tell-tale signs of the massive explosion. Diesel fuel was pooling on the surface of the water. It would be hard for passing ships to miss the oil, but hopefully they would attribute it to a minor spill from one of the massive tankers traversing the Strait every hour. He prayed that the incident would go undetected for the time required to maneuver through the Strait of Hormuz and get into position to launch a single cruise missile.

"Take us down to one hundred feet and proceed ahead at twenty knots. Stay alert—there may be more of a welcoming committee ahead," he advised.

Much to Nachman's relief, the Rahav encountered no additional deterrents. When systems indicated that they were on-target, the commander raised the ship to a depth of twenty meters and sent a coded signal via an extremely low frequency transmitter to the Bor. Moments later, the response, an electronic firing authorization, appeared on the weapons command console.

Nachman reached under the top button of his shirt and removed a chain with a key attached, as did his first officer. They approached redundant fire control panels that were separated by ten feet. On Nachman's order, they inserted their keys and turned them in synch. A red light on each panel turned green, indicating that the missile was hot.

"Fire on my orders," he barked to his weapons control officer as he began a count-down. "Three . . . two . . . one . . . fire!"

Flying at an altitude barely higher than the tree-tops, the Popeye cruise missile would take forty-two minutes to reach its target. A digital clock ticked off the minutes and seconds. It was the longest forty-two minutes of Nachman's life.

CHAPTER THIRTY-FOUR

And Then There Was Silence

LIVE IMAGES OF SEMNAN MISSILE COMMAND were transmitted in tandem to the White House and Bor by Space Satellite Command in Colorado Springs, providing Rabinovich and Conner with identical views of the ensuing destruction.

When the cruise missile went nuclear, the destructive force was overwhelming. Everything within 500 yards of the missile's point of impact was leveled. A fireball rose above the rubble, obscuring the view. When it finally subsided, charred bodies littered the area. There was no movement . . . no life.

"I don't think they will be communicating with the other silos, Mr. President," Rabinovich said with restrained glee. "Let's see what happens when the Jericho explodes."

"You're certain it will not impact the circuitry on the aircraft en route to their targets?" Conner asked anxiously.

"Don't worry, Mr. President. All of the circuits have been hardened to withstand an EMP—at least in theory."

"What do you mean in theory? You're risking the entire operation on theory?"

"When was the last time you witnessed an atmospheric detonation of a nuclear bomb, Mr. President? We've done everything possible to protect our electronics. I'm confident our actions will prove sufficient."

Then he added impatiently, "Mr. President, are we a go with the Jericho?"

Conner nodded his acquiescence.

Nachman contacted the Bor for further instructions.

"Good shot, Commander," General Simon responded. "One more to go. I'm transmitting the launch codes for the Jericho III ICBM as we speak."

Again, the weapons console came to life. A flashing red button indicated that the missile was now armed and fused, and the system awaited insertion of duplicate keys.

Once this was done, Nachman counted down from three. On his order, the weapons officer pushed the flashing button, unleashing the ghostly weapon that, up until that moment, had only been rumored to exist within Israel's arsenal.

"Return home, Commander. Your work is done," Simon communicated solemnly.

"Take us down to 150 feet, and let's get the hell out of here!" Nachman ordered.

Conner and Rabinovich watched a satellite feed as the missile broke the surface of the water in the Strait of Hormuz and began its arc over Iran. The camera lens widened to show the vast landscape of Iran. Less than a minute later, the screen went white as the warhead exploded high in the atmosphere.

There were no tornadic winds, no thermal or ionizing radiation at the surface . . . in fact, no real sign of what had happened other than a flash of light right before all power died.

A second satellite forwarded images of Tehran. Traffic had come to a standstill—cars and buses stopped as if frozen in time. And though it was largely invisible from space, the damage to Iran's power grid was massive.

There were casualties: hospitals lost all power and back-up generators refused to start; subway trains lurched to a stop, injuring some passengers; and all air conditioning and refrigeration systems went off-line on a day when the heat was predicted to exceed one hundred degrees.

"What is happening?" General Mohammad Ali Jafari shouted at his subordinate, Soleimani.

"We've had a massive power failure, General."

"Don't tell me the obvious . . . I want to know why!"

"I don't know, General, but I pray it is not Israel's way of preparing to attack."

The Ayatollah had sat silently while Ali Jafari erupted. Now, he commanded, "If the power is not restored within an hour, fire the missiles."

Soleimani and Ali Jafari each picked up a phone, but they were dead. "That may not be possible," Ali Jafari informed the Ayatollah.

"One hour, gentlemen, then our missiles must fly. That is what God has ordained, and it is your job to execute his orders," the Ayatollah intoned.

Jafari turned to Soleimani. "Find a jeep that's running—and get over to Semnan now!"

"That will take hours, General!" Soleimani knew he could never honor the Ayatollah's deadline.

"You're wasting time, General Soleimani . . . go now! And when you arrive, don't wait for my permission— send the launch codes the minute you arrive. Do you understand?"

Soleimani saluted and headed for the vehicle pool located underground. The surrounding concrete had sufficiently shielded the jeeps, allowing Soleimani to commandeer the first one he saw.

He knew that each passing minute might further imperil his country's ability to strike back at the Israelis. He threw the Jeep in gear, popped the clutch, and held on as the vehicle lurched forward. He weaved around thousands of stalled cars . . . careening down sidewalks with the horn blaring when necessary. When he finally cleared the outskirts of Tehran, he floored the Jeep and headed eastward. Semnan was still more than two hours away on Route 44.

"We are in the final stages of preparing for troop insertion," Simon informed Rabinovich with a smile, causing the prime minister to let out a long sigh of relief. "The F-15s are closing in on SAM batteries that appear to still be operational. As we anticipated, the Russians utilized hardened circuitry."

Rabinovich's heart, once again, began to race, and worry replaced relief.

"Don't worry, Avi, they won't be operational for long."

"When do the teams depart?"

"The C-130 has reached the staging area. The first team will depart as soon as the missile defense systems have been neutralized. I'm guessing within no more than thirty minutes."

"How will you know for certain that has happened, Moshe?"

"Their radar will go off-line. That will be our signal to launch the first team. As you know, the teams' departure times are staggered so that they arrive at their targets simultaneously. They have a lot of ground to cover, and still face the threat of hostiles—probably not the Iranian Air Force, but Russian or Syrian MIGs are a distinct possibility. The F-16s should be able to dispatch any threat."

"When will they be in position to launch their attack on the silos?"

"Within hours . . . unless they incur a higher level of resistance at the missile sites than we are anticipating."

"Isn't that what the Apaches are for?"

"Yes, Sir."

Captain Jacobson's F-15 had picked up faint radar pings emanating from a SAM battery approximately 140 miles from his current position. It was an advance warning—miles before a return echo would bring the surface-to-air missiles to alert.

He armed the 1,200-pound missile, a newly developed Rampage ALBMA, attached to the belly of his plane.

"SAM battery at 140 miles and closing. Requesting permission to light it up."

"Permission granted, Alpha Baker Tango. Shut it down."

Jacobson pressed the bomb release, then set a vector home. He watched as a video camera in the belly of the plane provided a ring-side seat to the impending explosion.

Four minutes later, only twisted metal remained of the missile defense system. Jacobson smiled, grateful to know that the new weapon had delivered on its promise.

Jacobson was not the only pilot scoring a hit. Every F-15 deployed struck its target with impunity—dramatically lowering the risk of a missile bringing down one of the helicopters. With the F-15s en route back to base, D-Day had arrived.

CHAPTER THIRTY-FIVE

Delilah

A THICK CLOUD OF DUST TRAILED from the landing gear as the massive C-130 touched down at Qaisumah Airport in Haf al Batin, 400 kilometers southwest of the Iranian border. Its cargo of fifty elite Special Forces hustled off the plane and into a holding area adjacent to where flight crews were readying five Blackhawk helicopters for departure.

Each UH-60L helicopter could transport up to eleven troops in addition to two pilots and two crew chiefs/gunners. Protection came from two M240 machine guns, as well as AGM-14 Hellfire missiles.

Because they would be pushing the outside limits of the Blackhawk's range, the birds had been fitted with external tanks. Hart's target, Bakhtaran Missile Base near Kerman Shahan, was 675 kilometers by air, making additional fuel a necessity.

As they stood in the 109-degree heat, Hart was surprised to see Major General Amikam Norkin approach.

"Commander Hart, did I startle you?"

"I'm just surprised to see you here, Sir, on the front line. I thought you would be at the Bor with Prime Minister Rabinovich."

"I think they have plenty of brass to fill the Bor. I'm a soldier, Commander, just like you. I don't want to sit in a sanitized conference room watching things play out on a video screen. I want to look my men in the eye as they depart on the most important mission of their lives."

"Yes, Sir. I understand, Sir."

"I know you do, Commander. In that way, we are brothers."

He handed Hart his orders. "Your team is third in line for departure. That means you need to be airborne ninety minutes from now. We've estimated your flight time at three hours and forty minutes, assuming you don't run into any unwelcome company. That puts you on target in just over five hours. Good luck, Commander."

"Thank you, Sir."

There were no signs of trouble for the first two hours of the flight. Shortly thereafter, the pilot informed his crew that they were entering Iranian airspace.

"We're not anticipating a welcoming committee, nor any active surface-to-air defense batteries, but keep your eyes open, gentlemen, and let me know if you see anything."

If they were attacked, it was doubtful they would have any forewarning. Most likely a fighter would sneak up from behind and dislodge an air-to-air missile from a distance of fifteen to twenty miles. Though the Blackhawk was a formidable killing machine, it didn't take much to bring it down. Hart knew this intuitively; still, the captain's words provided a needed distraction.

When they were less than an hour out from Bakhtaran, Hart began a methodical review of the planned attack, including a reminder to the captain and gunners that there was a good chance of encountering resistance while landing.

"Take out any unfriendlies fast with the M240s . . . don't wait for my command, and hold the Hellfires in reserve until absolutely necessary." Turning to the crew, he added, "If anyone goes down, your orders are to finish the mission before attending to your comrades!"

"Yes, Sir," the men shouted in unison, knowing the sacrifice the mission might require.

The Blackhawk had descended to an altitude of 500 feet when tracers lit up the airspace around the bird. Incoming rounds could be heard ripping past the aircraft. The pilot throttled up the twin 1560-horse-power engines to their limit, then banked hard right. He straightened out the helicopter, hoping for a clear shot at the location where the anti-aircraft fire appeared to originate.

The on-board gunners opened up—firing 950 rounds per minute and blanketing the landing area with bullets. Within seconds, all return fire stopped.

The pilot turned his head towards Hart. "I'm going in, Commander," then pushed the helicopter's stick forward in a rapid descent.

"Helmets on, guns locked and loaded. They sure as hell know we're here!" Hart shouted to the team.

Within seconds of touching down, all the men were prone on the ground, feet from the Blackhawk, scanning the surrounding area for remaining Iranian troops.

"It looks clear, but don't be fooled. I'm sure we'll encounter hostiles any minute. Now get moving!"

Three members of the Special Forces team fanned out to provide perimeter defense, while Hart and six others moved towards the entrance of the underground facility.

"On my count," Hart instructed a soldier holding a stun grenade. "Three, two, one" . . . he flung open the heavy metal door and the soldier tossed in the grenade.

Seconds later, a powerful concussion shook the ground on which they stood. As quickly as it subsided, Hart signaled his men to move in. There was no time to take prisoners. Threats had to be neutralized as they emerged, which meant a half-dozen Iranian soldiers, dazed and confused, were shot were they stood.

"Six minutes," Hart shouted—the time remaining to descend to the launching pad, plant the charge, clear the tunnel, and re-board the bird.

The men were moving fast and arrived at the launching pad in just under a minute. An ICBM was in firing position. Hart checked his dosimeter. It indicated a level of radioactivity that was far above normal background radiation.

"Looks like we hit the jackpot," he told the team as they planted a charge. "That's one down and four to go. Let's hope the other teams are having similar luck."

They placed the backpack nuke flush against a massive support beam in an effort to ensure the collapse of the subterranean facility and the absolute and complete destruction of the missile. It took another fifteen seconds to arm and fuse it.

"Let's get the hell out of here!" Hart bellowed as the men ran up four flights of metal stairs before emerging into the sunlight.

"Head for the bird, now!" Hart ordered, as he signaled to the men on the perimeter to relinquish their positions.

They had two minutes to board . . . anything longer would put the chopper at risk of being caught in the blast.

As the last soldier took his seat, Hart stopped to take a final look at the missile complex before climbing aboard. That's when it hit him—a single round from a sniper missed his heart by inches but left a gaping wound in his chest. He slumped to the ground.

The gunners responded with unremitting machine gun fire in the presumed direction of the sniper, as the medic and two of the infantrymen sprang from the helicopter and prepared to lift the commander to safety.

Hart shouted, "God damn it, leave me! Get this thing airborne and get the hell out of here!"

"You've got thirty seconds—then we're airborne!" the captain shouted.

The crew weren't about to leave him on the field of battle. They positioned themselves around Hart's body and heaved him into the belly of the helicopter. His chest was soaked through with blood, and his face was ashen. Hart felt his life slipping away. And then there was nothing.

CHAPTER THIRTY-SIX

The Hot-Line

ONCE SAFELY AIRBORNE, each unit reported in to the Bor. As hoped, the teams had uncovered five missiles loaded with nuclear warheads positioned on the launching pads of the targeted silos. Five backpack nukes were awaiting detonation.

The plan had come off flawlessly, with one catastrophic exception. Because of the soldiers' body cams and satellite uplinks, Rabinovich had observed Hart being shot in real time. There was little he could do at that moment, other than apprise President Conner of the situation and assure him that Israel would do everything in its power to save the life of the commander.

Rabinovich removed his cell phone from the pocket of his suit coat and brought it to eye-level. As he activated an app on the phone, it began performing a retinal scan. Once completed, a synthesized voice instructed him to speak his name. As he said, "Abraham Rabinovich," his words were instantly matched to a voiceprint. The final step required entering a seven-digit code given to him by Simon.

Five icons representing the five nuclear backpacks appeared on the screen. Small red and green buttons were adjacent to each device, allowing for their activation or deactivation. All were active. Rabinovich's thumb hovered over a single, large green button at the bottom of the screen.

"Are we certain that all of our troops are out of the theater of operations?" he asked Simon.

"Yes, Sir . . . they are close, but out of imminent blast danger."

Still, he hesitated, "You're sure, Moshe, absolutely sure?"

"Yes, Sir, I am absolutely sure."

Without taking his eyes off his general, Rabinovich pressed the large green button to trigger the devices simultaneously.

The monitors in the room were carrying images of the five installations. Set to a resolution of six feet, the field of view was wide enough to assess the damage once the blinding glare of white light subsided.

There was nothing left. Total and complete destruction. The conference room broke out in applause—everyone but Rabinovich.

Flying at the Blackhawk's upper limit of two hundred kilometers per hour, Hart's team was barely out of harm's way when the nuke detonated. Even though it was buried under forty feet of reinforced steel and concrete, its explosive force bathed the helicopter in a blinding light milliseconds before a shock wave rolled over the craft and nearly knocked it from the sky. When it passed, the captain reduced the airspeed to a sustainable 180 knots per hour.

The field medic had done her best to stop the suck-ing chest wound, but she knew that, in all likelihood, the commander would not survive the long flight back. Despite a strong sense of futility, the lieutenant started an IV, then broke out two ampoules of morphine. If Hart was going to have any chance of making it, the medic had to keep him from going into shock for as long as humanly possible.

Per the prime minister's instructions, the images of the destroyed silos were relayed to the White House Situation Room, where President Conner was on the phone with Russian President Vladimir Putin.

The call was momentarily interrupted as Putin received word of the nuclear events from his military aide.

"I warned you, President Conner, that Russia would not tolerate further use of nuclear weapons by the Israelis."

"Before you react, President Putin, listen to my words. This was a surgical strike by Israel with virtually no collateral damage. They had one objective—eliminate the imminent threat of annihilation by Iran, an objective they appear to have achieved."

As they were speaking, nuclear-armed B-52 bombers were approaching their fail-safe point near the Russian border; those planes still in their hangars were rapidly deployed. Missile silos began the sequence of events leading to launch, as did submarines carrying SLBMs.

Within seconds, the change in the status of U.S. nuclear forces was picked up by Russian satellites and long-range radar. The news was immediately conveyed to Putin.

"I see it's not only the Israelis that are prepared to use their nuclear weapons. Are you preparing for a first strike,

Mr. President?" Putin asked, doing his best to mask a surge of anxiety.

"No, I am merely honoring my obligation to protect my nation and its ally, Israel. Stand-down, Mr. Putin. Don't take this heavy burden to your grave."

"I will call you back." Putin disconnected the call.

Conner opened the comm line to Rabinovich and shared what had just transpired.

"We'll know soon enough whether we are at war with Russia. I'm putting you on speaker in the Situation Room, Mr. Prime Minister. I suggest we keep this line open for a while, if you are in agreement. I'm expecting our Secret Services to shuttle me out at any moment. Rest assured that I will do my best to remain in contact with you."

"Of course, Mr. President. There's one more thing that I must share with you, President Conner."

"And what would that be, Avi?"

"The mission resulted in one casualty, Mr. President. It was Commander Hart."

The blood drained from Conner's face. "Are you saying that Commander Hart is dead?"

"I don't know. He took a round to the chest from a sniper just as they were completing the mission. He's aboard the Blackhawk in the hands of a medic. When they last radioed in, I was told it did not look good. We'd like your permission, Mr. President, to modify their course . . . flying directly to one of your field hospitals in Baghdad. Our IAF will provide full air support until they are safely on the ground."

"I'll place a call to the MASH unit in Baghdad advising them accordingly. I know your men will do their best." Conner spoke these words as he was being escorted out of the Situation Room on his way to a safe bunker deep below the White House.

CHAPTER THIRTY-SEVEN

The Angel of Death Passes Over

THIRTY AGONIZING MINUTES PASSED before Conner re-established contact with Rabinovich.

"Forgive the interminably long delay, Mr. Prime Minister, but our protocol, when under threat of attack, is quite inflexible. Thank God, it appears not to have been needed. The Russians have had more than enough time to deploy their ICBMs against our countries. It appears they have blinked."

Just then, a Marine captain in full military dress interrupted the president. "I am sorry for the interruption, Mr. President, but I though you would want to know that the Russians have taken their missiles off-line, and it appears that their naval vessels are headed back to port."

"Thank you, Captain," Conner smiled and saluted the officer.

"I trust you heard that, Avi."

"Yes, Mr. President. Let's hope their submarines are headed back out to sea, too."

"Is there any word on Commander Hart?"

"Only that he's hanging on by a thread, Mr. President."

Conner wanted to put everything out of his mind with the exception of John Hart, but he could not afford that luxury. He knew that, though the imminent threat had been removed, the hard work of purging the remaining vestiges of the Shia Coalition was just beginning. He had to disassociate from the responsibility he felt for Hart's condition and pray for God's intervention. He would refocus on his friend as soon as possible.

"It's time for us to mobilize the Saudi coalition. Are you in agreement?" the president asked his Israeli counterpart.

"Full agreement, President Conner."

"Then, per our briefing with General Simon and Mr. Chaikin, we will begin working through the logistics of moving forward with deployment of a multi-national army in tandem with our new-found Sunni friends. I want to be crystal clear about our objectives. First, we will decapitate the theocracy and neuter the IRGC. Next, we will ensure a permanent end to the rule of the Assad family while bringing its leaders to justice. Finally, we will force Hamas and Hezbollah to capitulate and accept a tolerant but firm coalition government."

"That's a tall order, Mr. President. You know it's going to be a long and bloody war."

"The region has been engaged in a long and bloody war for more than two thousand years. Maybe this time, it will end once and for all."

"The 'war to end all wars,' Mr. President?"

"Something like that."

"I admire your optimism, President Conner."

"And I admire the tenacity of the Jewish people. Perhaps you will be surprised, Prime Minister, and it will be another Six-Day War!"

CHAPTER THIRTY-EIGHT

The Golden Hour

THE MEDIC REMOVED HER FINGER from Hart's carotid artery. His pulse was thready and fast. Three bags of IV saline plus plasma had brought his blood pressure up from 50 over 20 to 80 over 50 . . . a good sign. Yet the commander continued to drift in and out of consciousness.

"How long before we reach Baghdad?" the worried medic shouted at the captain.

The captain glanced at the flight computer. "We're forty-two minutes out. Can he hold on just a little longer?"

"We'll see."

An ambulance crew was waiting as the UH-60 touched down. For a moment, as he was being transferred to the vehicle, Hart regained lucidity.

"I've got to call my wife. I've got to call Liz," he whispered.

"Just rest, Commander. We'll get word to your wife."

"You don't understand . . . I have to tell her it's going to be alright."

The EMTs shared a look—a look that fortunately escaped the commander's attention.

"Sure, sure, buddy," one of them said as he began giving Hart a unit of whole blood matched to his blood type.

As soon as he was loaded, the ambulance rushed him to a MASH unit, where a team was prepared to take him straight into surgery. First, though, they needed x-rays of his chest to serve as a roadmap for the surgeon charged with repairing the vast damage to his torso.

"What's your name, soldier?"

Hart opened his eyes a crack—enough to see the nurse peering down at him.

"Hart, Ma'am, John Hart."

"You're pretty shot up, soldier. But you're going to have the finest thoracic surgeon in the region working on you. He arrived from Bagram a few minutes ago. I don't know who you are, but you sure as hell must be someone special to pull that kind of a favor."

"Just a grunt, Ma'am."

"Right. I'm administering a drug called Versed through your IV line. You'll feel sleepy pretty fast. When you wake up from surgery, we'll have you talk to your wife."

She had already pushed the drug before finishing her sentence. Hart started to speak, but he was out in an instant.

The anesthesiologist took one look at Hart's vitals and turned to the surgeon, a reservist from the Cleveland Clinic named Frank Holliday.

"Colonel, I don't think this man can endure the anesthesia, let alone the surgery."

"Captain, I appreciate your concern, but I received a call a few hours ago telling me that, come hell or high water, I had to patch this guy up . . . like I was Jesus Christ or something."

"Has your CO ever been in a trauma unit, Colonel?"

"The call didn't come from my CO . . . it came from President Conner. Shook the hell out of me—I thought it was some kind of a joke, but it wasn't. Our boy here is quite the hero—Commander John Hart."

"Hart—the guy who saved the nation during those terrorist attacks?"

"Yep, same guy."

"I wonder what in the hell he was doing in Iran."

"I didn't ask, and neither should you. Are you ready to proceed, Captain?"

"Yes, Sir."

The anesthesiologist had pumped potent drugs into Hart's system before intubating him. He began the flow of sedating gases through a mask covering Hart's mouth and nose.

"Is he ready?" Holliday asked impatiently.

"Yes, Sir, he's ready. But his pressure is hovering at 60/40. You know our patient is AB negative. They've only got three units to transfuse. There's more on the way from Bagram."

"Thanks for the warning, Captain."

A series of monitors arrayed above the surgical table carried different views of Hart's films. The bullet had passed through his ribs, narrowly missing the lower ventricle of his heart. It tore up his left lung before exiting a few inches from his spine. Holliday studied the x-rays carefully before picking up a scalpel. Job one was to determine if the lung was salvageable. No matter what, there was a lot of cleaning up to do.

Holliday addressed the surgical team. "Ladies and gentlemen, we are going to do a posterolateral thoracotomy on Commander Hart. I'll be going in over the fifth intercostal space, which should provide clear access to the pulmonary hilum. We'll make a decision then as to whether the patient needs a lobectomy or requires a pneumonectomy."

Holliday knew that a pneumonectomy, which called for the full surgical removal of a lung, would effectively end Hart's military service. It was a call he hoped not to make, but his first and foremost obligation was to preserve the commander's life.

The scalpel pierced the intercostal space on Hart's back. When he completed the arc, Holliday employed a rib spreader to widen out the incision. It was then that he began to see the trail of torn-up tissue.

"What in the hell did they hit him with?" Holliday exclaimed, not really expecting a response.

Peering over the Colonel's shoulder, the surgical assistant commented, "Looks like a .50 caliber, Sir. Not much else will do that kind of damage."

The surgical assistant was right . . . it had been a .50 caliber bullet fired from a single-shot Steyr HS that had felled the commander. He was part of an elite group—survivors of .50 caliber wounds—at least for as long as his heart was still beating.

"His pressure is dropping!" the captain called out from the head of the table where he was monitoring Hart's vitals. But before anyone could respond, the EKG flat-lined.

"God damn it," Holliday bellowed. "Roll him over now!"

As Holliday began CPR, the anesthesiologist pushed epinephrine through his IV.

No response. John Hart was dead.

A nurse wiped sweat from the brow of the surgeon. "Come on, God damn it!" he yelled at Hart as he rhythmically compressed his chest.

"Colonel, it's been almost two minutes. I don't think he's coming back, Sir," the captain said solemnly.

Just as the colonel considered removing his hands from Hart's chest, a single blip appeared on the monitor, then another, until normal sinus rhythm was restored.

"He's back!" Holliday exclaimed with cautious relief. "Let's get the job finished. I don't want him coding again.

"I'm proceeding with a lobectomy. He won't survive anything more invasive. We'll repair the other damage on the way out."

Hart lost an extensive amount of blood during the four-hour surgery. Fortunately, six units of whole blood arrived from Bagram before the most invasive phase of the surgery.

It would be several hours before he regained consciousness . . . if he regained consciousness. Frank Holliday hovered over his patient, saying a silent prayer to bring this man through.

A hand softly touched the back of his shoulder, "Colonel, I'm so sorry to interrupt you," the PACU nurse began, "but there's an important call for you. You can take it in the CO's office."

Holliday nodded and headed for General Crandall's office. He saluted as he walked in the open door. "Sir, I understand there is a call waiting for me."

"Colonel, it's the president," he said, as he picked up a receiver and handed it to the surgeon.

"I pray you've got good news for me, Colonel," Conner began, "because I'm not sure I'm ready to hear anything else."

"Yes, Sir, Mr. President. The patient is recovering in our post-anesthesia care unit. He's not out of the woods, Sir, but he's a heck of a lot better off than he was upon arrival."

Conner let out a long sigh. "Tell me about the surgery, Colonel."

"Yes, Sir. I accessed his wounds via an incision on Commander Hart's back. The bullet did a tremendous amount of damage, Mr. President. Midway through surgery, the patient coded on the table."

"You're saying his heart stopped."

"Yes, Sir. He was clinically dead for just under two minutes. But we brought him back. I decided not to push my luck and limited the surgery to a lobectomy, plus some clean-up on the way out."

"What are his chances, Colonel, and don't blow smoke at me."

"His condition is guarded, Mr. President. If he makes it through the next twenty-four hours, I think he'll be home free. If he codes again, we may well lose him."

"I know you are doing everything in your power, Colonel. Is there anything you need . . . anything that might make a difference?"

"I understand that you are a spiritual man, Mr. President. I would only ask that you join me in praying for our patient."

"I've been praying for Commander Hart since the second I learned of his injury . . . and will continue to pray for him until he is out of harm's way. Please keep me apprised of any changes in his condition. Your CO has been given 24/7 access to me."

"Yes, Sir." Holliday returned the phone to the General, saluted, and returned to check on his patient. He pulled a chair close to Hart's bed, slouching down to get a few minutes of sleep. He knew it was going to be a long fight.

CHAPTER THIRTY-NINE

Notifying Next of Kin

CONNER TURNED TO HIS PRIVATE SECRETARY. "Get Dr. Wilkins on the line, please."

A moment later, she returned. "Dr. Wilkins is on comm line 3. She sounds very upset, Sir."

Conner only nodded, then took a deep breath, exhaled, and picked up the phone.

"Liz, it's Jonathan Conner."

Conner heard a muffled sob.

"Is he dead, Sir?" her voice audibly trembling. "I assumed the only reason you'd be calling me, Mr. President, is that John is . . . "

"No, Liz, you are married to one tough cookie. But he's pretty beaten up. I'm sending a car for you. Take your time . . . the driver will be waiting when you are ready."

"Where is John, Mr. President?" her voice weak.

"I'll go over everything we know when you arrive at the White House. Then, together, we can decide on the best course of action. Have faith, Liz. It's carried you through some very dark times."

"Yes, Sir," she said bravely before hanging up the phone and collapsing in tears. There were few people with more emotional fortitude than Liz Wilkins, but the thought of losing the man she loved was overwhelming.

Liz let out a heavy sigh before slowly mustering the energy to lift herself off the couch and move towards the bedroom. She reached into the closet for a black dress, but then quickly withdrew her hand. She was not ready to wear black. Picking a conservative gray suit, she laid the clothes out on the bed while she freshened up.

When she looked in the bathroom mirror, she saw trails of mascara lining her face. She looked older, she thought, too old to manage the emotional turbulence created by her husband's career. Turning her eyes upward, she prayed. "Please God, let him pull through . . . then give him the wisdom to stop this insanity."

She glanced at her watch, feeling a bit panicky that the president was waiting for her. She touched up her make-up, ran a brush through her hair, then changed into the suit. Thirty minutes had passed by the time she descended the elevator and approached the black Suburban parked in front of the condo.

"I'm here to escort you to the White House, Ma'am," a Secret Service agent said as he opened the passenger door for Liz. They drove in silence.

Jonathan Conner was waiting at the entrance to the west wing as Liz approached. He walked towards her, arms open, and embraced her with a warm hug. She let out a single sob.

"I thought I was done with that for the moment," she said to Conner, pulling back and wiping her eyes.

"Trust me, you're not the only one shedding tears over what has happened. But I'm cautiously optimistic. Let's go to my office where we won't be disturbed and I'll bring you up to speed."

Liz entered the room where she, John, and the president had met on numerous occasions—perilous times when it was unclear whether the nation would survive. Now, it was one man's life hanging in the balance.

Once they were seated, Conner began. "Your husband is in a MASH unit on the outskirts of Baghdad. It was the closest field hospital to where he was injured."

Liz winced, dreading what might follow.

"And where was that, Mr. President? I thought he was acting as an advisor to Mr. Rabinovich—safely lodged in the Bor."

"His mission changed, Liz. And he was not at liberty to share that information with you. I'm sorry."

Liz cried, "God damn it!" She hid her face in her hands as she tried to stifle her hurt over the deception. After a moment, she raised her eyes to Conner.

"Can you tell me what happened, Sir?"

"The commander was drafted by Mr. Rabinovich to lead one of five teams of Israeli Special Forces that invaded Iran yesterday. Their mission was to destroy five missile silos from which Iran planned to launch a nuclear attack on Israel."

"Was the mission successful, Mr. President?"

"Yes, the destruction was total. The sole casualty was Commander Hart."

Fighting back what she knew would be an onslaught of tears, Liz asked, "What happened to John?"

"They cleared the area surrounding the missile silo, but somehow a sniper evaded detection. John was the last man out—standing by the helicopter, waiting until everyone else had boarded, when a bullet struck him in the chest."

Liz's hand jerked involuntarily to her face as she realized the severity of the injuries.

Conner reached across the table and took her other hand. "Your husband is the toughest human being I've ever met. And he has a great deal to live for—most importantly, you. Despite tremendous blood loss, he made it through major surgery that repaired much of the damage caused by the sniper's round. Right now, he's being closely monitored. I just spoke with his surgeon, who remains hopeful."

Conner chose not to share that Hart had coded for nearly two minutes on the table.

"Whoever he is, I hope he's good at his job!" Liz said with the first trace of relief that Conner had seen since greeting her.

"The best, Liz. I had him flown in from Bagram. Colonel Frank Holliday is a reservist whose day job is Chief of Thoracic Surgery at the Cleveland Clinic."

"I'd like to thank the colonel," she responded.

"I'll make sure that happens . . . but right now, let's let him do his job."

"Of course, Mr. President. Can you arrange for me to travel to Baghdad?"

"Yes, I can do that, but let me make an alternative suggestion, if I may. As soon as the commander is stable, we will be returning him to Israel, where we know he will get the best medical care possible. With Tel Aviv still in the midst of recovery, we plan to take him to Jerusalem."

Disappointed, she asked, "When would that be?"

"Not long. The next hours are crucial. Once he makes it through that window, his surgeon believes he will be stable enough for air transport in thirty-six to forty-eight hours.

"Would you like for me to make arrangements for you to stay in the White House until we know he is out of danger?"

"I'd like for you to help arrange transportation for me to be at his side, Mr. President. That's where I need to be."

"I'll have a plane standing by first thing in the morning. It will either fly you to Baghdad or, if John's stable enough to be transported to Israel, I'll have you taken to the hospital in Jerusalem. The best thing you can do for your husband right now is get some rest and be ready for the long road ahead."

Liz nodded her head without saying a word.

Conner picked up the phone. "Would you please ask Rebecca to join us?" he asked.

Although they had met briefly before, she did not expect Mrs. Conner to remember her. Liz instantly felt the warmth exuded by the First Lady.

"Liz, I'm so sorry for what you are going through," she said, opening her arms to give her a hug. "I think the last time I saw you was shortly after the attack in New York. I think we need to break the pattern—maybe see each other at a happy time."

"I'd enjoy that, Mrs. Conner."

The president addressed the First Lady. "Darling, Liz is going to be staying the night, then leaving early tomorrow morning. Would you help make sure she's comfortable and has whatever she needs—including for her trip tomorrow?"

"I'd love to," she said, extending her hand to their guest.

CHAPTER FORTY

A Voice from the Grave

"Why are they so damned quiet?" Rabinovich asked, unsettled by the Iranians' silence.

"We took out their entire communications network and power infrastructure. I'm not sure they can respond," Simon answered.

"Surely they have contingencies for such a situation . . . they are incredibly sophisticated despite their regressive theocracy."

"I'll grant you that, Mr. Prime Minister. I'm sure we'll be hearing from them any minute . . . probably chanting 'Death to Israel.'"

"Are you saying I should be careful of what I wish for, Moshe?"

Simon laughed and nodded, enjoying a brief moment of levity amidst the turmoil.

"Did I ever tell you about the dog that terrorized me as a child growing up?" Rabinovich asked with the hint of a smile.

"No, Mr. Prime Minister, you spared me that tale."

"When I was a little boy, long before we moved to Philadelphia, there was an old black lab with a gray muzzle that used to chase me on my way home from school. His name was Cleo, and he seemed to know exactly when I'd be peddling my bicycle past his house.

"As soon as Cleo would see me, he'd come loping after me in his arthritic way—teeth bared—that is, what teeth he still had. He was missing his top two incisors and had a bad under-bite."

"I'm getting the picture," Simon said, chuckling. "Did he ever bite you?" Simon imagined his dignified boss being chased around his bicycle by a decrepit old dog.

"No. One day I finally got tired of being harassed, and I jumped off the bike and gave it a hard shove in Cleo's direction. He backed off at first, but then turned and closed in. Fists clenched, I shouted and ran headlong at the beast."

"Surely he bit you then?"

"No, he took off running . . . and he never bothered me again."

"Our Iranian adversary is far from toothless, but I think you get my point, Moshe. They've taken off running, and I hope we never have to feel threatened by them again."

"Amen to that, Mr. Prime Minister."

But such was not the case. Six hours later, Ayatollah Khamenei appeared in front of a television camera, much to Rabinovich's chagrin. His location was not disclosed, and the neutral set gave little clue as to where the transmission was originating. As he spoke, a translation appeared in English at the bottom of the screen.

"Israel may think it has won a great victory, but the people of Iran know better. We have been locked in mortal battle with the Jews since ancestral times. What you witnessed today is nothing more than a minor skirmish . . . a momentary setback." The amplitude of his voice suddenly increased. "It does nothing to weaken our resolve to crush the Jewish state and its ally, the United States."

Khamenei stared into the camera as if he were looking into Rabinovich's soul. "Prime Minister Rabinovich, bask in the moment, for your defeat is already written by God. As I speak, Iranian Revolutionary Guard Corps troops are poised to strike. We will incinerate your people—finishing the job begun seventy years ago in Germany. This time, there *will* be a 'perfect solution.'"

Rabinovich was fuming, shouting obscenities at the cleric's televised image.

But Khamenei was not finished.

"I speak now to Muslims across the world—Shia and Sunni, Alawite and Wahhabists. The schism that has existed within our faith, driving brother to kill brother, must be mended this day. We are not each other's enemy. The enemy of Islam are the infidels . . . the Jews . . . the mongrels who inhabit Israel, the United States, and western Europe. Let us put aside our differences and work to cleanse our world of this filth. Let us usher in a new order and use the recent attack on Iran as our rallying cry!"

"That bastard. He's like a voice from the grave," Rabinovich muttered in disgust.

"Bluster and rampant anti-Semitism . . . that's all he's capable of, Mr. Prime Minister," Simon assured him.

"How do you know that, Moshe? All it would take is one nuclear missile to do unfathomable damage to Israel. We took out five of their missile installations—they have dozens more. And God forbid that his call for the unification of Shia and Sunnis is answered. Then we are really in deep shit."

"What are you suggesting, Mr. Prime Minister—the total and complete destruction of Iran? That's the only way to ensure that the Ayatollah's threat has been neutralized. How do you think the world would respond to such annihilation? And after that . . . do we take on the entire Muslim world?"

"It would be in self-defense for God's sake, Moshe!"

"What we did, we did in self-defense; and based upon early reports, that is how it's playing out on the world stage. I suggest we let the Americans, along with the Sunni Coalition, take the heat on what happens next. Our Sunni and Wahhabi friends are not going to be fooled by Khamenie's rhetoric. Their hatred for the Shias exceeds anything we can imagine."

"Then get President Conner on the phone. I want us in lock-step regarding further actions against Iran. And secure our borders. I don't care what level of force is necessary. Crush any sign of insurrection—be it in Gaza, the West Bank, or our northern and eastern flanks."

Moments later, he was connected to Conner.

"Has there been any change in Commander Hart's status, Prime Minister?"

"No, I'm told it remains guarded. I promise you we will call if anything does change. With your permission, we've made arrangements to care for the commander at Hadassah Ein Kerem as soon as he can be safely transported."

"Thank you, Avi."

"There's an equally pressing matter that we must discuss, Mr. President."

"The Ayatollah's speech?"

"Yes, you heard his invective-filled rant. What does your intelligence community make of his threats?"

"Mainly idle bluster, but not without substance. The DCI and Secretary of Defense are united in their opinion—we need to crush the IRGC, and the sooner the better. I trust we would have your support?"

"That's music to my ears, Mr. President. We will, of course, fully back such an action."

"We need an invasion plan. I think it best if Israel's contribution comes in the form of military strategy rather than boots on the ground. Let us and the Sunnis take the heat for the occupation of Iran . . . I assume you are in agreement?"

"We were just discussing the matter and came to the same conclusion," Rabinovich told him.

"Is General Simon with you?"

"I am here, Mr. President," Moshe interjected.

"We are arranging a teleconference with the Sunni Coalition for 14:00 hours GMT. I think you will find that the Jordanians and Saudis have great respect for you, General, and will welcome your direction."

"Thank you, Mr. President."

When the call ended, Rabinovich rested his hand on Moshe's shoulder, and, with eyebrows raised, asked, "Did you ever think you'd see the day when we were allies with the Arabs? I sure as hell didn't. Well, I'd better bring David up to speed. I'm going to want him on the call, too."

Rabinovich patted the general's shoulder as he took his leave and searched out his chief spook.

"Can we have a moment in private, David?"

"Of course, Sir. Shall I meet you in your office in five minutes?"

"That would be good."

Once sequestered from the group, David dropped the formality with his old friend. "What's on your mind, Avi?"

"I need you in a teleconference at 14:00 GMT with our U.S. counterparts and members of the Sunni Coalition. Moshe will be taking the lead in outlining an invasion strategy."

"That's fine . . . but you could have told me that in the conference room. There must be something else you want."

"Yes, I want Mossad to extricate the Ayatollah and bring him to me."

"Are you serious? Are you reacting to that crazy rhetoric he was spewing?"

"No. But I am dead serious. I want to eliminate any threat from that son-of-a-bitch. No one can know of the mission or that Khamenei is our prisoner—assuming you succeed." He paused. "Can you deliver him to me, David? It shouldn't be any more difficult than assassinating their top nuclear scientists . . . and you did a great job of that."

Chaikin chuckled as he remembered a series of grisly murders attributed to Mossad . . . killings that significantly slowed Iran's progress towards the bomb.

"Normally, I would say it's impossible. But with the disarray in Tehran, and the fact that we were able to tri-angulate the location of his television broadcast, I'd say the odds have improved greatly. Does he have to be breathing when we deliver him to you?"

"That would be highly preferable. We're not looking to create a martyr, David, nor leave a trail that suggests a kidnapping. The Ayatollah must simply vanish . . . and it needs to happen before Tehran falls."

"Then I need to mobilize a team quickly. The IRGC knows they take a risk every time they move him, so my guess is that he will remain at the studio and continue his hate broadcasts for a while."

"Do it."

Chaikin nodded briskly and walked out.

There was no time to assemble assets in Israel and transport them to Tehran. Chaikin would have to cobble together agents already on the ground—putting a vital component of Mossad's human intelligence at risk. But he knew the potential pay-off would be immense.

If it was going to be a bloodless extraction, he needed a powerful diversion to capture the attention of Khamenei's bodyguards, and he had an idea of just how to make that happen.

A minute after he sent a coded text, Ebrahim Ghorbani called on Chaikin's encrypted satellite phone. "The tension here is high. I suggest we only talk a minute, Sir."

"I need you to pull together a team for the extraction of a high value target . . . and it needs to happen within hours."

"The target?"

"Khamenei."

"Do you have a plan, Sir?"

"The rudiments of one . . . you can work out the details on the ground. We know where he is, or at least where he was when he made the last televised broadcast. We'll assume that he's still there. The building is in the eleventh district at the intersection of Hashemi and Abu Sa'id."

"And how do you suggest we relieve him of his body-guards without a bloodbath?"

"There's an herb shop down the street. It will be closed in a few hours. I think a couple of kilos of Semtex planted in the store's bathroom might buy you a few minutes of intense distraction. If his bodyguards follow protocol, they'll whisk the Ayatollah out the back door and into an armored transport."

"Yes . . . if he is there . . . if his guards follow protocol . . . and if we can intercept the transport . . . it's a good plan, Sir."

"I can almost see the sarcasm on your face, Ebrahim. We have no choice; these orders come straight from the PM."

"Understood, Sir. And once we have secured the target?"

"We'll transmit the coordinates for a safe-house. It has a deep bunker in which our guest will ride out the storm that's about to hit Tehran. After the city is occupied, we will transport him back to Israel. No one, outside of your team and the transport team, will know of his capture."

"I understand, Sir."

Chaikin hung up. The wheels were now in motion.

CHAPTER FORTY-ONE

Later That Day

At 14:00 GMT, just as the Sunni Coalition conference call was being convened, a powerful blast rocked the Iranian capital. Placed in a storefront shop, the bomb leveled the building. Fortunately, no one was on the sidewalks at the time, or they would have been eviscerated by what was thought to be a suicide bomber.

A block away, windows exploded inward and structures shuddered under the force of the blast. The building acting as a refuge for the Ayatollah sustained significant damage. However, Khamenei was resting in an interior room towards the rear of the house at the moment of detonation, which spared him serious injury, although he was thrown to the floor by the blast wave. His security detail scrambled to help him to his feet before forming a human shield that moved cautiously towards the rear of the building.

One of the IRGC bodyguards removed his 9 mm pistol as he slowly opened a rear door that exited onto the alley. He checked it methodically. Empty . . . no cars . . . no bicycles . . . no people. He returned the gun to its holster and reached for his radio, continuing to scan the street for any activity.

His voice was halting and laden with anxiety as he shouted into the device. "I need safe transport, now! The Great Leader is at extreme risk!"

"Transport arriving in less than two minutes," came the instantaneous response—not from headquarters, but from a Mossad agent who had intercepted the transmission.

As promised, a heavily armored Toyota Land Cruiser careened around the corner, not slowing down until it screeched to a halt directly in front of the men. Inside the vehicle were three IRGC officers, two of them armed with Tondar sub-machine guns.

"Get him in the back, now!" the colonel riding shotgun ordered.

"Yes, Sir!" The bodyguard detachment shouted in response and shepherded the cleric into the back seat and slammed the door. The tires squealed as the car sped away.

"Where are you taking me?" the Ayatollah demanded to know, but before he could hear the response, a needle pierced his skin, and a strong sedative flooded his system. He was out cold.

CHAPTER FORTY-TWO

Psy-Ops

THE ASSAULT ON IRAN BEGAN, not with the deafening sound of exploding bombs, but with a whisper . . . as leaflets gently floated down from the sky. Tehran, Mashad, Isfahan, Karaj, Shiraz, Tabriz, Ahvaz, and Qom were blanketed with sheets of paper dropped from low-flying aircraft warning that a massive retaliatory attack was imminent. Iran was to be punished for the Theocracy's attempt to destroy the Jewish state.

Led by the Sunni Coalition, the assault would focus on governmental and military installations. Its intent was not to kill innocent civilians, but to strip the Theocracy of any remaining power. Accordingly, people were advised to take shelter within the hour and be prepared to remain sequestered for upwards of a week. It concluded with the statement, "The Iranian people are not our enemy. We do not wish any harm to come to them."

A leaflet landed at the feet of Amir Kabirii. The old man slowly bent down and picked it up. He tilted his head until the reading portion of his bifocals brought the words into focus. As he read it, his body began to move from side to side in agitation.

"What is it, Amir?" Leilia, his wife of 52 years, asked.

Amir handed her the leaflet. "I don't know, Leilia. It says that we are to take shelter. That an invasion of our city is about to occur and no one may remain on the streets or in their houses."

"Is it from President Rouhani or from our Great Leader?"

"I don't know who it is from." He seemed confused.

She snatched it out of his hand, reading it slowly: Tears welled up in her eyes.

"Do we leave our home for a shelter—not knowing what will remain when we return?"

Amir put his arms around the love of his life and hugged her gently, then wiped away the tears. "My beautiful princess, don't cry. I will protect you."

She smiled at the thought. "I don't mean to laugh, Amir, but there is little you can do to protect me, let alone our entire family. I think we should heed the warning, gather our children and their children . . . and go to the shelter."

Iranian Civil Defense had learned many lessons from the Israelis, including the importance of constructing hundreds of shelters in major metropolitan areas. But the architects and engineers failed to anticipate the meteoric population growth in some cities. Greater Tehran had mushroomed to nearly fifteen million inhabitants, but the number of shelters had not changed. Amir knew they would fill quickly.

The couple walked as briskly as their arthritic bodies would allow. Arriving at their residence, Amir and Leilia were greeted by their sons, daughters, and grandchildren—all of whom had seen the papers falling from the sky.

"Your mother and I have decided that we all must go to the shelter, now, while there is still room."

No one resisted.

"Gather your things and meet back in here in thirty minutes—no later!"

When they arrived, the shelter was already nearing capacity. The Civil Defense commander overseeing access recognized Amir's sons and immediately welcomed three generations of the Kairii family into his safekeeping.

Slightly claustrophobic and more than a bit impatient, it did not take long for Amir to grow restless. Looking for something to do, he spied a group of his peers engaged in an animated discussion. He wandered over.

"May I join you?" he asked respectfully.

The circle of elders widened to accommodate him. He knew several of the men from the neighborhood and introduced himself to others.

"Manu, here, thinks this is all a ruse," a rail-thin man said as he pointed to a man who was nodding his head.

"It *is* a ruse!" the man insisted.

"And what evidence do you have of that?" Amir asked.

"Have you heard a single bomb go off?"

"No," Amir admitted, shaking his head.

As if on cue, what sounded like a muffled blast could be heard in the distance. Though it was frightening, it paled by comparison to the explosion that followed seconds later. The thunderous blast rocked the shelter and shook its inhabitants to their very core.

"I guess you were wrong," Amir said.

An IRGC officer was weaving rapidly through the crowd, trying to ascertain if anyone had been injured. As he approached the group, Amir stopped him.

"I've never heard anything like that, Major. What just happened?"

"It sounded like a thermobaric bomb. If so, be grateful you are in this shelter and have pity on anyone still on the streets!"

Wave after wave of explosions followed. Children screamed, their mothers wailed, and men sat glassy-eyed, unable to do anything about it. More than a hundred people huddled together in the dimly lit fluorescent room, which was bare except for cots and the blankets covering them.

The two bathrooms, if one could call them that, were grossly insufficient for the mass of humanity hunkered down in the shelter. The air had taken on a putrid smell, and people covered their faces with bandanas to keep from gagging. Between the conditions of the shelter and the near constant bombardment, sleep was virtually impossible.

Finally, after three days of hell, the noise stopped. A small cadre of men, including Amir, slowly emerged from their life-saving bunker and took in their first glimpse of a ravaged city.

The old man shook his head as if to dispel a bad dream. Nothing recognizable remained. The major buildings that had defined the skyline of Tehran lay in ruins. Milad and Azadi Towers—gone; Niavaran Palace—gone; Shah Abdul Azin Shrine—gone. Smoke rose from hundreds of fires dotting the city. Bodies lined the streets—men, women, and children who had either ignored the leaflets or been denied access to overcrowded shelters.

Even a nuclear bomb wouldn't do such damage, Amir thought to himself before returning to the somber, dark world of the shelter.

The Major summoned everyone's attention. "The bombing may be over, but I've been told that there is a large military force en route to Tehran—presumably with the intent of occupying our capital. You must remain in the shelter until we know it is safe to return to your homes. If you are on the street, you risk being shot, taken prisoner, or raped."

Saudi and Jordanian forces, as well as a small contingent of U.S. advisors, arrived within hours. Following a plan outlined by Moshe Simon, they systematically quelled any remaining resistance. A field command center was established, as were MASH units. A similar scenario played out in every major city in Iran.

One agonizing week later, the Kabirii family returned to what was left of their homes.

CHAPTER FORTY-THREE

Putting Humpty Dumpty Together Again

LIZ SPENT A SLEEPLESS NIGHT tossing and turning while images of her dying husband flooded her mind. Exhausted, she finally collapsed into a deep sleep at 5:15 in the morning, only to be awakened an hour later by a sharp rap on the bedroom door.

"Come in," she said apprehensively, pulling the bed sheets up to her neck.

The First Lady entered and walked towards the bed. Liz's eyes widened, looking for signs of the news she was about to hear. The First Lady sat on the edge of the bed, took Liz's hand in hers, and began to speak.

"I have good news for you, Dear. It looks like he's going to be okay."

The pent-up angst stored in every cell of her body was released in a torrent of tears. Liz's body shook as she tried to comprehend the magnitude of what she had just heard.

"He's okay, my John is okay?" she stammered out between sobs.

"Yes, your John is going to be okay . . . still pretty beaten up, but it appears that he's out of the woods."

Liz closed her eyes and thanked God for answering her constant prayers.

"When can I see him?" she asked urgently.

"He's being flown to Jerusalem as we speak. The president has a plane waiting for you at Andrews. If you don't mind helicopters, Marine One is standing by on the south lawn. Shall I help you get ready?"

"You've already done so much! Please tell President Conner how grateful I am to you both."

"I think you'll have a chance to tell him yourself. He plans to see you off as soon as you're ready."

There was little for Liz to do other than put on some comfortable clothes for the long flight to Israel. Thanks to the First Lady, everything she would require for an extended stay had been gathered from the condo, neatly packed in a bag, and delivered to the White House.

As soon as she was dressed, she opened the door to the expansive suite and stepped into the hallway. A female Marine awaited her.

"If you will please follow me, Ma'am, I'll escort you to Marine One."

As they approached the helicopter, the young Marine saluted the Commander-in-Chief, who discharged her of her obligation.

"Liz, when you get to Jerusalem, tell John how grateful I am that he is on the mend, and that I look forward to speaking with him shortly."

"I will, Mr. President. You know how devoted he is to you."

"And to you, my dear. Best of luck. We'll be in touch." He gave Liz a quick hug before directing her up the gantry. Seconds later, she was airborne.

"It's a quick ride to Andrews, Ma'am," the Captain said. "The president has arranged for a G5 to take you the rest of the way. It should be a very comfortable trip, Dr. Wilkins."

"Thank you, Captain."

"Ma'am, would you mind telling Commander Hart how proud the Marines are of him. I'd sure be grateful."

"That's very kind. Of course, I will, Captain."

The front half of the G5 was configured with over-sized leather chairs and two small couches. The back of the fuselage contained a bedroom and bathroom. A flight attendant quickly acquainted Liz with the plane's features before making sure she was strapped in for take-off.

"Our flight time to Jerusalem is approximately nine hours, Dr. Wilkins. After take-off, I'll turn back the bed in case you want to sleep. Please let me know if there is anything I can get for you."

"That would be wonderful. I'm afraid I didn't get much sleep last night. Thank you for taking such good care of me," Liz smiled.

She never made it to the bedroom. Ten minutes after reclining her seat, Liz fell fast asleep. When she finally awakened, they were two hours from touchdown.

As she exited the plane, Liz was shocked by the sight of her welcoming committee. Never in a million years would she have expected the prime minister of Israel to personally greet her.

"Welcome to Israel, Dr. Wilkins," he said, taking her hand warmly in his.

"You are very kind to greet me, Mr. Prime Minister. It's not something I would have expected, with everything that is happening."

"Please, my friends all call me Avi." Gesturing to his left, Rabinovich said, "A car is waiting to take us to Hadassah Ein Kremen Hospital, where some of the finest doctors in Israel are caring for your husband. Are you ready?"

He climbed in beside her for the twenty-minute drive.

As they approached the hospital, Rabinovich cautioned her. "It's a miracle your husband survived a .50 caliber round from a sniper's rifle. He looks like he's been through hell. But you know, John's been to hell and back before. Have faith, Liz, but don't expect too much too soon."

She nodded, wondering just how bad it would be.

Heavily sedated, John lay motionless as Liz and the prime minister entered the room. The sheet concealing his badly wounded body raised and lowered in synch with the rhythmic sound of a respirator. IV bags slowly discharged their contents through multiple lines running into his veins. A flat panel displayed his vitals, including his heart rhythm.

A doctor entered the room and introduced himself. "You must be Dr. Wilkins." Without waiting for confirmation, he thrust out his hand. "I'm Michael Kaplan. I'm in charge of your husband's care while he is with us."

"How is he . . . is he . . . "

"Yes, he's going to be okay, but you must be patient. Your husband sustained an injury that would have killed most mortals. Frankly, I don't know how he survived it."

"How long will he be here, Dr. Kaplan?"

"That's up to God and to your husband. My best guess—a couple of months."

"Oh!" Liz exclaimed, caught off-guard by such a lengthy estimate.

"We will send him home as soon as we can, Dr. Wilkins. You have my promise," Kaplan told her.

"Can he hear me, Doctor?"

"He's pretty deeply sedated, but I wouldn't entirely rule it out . . . particularly with your husband. I'll check on him later. It's nice to meet you, Dr. Wilkins. Mr. Prime Minister."

"Thank you, Doctor," Liz and the prime minister said in unison as Kaplan exited the room.

"That's my cue, too. I think you need to have some time alone with the commander. I'll be returning to Tel Aviv, but I'm only a phone call away. Don't hesitate, my dear, to call me if you need anything." Rabinovich handed her a card on which he had written his personal cell number.

Liz nodded, accepted a brief hug, and then turned her attention to John. She scooted a heavy chair close to the side of the bed—close enough to stroke his hair and squeeze his hand.

As their skin touched, tears began flowing down her cheeks.

"You told me not to worry, Cowboy, and this naïve little girl from Carolina took you at your word. I don't mean to scold you; I'm just so afraid, so deathly afraid of losing you!"

Liz paused to collect her thoughts. She needed to say her feelings aloud—whether John could hear her or not. "I'm with you now . . . I'm with you forever."

Her brief moment of reflection ended when a nurse knocked lightly on the door.

"I'm so sorry to intrude, Dr. Wilkins, but it's time for the commander's medication. It will only take me a moment."

The nurse hung a 200 ml bag containing vancomycin on the IV pole, then connected the potent antibiotic to the saline flowing into his body.

"Let me know if there is anything you need," she advised Liz on her way out the door.

Still holding John's hand, she thought she felt a slight squeeze. No, she told herself, don't get your hopes up.

CHAPTER FORTY-FOUR

A Ghost

As TEHRAN TEETERED ON COLLAPSE, the IRGC performed one of its final official functions: it corralled and transported the country's most senior leaders—religious, political and military—to a remote shelter near Zahedan in eastern-most Iran, close to the Afghanistan/Pakistan border. From there, they would form a shadow government until the Ayatollah summoned them. Tensions mounted as they awaited news of the Great Leader.

"I'm tiring of your incompetence, General," Hossein Taeb snarled at Mohammad Ali Jafari. "Men such as the Ayatollah do not simply disappear. It was your IRGC who were guarding him at the time. Where have they taken him?"

"They have not taken him anywhere," Jafari responded with little affect. "I understand your anger, but it will not hasten the return of our Great Leader."

"If the IRGC does not have possession of the Ayatollah, then who does?" Rouhani demanded.

"We believe he may have been abducted by the Jews," Jafari responded half under his breath.

"That's absurd!" Rouhani said in disgust. "How would they gain access to him when he is surrounded by men who would gladly give up their lives in his defense?"

Before Jafari could answer, Rouhani continued, "And why weren't his guards killed during the so-called 'abduction'? These are not rhetorical questions. I'm waiting for your answers, General. And, while you are at, tell me how they removed the Great Leader from Iran without detection."

"I don't have answers to your questions, President Rouhani, not yet. As for Israel's role in the Ayatollah's disappearance, why is it so far-fetched? It could have been their agents, dressed as IRGC officers, manning the car that picked up the Ayatollah following the explosion in Tehran. The Israelis are smart . . . they would have laid low until occupation forces captured the city, then transported him to an unknown location in Israel."

"Or killed him!" Taeb's tone was defiant.

"No!" Jafari stood and pounded his fist against the table. "Why would the Jews create a martyr and relinquish control of such a grand prize? They would hide our leader . . . hoping we would eventually give up the search." He shot a harsh look at Taeb and Rouhani before striding furiously out of the room.

After leaving the hospital, the prime minister's security entourage headed west on Highway 1. They had been traveling for nearly an hour when Rabinovich informed his driver that he intended to make an unscheduled stop.

"Where, Sir?"

"Ramla. Take me to Ayalon."

Formerly known as Ramla Prison, Ayalon had been home to some of Israel's most notorious prisoners, including John (Ivan) Demjanjuk, a retired U.S. autoworker accused in the deaths of more than 28,000 Jews at Treblinka and Sobibor concentration camps, and Yigal Amir, the Israeli who assassinated Yitzhak Rabin in November 1995.

Rabinovich instructed his bodyguards to remain outside—a departure from protocol but an essential step in maintaining compartmentalized knowledge about the prisoner Rabinovich was here to visit. The warden met him at the door, then escorted the prime minister through numerous layers of security until they finally arrived at Unit 15, where the worst of the worst were housed.

Stopping in front of a metal door, the warden explained. "Your prisoner is being held in the isolation cell we built for Yigal Amir. As you will recall, it was also a temporary home for Prisoner X." He was referring to Ben Zygier, a former Mossad agent turned spy who committed suicide following his imprisonment.

"I want you to let me in and then leave us. I will pound on the door when I want to be released. Am I understood?"

"Yes, Mr. Prime Minister, but I don't think that's a very good idea. He may be a cleric, but he is also a fanatic committed to the death of our country and its leaders."

"Thank you for your concern, but I will be fine. The Ayatollah has always relied on proxies to kill men. I've had to rely on my own two hands."

Rabinovich's twenty-year service in the Israeli military was legendary. As was his ability to take care of himself.

"One more thing. The Iranians are undoubtedly pulling out all the stops to find their beloved leader. We can never let them know that he is in our possession . . . even if it means putting a bullet in his head and incinerating the body. My hope is that it never comes to that, but you need to be prepared."

"Understood, Mr. Prime Minister."

Rabinovich entered the six-foot by ten-foot room carrying nothing but a thin stainless steel attaché. The prisoner was prostrate on a rug facing east towards Mecca, reciting his prayers. Rabinovich did not interrupt him, sitting quietly on a stool. When he finished, the Ayatollah slowly rose to his feet.

"Aren't you afraid to be alone with me?" the cleric asked as he stood a few feet from the prime minister.

"Please, have a seat," Rabinovich gestured towards the stainless steel slab bed. "You are a man of God, and though you have the blood of thousands on your hands, I don't think you are eager to wage a personal war against me."

The Ayatollah laughed. "There is nothing that would give me more pleasure than killing the head of the Jewish state, surely you know that."

"What I know is that your country has been decimated, its extremists killed or driven into hiding, and its government decapitated."

"You will have to forgive me . . . I don't get much news down here. What exactly are you saying, Mr. Rabinovich?"

"Iran has been occupied by a Sunni coalition. Your president, chief clerics, and IRGC generals are all in hiding. We will ferret them out. You can count on it."

"You speak as though you have won, Prime Minister Rabinovich. So why are you here? Why not just let me rot in this prison cell?"

"As you said in your televised address to the world, our peoples have been at war for millennia. And, yes, we have won the latest skirmish in a seemingly eternal battle. So why am I here? Probably on what will prove to be a fool's errand. I am here to negotiate a permanent peace that will long outlast us both."

The Ayatollah rose slowly from the metal bed and approached Rabinovich, stopping inches from the prime minister's face.

"There will never be peace until the final drop of Jewish blood is spilled and the scourge of your people is wiped forever from the face of the earth. Then, and only then, will heaven on earth be restored . . . and the lamb and the wolf lie together."

"I don't know who is the lamb and who is the wolf, but I believe peace is possible between our people despite your rantings. Your holy book, the Koran, allows for multiple interpretations. You have chosen the most insular. Why not choose the most enlightened?"

"Don't lecture me on the Koran, a subject about which you are ignorant. The message of our prophet is as clear today as it was a thousand years ago: 'When you meet the infidel, strike off his head.'"

"And our holy book, the Torah, calls for *an eye for an eye*. If I took it literally, I would have you gassed just like you gassed the people of Tel Aviv. But I believe those laws were set down by man, not God, and that man has evolved over the two thousand years since such laws were written."

"Your people are descended from apes. My people are descended from the prophet. That is my final word on the subject, Mr. Prime Minister." The Ayatollah glared at Rabinovich for a several seconds before finally breaking eye contact and returning to his seat on the bed.

"Your hatred is infectious, but I am not going to be taunted by you. No, I'm simply going to provide you with some facts before I leave. It will give you something to think about . . . a parting gift from one ape to another.

"The assault on your country was led by a coalition that included Israel, the United States, Egypt, Saudi Arabia, and Jordan. Kuwait, Iraq, Bahrain, and Qatar chose to remain on the sidelines. As of today, every major city in Iran has been reduced to smoking rubble."

"You accuse us of mass murder. What would you call your actions, Mr. Prime Minister?"

"The people of Iran were warned to take shelter well in advance of the bombings—warnings that were heeded by the majority of the population, according to our intelligence. Schools, hospitals, and neighborhoods were largely spared. Government facilities, military installations, and your precious theocracy were leveled. I would call it a surgical intervention, not murder."

"The IRGC will rise again from the ashes. You have not defeated them; they've only retreated in order to regroup."

"General Mohammad Ali Jafari—presumed killed in battle; General Qasem Soleimani—presumed killed in battle; General Hossein Saleh—MIA; Hossein Taub—whereabouts unknown. Would you like me to continue, Ayatollah Khamenei?"

"For each of the men you have mentioned, there are tens of thousands of soldiers loyal to their command. Don't tell me you've killed them all."

"Actually, many of them lay down their weapons, raised their arms, and surrendered. Even your awesome Qud forces showed their true colors and chose to be prisoners of war rather than die on the battlefield."

"It takes very few men to fire our missiles. Your people destroyed five of our silos, and you know that many more remain."

Rabinovich opened the attaché and removed a folder containing more than a dozen photos—some taken by satellite, others providing a ground-level view. He tossed them to the Ayatollah.

"Don't take the word of this Jew . . . have a look for yourself," he said, baiting the cleric.

The Ayatollah studied the massive destruction that had been inflicted upon his country, his head slowly sinking towards his chest.

"Talks have begun between Shia and Sunnis across the region. Long-festering wounds are beginning to be healed."

"You really believe that's possible, don't you!" the prisoner seethed.

"I drive a Mercedes . . . the product of a nation that attempted to systematically eliminate my people. Do I hate what the Nazis did? Of course, but do I hate the German people? No. I realize that the darkness that overtook Nazi Germany exists wherever it is allowed to take root. The goal is to extinguish darkness . . . to bring forth the light."

"As your country has done with Palestinians, Mr. Rabinovich? I'm not interested in listening to your hypocrisy."

Rabinovich's tone was now sharply vindictive. "Cling to your hatred, cling to your Prophet, and go straight to hell . . . but know that your reign has resulted in nothing but death, anguish, and destruction. We're done!"

He snatched the photos out of the cleric's hands, deposited them back in the attaché, and snapped it shut. He called for the guard.

"I'm finished in here," he said to the soldier through a slit in the door.

"Wait!" The Ayatollah beckoned.

"For what? More of your hatred? No, you stew in your own vitriol. We're done."

CHAPTER FORTY-FIVE

Waiting for a Miracle

A WEEK AFTER LANDING IN JERUSALEM, Liz had settled into a routine. She spent almost every waking hour at her husband's bedside, waiting for any sign that John was improving. But his condition remained largely unchanged.

Each night, she walked the few short blocks to her hotel to shower and change before returning to the hospital. She spent the balance of the evening reading, stroking her husband's head, and praying that the nightmare would soon end. When exhaustion finally overtook her, Liz would curl up in a recliner. She would try to eke out a few hours of dreamless sleep in between nocturnal visits by nurses checking John's vitals or administering medications. The routine was taking a toll visible to everyone in her orbit.

"I don't know who I'm more worried about, the commander or you," Rabinovich told her ten days into the ordeal. "You know this isn't healthy, Liz. Please let Rachel and me take you out to dinner. A break would do you good, and John will forgive you if you skip a meal with him."

She thanked the prime minister for his concern, but politely declined the invitation. She insisted on taking every meal with John, although he remained unresponsive.

On the fifteenth day of his hospitalization, doctors removed the tube from the commander's throat, allowing him to breathe on his own. Liz had envisioned him taking in a deep breath that filled his lungs, then opening his eyes and gazing at her. But that's not how it played out. There were still no signs of conscious awareness.

"I'm not one to give up, Dr. Kaplan, but I'm getting discouraged. Why hasn't he opened his eyes? Why hasn't he spoken to me?" she pleaded.

"Your husband is trying to heal. Be patient just a little while longer. I'm actually quite pleased with his progress. Even though it isn't readily apparent, there have been clear indications that he will walk out of here one day soon."

"Forgive me, Doctor, but that's hard for me to imagine right now. Help me understand how you can be so optimistic when I don't see a single encouraging sign."

"But we do. Take his pain, for example. We can now control it with short-acting narcotics."

Kaplan continued. "There have been no cardiovascular irregularities. His perfusion is strong. He's avoided an infection that could have easily claimed his life. Is that sufficient, Dr. Wilkins?"

"Yes, and thank you." She reached for his hand.

He held her hand between his two large ones. "Keep an eye on your husband, say a prayer, and know he's coming back to you," Kaplan said confidently before leaving.

Once again alone with her husband, she stroked his cheek, "Are you coming back to me, Cowboy?" Bending over him, Liz closed her eyes as her tears fell silently on John's cheek.

"Oh, my God!" she suddenly exclaimed, "You squeezed my hand!" Her eyes opened wide as she stared at her husband.

"You heard me talking to the doctor, didn't you, John?"

He squeezed her hand again, this time with a bit more strength. Then his eyes fluttered and his lips began to move. Liz moved her face to within inches of his, straining to hear what her husband was struggling to say.

In a weak voice, he responded, "I'd squeeze your ass if I could reach it."

She broke out laughing. It was the first moment of unadulterated joy she had experienced since receiving the news that John had been shot.

"You really are incorrigible, Cowboy!"

Whispering again, he responded, "That's why you love me, Darling," before relaxing his grip and drifting back to sleep.

The walls of the hospital room no longer closed in on Liz. She knew that, sometime in the near future, they would be leaving . . . her husband would be coming home. She leaned back in the recliner, closed her eyes, and when she opened them again, the day had turned to night.

At five o'clock, Avi Rabinovich arrived to check on Hart. He immediately noted that something was different. The storm cloud that had hovered over Liz for days seemed to have lifted.

"So how's our boy doing?" he said with a tentative smile.

"He opened his eyes and spoke to me!"

"When?"

"Shortly after Dr. Kaplan made rounds this morning. I told him I was pretty demoralized and he told me to have faith and pray."

"And you did?"

She smiled and nodded. "I was holding John's hand when I felt a gentle squeeze. At first I thought it was my imagination, then I saw his lips starting to move."

"What did the commander say?"

Liz blushed, choosing to deliver a sanitized version of the commander's words. "He told me he loved me."

"What else would enable a man to survive a near fatal injury hundreds of kilometers behind enemy lines! He had to have something precious to hold onto, and that was you."

"John and I owe you a great deal, Avi."

"Nonsense. It is my country that is indebted to you and the commander. Maybe, someday, you and John will tire of Washington and join us here. I think you'd both like Jerusalem."

A faint voice caused them to turn towards the commander.

John spoke ever so slowly. "I was thinking more of a kibbutz."

"Shot to hell and he hasn't lost his sense of humor," Avi laughed as he turned towards the commander. "Welcome back, John."

"Thank you, Sir," he said in a subdued and gravelly voice, then slowly raised a finger and pointed to a cup of water.

Liz held the straw to his mouth. "Just a little at a time, Cowboy. I don't want you to choke." She gradually pulled the straw away.

"So she calls you 'Cowboy.' Seems fitting to me."

"John grew up on a ranch in Montana," Liz explained, "So his nickname isn't just about his attitude . . . he really is a cowboy."

"Why should I be surprised," Avi mused. "Now, my wonderful friends, I must leave and share your good news with President Conner. He's been waiting anxiously for this moment. I will see you both tomorrow."

Before leaving the hospital, Avi Rabinovich had one more stop to make. Two floors below, on the oncology unit, his wife, Rachel, was recovering from surgery. He had been there throughout the day—wanting to ensure that there were no complications during her bilateral mastectomies—before finally allowing himself to go home and sleep for a few hours.

Her face, still ashen from the shock of surgery and the after-effects of anesthesia, gave way to a warm smile at the sight of her husband. She extended her hand slowly, as if to guide Avi to her bedside.

He took her hand in his and kissed it gently, then pulled a chair close to the head of her bed.

"Are you in a great deal of pain?"

Avi kissed her cheek then whispered, "You know you look beautiful."

"Only you would tell me that, and though it is not true, it feels so good to hear you say it."

"I'm going down to the car to make a secure call to President Conner. I owe him an update on Commander

Hart. Thank God, I've got good news to share. The minute I'm done, I'll be back."

"What for? Go home . . . relax!"

He gestured to a recliner. "No, I'm staying the night. I've been gone enough."

CHAPTER FORTY-SIX

The Long Road to Recovery

SIX WEEKS HAD PASSED since John Hart had been cata-strophically wounded by a sniper's bullet. After two weeks in a coma, he had awakened. Since that moment, it had been a non-stop march towards liberation—regaining his strength and then his freedom.

"I don't need the walker!" he insisted, but the physical therapist wasn't taking no for an answer.

Liz interceded, "I don't think you know my husband. When he says he doesn't need something, he means it."

"If he falls, he could re-open his wounds. That's not happening on my watch."

Hart suddenly burst out in laughter.

"What's so funny?" Liz demanded.

"I survive a nuclear detonation, exposure to smallpox, and .50 caliber round ripping my chest apart, only to be told by my physical therapist how the world rotates."

"I'm glad we've come to an understanding," the therapist said, mistakenly believing that the commander was capitulating.

"No, Ma'am, there's no understanding," at which point he stood erect and began walking across the floor. His steps were slow and halting, seeming to take an inordinate amount of strength and determination. When he reached the far wall, he turned and walked back.

The therapist shook her head and stated, "Dr. Wilkins, he's your problem now," before walking off.

"John, stop fooling around!"

"I'm ready to go home, Darling. I need a change of scenery. We've been in this damned place for forever. The walls are beginning to close in on me."

"I know the feeling," she said, relieved at the idea of going home.

John acquiesced to Liz's insistence on pushing him in a wheelchair back to the room. When they arrived on the fifth floor, he announced to the nursing staff his intention to leave shortly.

"We don't have any orders to that effect, Commander," the head nurse responded in surprise.

"Here we go again," Liz said under her breath, choosing to simply smile and quickly push John's wheelchair past the nursing station.

"Start packing, Darling," he instructed her as they entered his room.

"Last time I checked, you were not the boss and I was not the little woman. I'll pack when your doctor tells me it's time to take you home, and not a minute sooner. Got that, Cowboy?"

"Yes, Ma'am. Loud and clear, Ma'am."

It was towards the end of the day when Dr. Kaplan knocked on the door of Hart's room.

"I hear you're planning to leave us, Commander."

Liz jumped in. "He doesn't understand the chain of command, Dr. Kaplan. And I don't need to tell you that John can be a little headstrong."

"Guilty as charged, Doctor," Hart added.

"Be grateful for that spirit . . . it's what helped you get through this ordeal," Kaplan advised.

"I thought it was having the finest care available in Israel," Hart countered.

"The finest care in the world, Commander," Kaplan corrected him.

"Dr. Wilkins, I think the time has come for you to take the commander home. We're going to run a few quick tests in the morning, but I can't make an argument for keeping him here any longer . . . other than for amusement. So what do you say, Commander Hart—ready to hop on a plane and head back to Washington?"

"Yes, Sir . . . right this minute, Dr. Kaplan. I don't need any tests to confirm I'm okay."

"Let me be the judge of that, Commander. You're still my patient until I discharge you. I'll plan on signing the papers the day after tomorrow, assuming you get a clean bill of health. I'll notify Mr. Rabinovich, who will be in touch with President Conner."

"Thank you, Doctor, for all you've done for my husband. Six weeks ago, I didn't think this day would ever arrive. I'm so grateful."

Hart couldn't resist spoiling the moment. "Darling, it was just a scratch. You're giving Dr. Kaplan far too much credit. Hell, a first year medical student probably could have pulled me through. Right, Dr. Kaplan?" Hart asked with a wink.

"On that note, Commander, I'll take my leave. I'll see you both bright and early."

True to his word, Kaplan returned at 6:15 a.m. accompanied by an RN. "Nurse Helm is going to take you down to radiology for an MRI, as well as a CT. Then you're heading to the lab. You'll finish the morning in the pulmonary clinic, where they will clear you to fly."

"How many CTs have I had, Doctor? You know I already glow in the dark, thanks to that damned nuke I had to babysit in New York."

"We're only irradiating a small section of your chest and back. I'm pretty confident you won't die from the exposure, Commander. I'll have the results back late in the afternoon and meet with you before supper."

Within minutes of his departure, another guest appeared at the door. It was Avi Rabinovich.

"I understand that congratulations are in order . . . you are leaving us shortly."

"If Dr. Kaplan gives John a clean bill of health," Liz added.

"*When* Dr. Kaplan gives me a clean bill of health tomorrow," John said emphatically, staring at Liz.

"I have great respect for you, Dr. Wilkins. You have your hands full with this one!"

"Most of the time, he's wonderful. Some of the time, he's like a petulant child."

"Yes, I can see that," the prime minister chuckled.

Hart lay on the raised bed with his arms crossed and face scrunched in protest.

"Come on, Commander, we've got to have some fun with you. You've been a most interesting guest for many weeks now. You are going to be missed by everyone here . . . well, except for one physical therapist who refuses to set foot in your room."

"Have you spoken to the president, Sir?" Hart's tone was now serious.

"Yes, shortly before I came over. He wanted to be certain that you were up for the travel. I explained that Dr. Kaplan was running a final battery of tests before releasing you. He will have a plane standing by the day after tomorrow on the assumption that you're good to go."

He added, "I need to talk with you privately before you depart, Commander. I hope you will forgive me, Dr. Wilkins, if I ask for a few minutes alone with your husband tomorrow following his tests."

CHAPTER FORTY-SEVEN

Rabinovich's Revelation

"Tip-top shape, all things considered, Commander," the pulmonologist told Hart after reviewing his imaging studies and checking his respiratory function. "Dr. Kaplan, of course, has the final word . . . but I think he'll be giving you good news later today. It's been an honor to help care for you, Commander."

"It's been my honor to serve your country," Hart responded as he shook the physician's hand.

When he arrived back at the room, the prime minister was waiting for him.

"I'm going down to the cafeteria for a while. Can I bring either of you anything when I return?" Liz asked.

"You are far too nice a woman to be married to this man!" Rabinovich proclaimed.

"I know, and he knows it too," she said, pointing to her husband. "I'll be back in an hour . . . I assume that's enough time?"

"More than enough, and thank you." Rabinovich walked her to the door.

The prime minister paused before motioning to a man seated down the hall to join them. Rabinovich closed the door behind them. The man opened a briefcase, removed a device with a large meter, and swept the hospital room for any RF signals.

"It's clean, Mr. Prime Minister."

"Can you block any possible electronic intrusion?"

The man removed a second device, which he placed in the center of the room. He switched it on, causing a red light atop the unit to glow. "You are covered, Sir."

Rabinovich thanked the man and asked that he return to the hall.

"I have something important to share with you, Commander."

"No, shit." Hart caught himself. "I'm so sorry, Sir, that slipped out."

Rabinovich was laughing. "I'm glad to see you're as human as the rest of us, Commander."

"It must be one hell of a secret, Sir, for you to take such measures," Hart said by way of correction.

"I need your advice, Commander. You see, we are holding a very valuable prisoner of war, and we're not sure what his disposition should be."

"Are you talking about an IRGC officer, Mr. Prime Minister?"

"No, I'm talking about Ayatollah Khamenei, Commander."

Hart was visibly startled by the news. "You are not serious, Sir?"

"Dead serious, Commander. He was picked up by Mossad prior to the fall of Tehran."

"I appreciate your confidence, Mr. Prime Minister, but I assume you've solicited the president for his opinion."

"President Conner doesn't know, Commander."

"Mr. Prime Minister, why have you kept this information from your greatest ally?" Without waiting for a response, he continued, "I suggest you rectify the situation immediately with a phone call to the White House, Mr. Rabinovich." Hart's tone was firm, not at all similar to his easygoing manner of a moment before.

"Before you get too self-righteous, my friend, let me remind you that there are secrets in every relationship."

"Not of this order of magnitude," Hart responded.

"Really, Commander? You are not naïve. Would you consider the fact that Osama Bin Laden is the sole detainee in Langdon Prison any less pernicious a secret?"

"I don't know what you are talking about, Sir."

Rabinovich studied Hart's face, trying to determine if there was any attempt at deception.

"I believe you, Commander. I'm sure President Conner would take you into his confidence on any and all matters related to the security of America, but he's not the only voice on such matters. What I am revealing to you, I do so with absolute knowledge of its validity."

"So you are saying that the government of the United States of America faked Bin Laden's assassination. I know the men on SEAL Team 6, and they described every minute of the operation to me . . . including the kill shots."

"They told you what they were obliged to share—a methodically constructed story that would hold up under scrutiny. I imagine it gave them great displeasure to lie to a fellow SEAL. But no one understands orders better than you."

"Why lie . . . why not bask in the glory of capturing the world's greatest terrorist, and slowly extracting each of his secrets?"

"Because your government wanted the best of both worlds—long sought retribution that helped restore American's sense of pride and justice, while quietly torturing a prisoner to eke out what has proven to be increasingly irrelevant information about future terrorist plots."

"Why are you telling me this, Mr. Rabinovich?"

"Because I am in a quandary about what to do with the Ayatollah. If we hold a trial, he will be found guilty of war crimes and executed. That will only up the ante with all Shia Muslims. If we allow him to die quietly in prison, what have we accomplished through his capture?"

"May I be the one to share this information with President Conner?"

"That's why I am sharing this information with you, Commander. I owe it to you. Determine the best way to use it."

"Understood, Sir."

Rabinovich looked at his watch. "Liz will be returning before long."

He summoned the agent from the hall, who quickly removed all traces of the electronic jamming equipment.

"I'll say goodbye in the morning, Commander. Forgive me for leaving before Liz returns, but I have a speech to give."

CHAPTER FORTY-EIGHT

Crafting a Lasting Peace

THE HOT GLARE OF STUDIO LIGHTS beat down on Rabinovich as he prepared to address the world. The broadcast was being carried live by CNN, BBC, and Al Jazeera, as well as dozens of smaller networks. He would speak, not only for Israel, but also for the Sunni Coalition.

"It is estimated that over two billion people have tuned in to hear what I am about to say. That affords me a unique opportunity to share what is in the hearts and minds of my countrymen, as well as my allies.

"The Middle East has been a point of friction throughout the long history of civilization. Countless empires have risen and fallen—with countless lives lost in each transition of power. It has been a constant ebb and flow of power between opposing sides—who see their enemy as soldiers of the darkness, but fail to see the darkness within their own hearts.

"It is that darkness that drove Iran's leaders to chant 'death to Israel,' and then attempt to make it a reality. And it is that darkness that stoked our response—reducing the once proud and mighty country of Iran to rubble.

"There is no victor in such calamities, only victims.

"Israel and our coalition have been united by a common enemy. It is now time for us to put aside our weapons and call for peace across the region. Hatred must be supplanted by an understanding that we are one people—Shia and Sunni, Jew and Gentile. We may worship differently, hold different customs sacred, but we belong to one God . . . a God that has commanded us to love our neighbor as ourselves.

"Israel, in tandem with its allies, will begin reconstruction efforts in Iran immediately. As part of this process, we will facilitate the holding of open elections for a new Iranian government—a government of the people. The only restriction we will impose is that Iran not re-arm itself.

"Arabs, Jews, and Christians can peacefully co-exist. That is not mere rhetoric, but well-demonstrated fact. It requires an open mind, a loving heart, and a degree of self-sacrifice. This is what I ask of everyone who calls himself or herself an Israeli.

"Just as we are rebuilding Iran, we will also work assiduously to create a home for Palestinians by resuming anew discussions with multiple factions representing the Palestinian people. I pledge that Israel will work towards a palatable solution within six months. This is not political propaganda . . . nor an action that will endear me to my party. I am impelled to seek peace after being party to so much death.

"Our American friends are fond of saying, 'The proof is in the pudding.' So let's get at it and prove that light and love can dispel the darkness."

"That was a stirring speech you gave today, Avi. Everyone in Israel is proud of you."

"I wouldn't be so sure of that, Rachel. The hard-right portion of our party thinks I've gone soft. Some even say that our defeat of the Syrian Coalition was at the expense of my balls."

"Well, I can tell them that you are just fine in that department!" This elicited a hearty laugh from her husband, before his expression turned serious.

"You are an extraordinarily strong woman, Rachel, you know that."

"How do you think I manage to live with you, my Darling?"

CHAPTER FORTY-NINE

A Change of Hart

"John, for God's sake, let me push your wheelchair out to the plane. And don't give me that look!" Liz said in mock annoyance as the small group congregated on the tarmac near the parked Gulfstream.

"I stepped off the plane when I arrived in Israel and I'll step onto the plane when I leave Israel." John pushed himself up out of the chair on wobbly legs.

Liz turned to Rabinovich, who simply shrugged his shoulders. Moshe Simon smiled knowingly, empathizing with the wounded warrior returning home from battle.

Hart turned to the two gentlemen and snapped a salute. "I'd either be lying face-down in the dirt at an Iranian missile complex or being sent home in box if wasn't for you and the men under your command. Liz has told you how grateful she is for all that you have done, and now it is my turn. You are my brothers, always. My debt to you is immense. Whatever I can do to repay your kindness, know that I will."

"You owe us no debt, John," Rabinovich said. "You almost gave your life for Israel, and you are not even a Jew!"

A boyish smile emerged as Rabinovich reached into his coat pocket and extracted a brand new yarmulke. Unfolding it, he placed it on the crown of John's head.

"Moshe and I have decided to make you an honorary Jew. Remember the Sabbath Day and keep it holy . . . oh, and don't forget you owe me an answer to a very important question."

"Shalom, my brothers," John said with a warm smile. "I am honored." He turned to Liz.

"Are you ready, Darling?" John locked arms with Liz and walked the short distance to the waiting Gulfstream.

Safely buckled in, Liz turned to John. "What was the answer the prime minister was referring to?'"

John was already reclined in his seat with his eyes closed—the short walk had been more taxing than he had anticipated. Opening his eyes a crack, he turned his head towards Liz.

"Oh, that . . . I'm going to call the president in a few minutes regarding Mr. Rabinovich's question," he answered nonchalantly.

"Don't play games with me; just tell me what's on the prime minister's mind."

"Be patient, Darling. Ten minutes . . . that's all I ask."

Twelve minutes into the flight, the captain announced that they had reached cruising altitude. The flight attendant stopped to check on her only passengers.

Hart returned his seat back to its upright position, and assumed a formal tone. "Dr. Wilkins and I are quite comfortable, but I need you to do something for me."

"Of course, Commander."

"I am going to place a call to the White House and I need absolute privacy. Would you please inform the captain that I've asked you to ride up front for the next fifteen or twenty minutes? I'll signal you with the call button as soon as I'm off the phone."

"Yes, Sir."

"This is serious," Liz said as soon as they were alone.

"You might say that," John responded.

He removed an encrypted satellite phone from his carry-on. As soon as he had a signal, Hart pressed a speed dial number that connected him directly to the president.

"Commander?"

"Yes, Mr. President."

"I wondered when I'd hear from you."

"The hospital was not a secure environment, Sir. I'm sorry, Mr. President, but I needed to wait until we could speak privately . . . and I knew that the prime minister was in daily contact with you. Is this a good time, Sir?"

"I'm scheduled to meet shortly with the Secretary of Defense. I'll push it back if needed."

"Thank you, Sir. Before we departed, Mr. Rabinovich had an interesting conversation with me. It appears that Israel is holding a high-value prisoner but is at a loss as to how to manage the disposition of the POW. He requested my input."

"Who is the prisoner, Commander?"

"The Ayatollah, Sir."

There was a prolonged silence as Conner considered the ramifications of what he had just heard.

"Why didn't Avi share that information with me?" Conner demanded.

"I asked the prime minister the same question, explaining that he had put me in a very difficult position."

"You are not in any jeopardy, Commander, but I resent our ally keeping such matters secret. We would never do such a thing! You understand that I will have to speak with the prime minister about this issue at my earliest opportunity."

"Before you do, Sir, there's one more piece of information I need to share."

"What is it?" Conner's tone was impatient. He didn't like surprises.

"When I expressed my concern over the Israeli's concealment, he chastised me for being self-righteous and duplicitous."

"That's absurd! I would never ascribe such attributes to you."

"Apparently, Mr. Rabinovich assumed that I was privy to the fact that we, too, are secretly holding a very high value prisoner."

"And who might that be?" Conner asked.

"Osama Bin Laden, Sir."

Once again, there was silence on the line. Hart turned his head to see if Liz was taking it all in. The look on her face gave him the answer.

"Commander, only a handful of people in the world— including the DNI—know about our prisoner."

"And Mossad, Sir. They know."

"How in the hell did Israeli intelligence get that information . . . or was it just a hunch that Rabinovich was floating with you?"

"Sir, he told me where Bin Laden is being held. Plus, he had details of how the deception was created. I believe he had his facts straight."

"I assume that Dr. Wilkins is seated next to you, Commander?"

"Yes, Sir."

"Explain to Dr. Wilkins the potential consequences of such information becoming public. The fallout from deceiving the American people would do untold damage to the credibility of our government."

"You don't have to worry about Liz, Sir. May I ask why we would take such a risk, Mr. President?"

"That's a damn good question. I've asked myself the same thing on numerous occasions. Suffice it to say that I was under heavy pressure from our intelligence leaders, who were dying to get their hands on Bin Laden. They were convinced that he would be a treasure trove of secrets. By faking his death, we were able to transport him to a maximum security cell where daily interrogations began shortly after his arrival. But I can't blame the CIA. As Truman said, 'The buck stops here.'"

"Did Bin Laden live up to your hopes, Sir?"

"He has said very little, Commander, and nothing of value, despite enhanced interrogation techniques. I'm pretty convinced he will die before he gives up any meaningful intelligence."

"And I believe the same can be said of the Ayatollah, Sir. His rewards are in heaven, not on earth. He will never kowtow to a human being, and certainly never to a Jew."

"So what do you think we should recommend to Prime Minister Rabinovich?" Conner asked.

"I believe the Ayatollah should be tried in secret for crimes against humanity. The proof is self-evident. Once found guilty, he should be put to death. It's that simple."

Liz squirmed in her seat, uncomfortable with how nonchalantly her husband was suggesting the execution of another human being.

"Nothing is simple, John. You can try to bury secrets, but they have a way of emerging over time . . . and they get uglier and more insidious with age. We can eliminate Bin Laden and the Ayatollah, but even in death, they cast a long shadow."

"What would you like me to say to Mr. Rabinovich, Sir?"

"I think you should tell him that we have no magic answers, but empathize with his dilemma. I would be very interested to know how Mossad found out, but that's not something Avi will be quick to share . . . with anyone."

"Yes, Sir."

"I will see you and Dr. Wilkins after you arrive. Safe travels, Commander."

"Thank you, Sir."

Hart reached for the call attendant light, but Liz intercepted his arm.

"Wait just a minute, Cowboy. That was a hell of a lot for me to digest, and some of it is not sitting so well."

She continued, "Let me get this straight. The U.S. is holding Osama Bin Laden, having captured him after creating a mock assassination; and Israel is holding Ayatollah Khamenei."

"Yep."

"And the prime minister has asked for your opinion on what to do with Khamenei."

"Looks like you got the drift of things, Darling."

"Yes, including your recommendation to execute a religious leader."

"Oh, don't go soft on me, Liz. That man is about as close to God as a snake. His religion is nothing more than a cloak concealing his imperialistic vision for regional domination." Hart was on a roll.

"Holy men don't attack innocent civilians with deadly nerve gas. They don't threaten the total and complete annihilation of a nation. Death may be too kind a gift for a man like the Ayatollah. Maybe it would be more fitting to lock him in a cell, never to see the light of day . . . and facilitate his slow descent into madness. I'll have to give it some thought."

"Are we any better?" Liz responded, shaking her head in disbelief. "We kill with impunity—and don't tell me we aren't the most imperialistic nation ever to exist on the face of the earth. The Ayatollah sought conquests in the name of religion. We do it in the name of democracy."

"Now you are sounding like one of those wide-eyed liberals marching in Lafayette Park. Come on, Liz, you're far too smart to take such a position."

Frustration turned into sadness, as a tears formed in Liz's eyes and overflowed onto her cheeks. John reached to wipe them off, but she slapped his hand away.

"Don't do that," he said firmly.

"Don't touch me," she responded.

Hart reached up and turned on the call light, initiating the prompt return of the flight attendant.

"May I get you anything?" she asked with a perky smile.

"I'll have a scotch—single malt if you've got it—and Dr. Wilkins will have a vodka martini."

As soon as the flight attendant turned her back, the forced smile evaporated from Liz's face. "You son of a bitch . . . you're not going to calm me down with alcohol."

Half of Hart wanted to let her have it, while the other half knew it was best to apologize as fast as he could. The question was which half would win out.

"I can't believe I'm fighting with you, Darling. I'm so sorry . . . so very sorry." He reached to take her hand in his. It was cold and limp.

Hart paused. "What more do you need to hear from me?"

"I need you to acknowledge my feelings . . . to demonstrate to me that you understand why I am hurt. That would be a good place to start, John."

Taking a deep breath, he sighed. "Okay, I'll try. I'm sorry that you observed me responding like a warrior—a man trained to kill his enemies before they can kill him. Empathy doesn't work well on the battlefield, Liz. If I thought about my targets as human beings, I could never pull the trigger. To survive, I've had to believe that our causes were just, and our combatants were evil."

"You are not on the battlefield now, John. You have the time to take everything in . . . to process what you've observed without the threat of death hovering over you. How you resolve the dilemma regarding the Ayatollah will speak loudly about what is in your heart, and what will likely remain there long after your final battle. I pray—for us—that you can leave your hatred behind and channel all of that life-force in an affirming direction. Think about what Mr. Rabinovich said yesterday in his speech."

Hart started to respond, but Liz put a finger to his lips. "We've talked enough. I'm no longer mad at you, just very concerned. I'd like to get some sleep, John." She turned away, braced a pillow against the window, and closed her eyes.

Mad would have been better, Hart thought. It was easier territory to navigate than Liz's obvious disappointment in him. What if she was right, he wondered. What if he was so indoctrinated in U.S. propaganda that he had lost the lens of objectivity? And what if his hatred of the enemy was ultimately what fueled him . . . what then? He closed his eyes, but even with the help of Macallan, sleep was not to follow.

As he lay in a nether land, somewhere between wakefulness and sleep, he heard something—not with his ears, but within his mind. It was a voice that he not heard in decades . . . a voice that had comforted him on the sleepless nights following his younger brother's death.

Images appeared, as though playing on a screen in his mind . . . vivid reminders of the missions he had led . . . the men he had killed. These phantoms seemed all too real—muttering unintelligibly as they struggled to cling to life. Then he saw families of the fallen—women and small children crying out in desperation at the news of their loved one's death. He felt the depth of their overwhelming anguish. It washed over him like a break-tide and pulled him under. Their suffering was so much more grievous than anything he had ever experienced during all of his military missions. He tried to break free of the ghosts, but something kept him tethered to the pain.

The images slowly faded, replaced by pure darkness. "This must be hell," Hart thought. "Well, I knew I'd get here someday."

Then a light appeared. It was like a candle burning in a distant window.

"Move towards the light, John," the voice seemed to say.

As he focused on the light, it began to grow in intensity . . . pulsing as if alive. As he inched closer, the light suddenly enshrouded him. But it was much more than *light*. It was the antithesis of death and anguish. It felt alive, as though it was imbued with a presence . . . a pure love unlike anything he could have imagined.

Every burden seemed to melt away in the light. Tears began streaming down his face, yet he smiled. It came without volition—a sign of the ineffable power of God.

He slowly opened his eyes, beaming. He could not stop smiling.

Liz was staring at him.

"Are you okay, Cowboy?" Liz asked with concern on her face.

Had it all been a dream? he wondered.

No, it had been stunningly real. More real than anything else he'd ever experienced.

Hart looked at her with love. "I'm sorry. I'm not sure what got into me, but I didn't have a right to speak to you that way. Please accept my apology."

Liz did not respond directly to the apology. "What are the tears about, John? I don't remember the last time I saw you cry."

"Just a powerful realization that life is a precious gift."

Liz raised her eyebrows in surprise. "What are you saying, John?"

Hart held off describing what could only be called an epiphany, choosing instead to focus on the transformation in his thinking. "I've spent two decades blindly following orders, killing men, then rationalizing away any guilt based on the belief that my actions were justified. Call it my judgment day, Darling . . . or maybe a second chance to embrace life in a very different way."

"I can't believe I'm hearing this from you, Cowboy. Are you sure you're okay?"

"I'm more than okay. You delivered a hard slap against my face just when I needed it most. You cracked something open, Liz. I'm not angry. I'm grateful."

Liz slowly nodded her head, while she tried to take in what she was hearing.

"I'm done, Liz."

"What do you mean, you're 'done'?"

"I'm done killing. I'm not a savior. I'll leave that task to someone whose motives are pure—Christ."

"Now I know there's something really wrong with you. John Hart is going to die with his boots on. I realized that when I met you and when I married you. So don't pretend with me just because we had a minor skirmish after an exhausting ordeal."

"Fine," Hart surrendered.

He looked different—this man she loved—as though he glowed from the inside, Liz thought. Something immensely powerful had touched his soul, and John Hart would never be the same.

CHAPTER FIFTY

Washington

THE SMILE WAS STILL PLASTERED on his face when they disembarked in Washington.

"Cowboy," Liz whispered, "You might want to lose that grin. It doesn't quite go with your image. You look like a holy roller who's just been touched by the Spirit."

But it was immutably mapped across his face—recognition of something divine, a grace long overdue. "It's okay, Darling," he assured her. "I'm not too worried about my macho image."

A Marine sergeant approached the couple and saluted. "Commander, I've been ordered to bring you and Dr. Wilkins to the White House. The president advised that I was to stop at your condo en route if requested, Sir."

Hart returned the salute. "At ease, Sergeant. Would you please inform the White House that Dr. Wilkins and I need a day to recover? We ask that you drop us at the condo, and we will make arrangements to meet with President Conner at his earliest convenience tomorrow."

Sensing hesitancy on the Marine's part, Hart added, "It's okay, Sergeant, the president will understand."

Forty-five minutes later, they were finally back in their Washington home. It seemed oddly foreign after so long away and yet still comforting. So much had transpired. So much had changed. Hart collapsed onto the couch, then extended his arms fully towards Liz. Carefully she climbed atop his massive frame, careful not to put pressure on his wounds.

"I wanted time to think, Liz, before I speak to the president."

"You are serious, aren't you . . . I mean about leaving this life behind."

"Dead serious. I've never experienced an epiphany before . . . I thought it was all touchy feely bullshit . . . you know, that Amazing Grace stuff. Well, if ever there was a wretch to be saved, it was me."

Liz laughed. "I'm glad to see that the conversion was not complete . . . and you remain mortal. And I'm glad you can sort through your thoughts before laying your cards on the table with President Conner. On a more mundane note, though, what would you like for dinner, Cowboy?"

"I'd love a steak, bloody. Some taters and a salad, but I don't want you to have to cook. Let's go down to Capitol Grille for an early meal."

"Now you sound like the man I married." Liz draped her arms around him. "I'd love to fix dinner . . . it will feel good to be the one taking care of you for a change."

Liz uncorked a bottle of Chateau Brane Cantenac that they had been saving for a special occasion. Before leaving the kitchen, she set the oven to 400 degrees.

"I'm going to run down to the store and pick up a few things . . . I'll be right back. And don't get into that wine without me!"

"Yes, Ma'am," the commander responded with a half-salute.

Liz set the table with their fine china and sterling. She wanted to re-create a dinner that they had shared when they had been courting—a dinner that had forever cemented her love for him.

With the food well underway, it was time to take a break. She stealthily retreated into the bedroom, emerging a moment later in a pale blue chemise that left little to the imagination. As she walked into the living room, a slumped commander suddenly sat upright on the couch.

"My, oh my, that's what I call 'dinner'!"

"Now remember what the doctors told you, Cowboy. You're not supposed to fool around until your wounds are completely healed."

"Don't tell me that, Darling, after coming out looking like a goddess!"

"I didn't say we couldn't play . . . just let me do the work this time . . . all you have to do is lie back and enjoy."

After months without sex, Liz's touch was overpowering. When she began to kiss his chest, slowing moving towards his navel, John moaned so loudly she was certain the neighbors had heard.

"Oh, Darling, don't stop!" he kept repeating like a mantra, until words could no longer contain his ecstasy. All of the tension flowed out of his body and his heart rate slowly returned to normal.

"So how was that, Cowboy? As good as you remember?"

Hart laughed. "It was far better!"

"Okay, enough fooling around . . . it's time for your grub. I'll have dinner on the table in about ten minutes." She winked at him before disappearing, returning a moment later in a more modest robe.

After lighting the candles and dimming the lights, she invited her lover to join her. Dinner was a reunification—a celebration of the love they felt for each other despite immense differences in their histories and personalities . . . each grateful to have found the other.

"So what are you going to say to the president tomorrow?" Liz asked.

"Exactly what I told you . . . that I am done. I'm leaving the government and don't plan to return."

"He's not going to accept your resignation . . . you know that. You're too important to him, John. He'll chalk up your feelings to transient battle fatigue—fully understandable under the circumstances—and tell you that it will pass. He may even suggest a few months of R&R."

"He'd be partly right . . . I am fatigued. I'm tired of all the killing. But my feelings are not going to change . . . not in a day, a week, a month, or a year.

"I've been the good soldier—never questioning my orders, or the assertion that my job was to 'help bring forth the light that dispels the darkness' . . . to claim the moral high ground for the United States and its allies, while decimating its enemies."

"And you no longer believe that?"

"That's right. We all feel our causes are justified and our actions are rooted in morality—whether we're a Navy SEAL or a Taliban fighter. We see the inhumanity of our enemy, not our commonality. Without such emotional distance, how could we ever pull the trigger and claim a life? So we operate under an illusion that justifies our involvement in conflicts that rage in distant lands."

Liz was quick to counter. "Tell me, John, what we have in common with a terrorist organization that plants a nuclear bomb in the heart of New York? Talk to me about the shared humanity of men who unleash a deadly virus capable of destroying the civilized world. So, while I understand your point in principle, I think you've taken things too far. There is good and evil, and I choose to believe that we are on the right side."

"And that is your choice to make, and I respect it. I ask that you respect that I'm done killing."

"I, and every other American, would call it *defending*."

"Thank you, Doctor, for the salve upon my soul. I'd like to move beyond semantics. This warrior is lowering his shield and dropping his sword. Perhaps there are ways that I can even help move our world towards peace."

"Peace is not in our DNA, John. There's no better evidence than the Middle East, where people have fought since the dawn of time. Conflict is part of the human condition. Our primordial ancestors set us on this path . . . aided by a serpent. God promised that there would be no return to the Garden, and I'm taking his word for it."

"Liz, I know it's going to sound hokey, but I felt God's presence on the flight back from Israel. I can't really put words to it, but it was the most powerful experience of my life. Our president is right, there is a light . . . but it does not separate men, but rather unites all of humanity. It is a light of pure love. That may sound over the top coming from a career soldier, but it's why I can't do it anymore. It's time to become a true agent of the light . . . not one of the federal government. That's what God was communicating to me."

"Are you going to share your experience with the president?"

"No. Sharing it would only convince him that I had lost my bearings. Our president is a great man faced with enormous challenges. Far better that I help him identify a suitable replacement than share my moment of conversion."

"Agreed."

CHAPTER FIFTY-ONE

The Oval Office

"I'm delighted to see you made it home in one piece, Commander." President Conner took Hart's hand and pulled him into a man-hug. "And welcome back to you, too, Liz!" he said, embracing her warmly.

"Please, have a seat." He gestured to one of the two familiar white couches in the Oval Office. "I just hung up from Avi Rabinovich, who couldn't rave enough about you, John. You know he gives you much of the credit for the survival of the Jewish state."

"The prime minister has a tendency towards hyperbole," Hart said with genuine humility.

"Your husband fails to see that he's a hero, Liz. I have to say that, in a town driven by ego and narcissism, John is a breath of fresh air!

"So tell me, Commander, how are you . . . I mean really. I don't know a single man who could have survived a wound like that."

"I'm fine, Sir. A little short of breath, but the doctors tell me that will improve with time."

"Liz, is he telling me the truth?" Conner asked, only half in jest.

"Mr. President, my cowboy may have gotten thrown from his horse, but he climbed right back on."

"It sounds like you are already thinking about your next assignment, Commander."

Hart shot Liz a glance. She winced, realizing that she had implied that the commander was readying himself for duty.

"Well, Sir, that's something I need to discuss with you when the time is right."

"Now is as good a time as any, Commander . . . but I suddenly have a sense of foreboding."

Hart didn't respond with words, but rather reached into the lapel pocket of his formal Naval uniform and extracted an envelope.

"A request for time-off? Approved . . . take as much you need." Conner said without looking at the contents.

"No, Sir, it's my letter of resignation."

"Let me see that," Conner instructed the commander. Taking it from Hart, the president tore the envelope neatly in two without ever removing the letter. He handed the pieces to the commander.

"Denied!" Conner said without any hint of humor.

"Sir, you know that it is within my right to resign my position with appropriate notice. I am giving you that notice today. I'm sorry, Sir, but it's not negotiable."

Conner, who had been leaning forward as if ready to pounce, sat back on the couch, his hands folded. He closed his eyes. "Give me a moment."

Liz looked at husband and mouthed, "I'm sorry."

"I know," he said under his breath, his look one of forgiveness.

After a moment, Conner opened his eyes, leaned as far forward as he could, and spoke directly to the commander.

"The world stood on the brink of war . . . a war that could have resulted in unimaginable death—at home, throughout the Middle East, and in Russia. Thanks to you, that war was averted . . . at least for now. That's an awesome amount of responsibility to fall on the shoulders of one man. I can think of only person whose shoulders are wide enough to bear such a burden—you, Commander.

"Serving your country is not something you were elected to do . . . it's who you are at your best. That's why you cannot abdicate your responsibilities . . . only take a reprieve from them."

"Sir, there are many men capable of shouldering heavy loads—whether in battle or in peace. I have a list of names for you . . . men who would serve you, as I have."

Hart started to reach into another pocket, but the president stopped him.

"I'm not interested in a replacement, Commander . . . not as long as you are breathing."

Hart waited a moment, then pulled the list of names from his pocket and placed it on the table.

"Dr. Wilkins, I need your help here. I think this last deployment was pretty hard on your husband. Can you help me communicate that, whatever is troubling him, it will pass . . . and that he's exactly where he belongs."

"I would love to, Mr. President, but I learned a long time ago not to try to bend John's will. Part of what you admire in him is his steely determination.

"John and I have talked, and I respect the decision he has come to, albeit with my own reservations."

"Okay, so it's going to be two on one," Conner said in an attempt to lighten the mood. "Can you at least help me understand, Commander, what's driving this decision?"

"Yes, Sir. I can no longer kill people with impunity. That makes me a danger to any mission. You need someone who doesn't flinch when confronted with a threat. That's who I was, not who I now am."

"Did that bullet damage you in ways that were beyond the doctors' ability to repair? Why this sudden crisis of conscience?"

"I don't know, Sir. Lying in that hospital bed, I had weeks to reflect on matters . . . and this is the result."

"Why don't you just take some time off, Commander? If, in ninety days, you still feel so convicted, I will accept your resignation."

"Sir, time will not heal this wound. Please accept my resignation and allow me to leave the government feeling good about my service to our nation."

"That is something I would never deprive you of, Commander. On three separate occasions, this country would have suffered irreparable damage were it not for you and Dr. Wilkins. Words like bravery, selflessness, hero are grossly insufficient to describe you and your contribution." Conner extended his hand. "I'll take your letter—both pieces, please.

"My God, you'll be missed," he said, slowly shaking his head as if denying the reality of Hart's resignation.

"Thank you, Mr. President. It's been an honor to serve under you, Sir." Hart stood and saluted his leader.

"So what's next?" Liz asked once they exited the White House.

"I don't know, Darling. I haven't planned much past breakfast." He stopped, put his hands on her shoulders, and looked deeply into her eyes. "How would you feel about chucking this life and buying a ranch in Montana . . . someplace close to where I grew up outside of Whitefish? It's beautiful there, Liz. God's country."

EPILOGUE

"Have you called this meeting simply to chastise me once again? If so, I'm not interested in what you have to say," General Mohammad Ali Jafari warned Hossein Taeb before he could speak. President Rouhani shifted uncomfortably in his chair.

"If I thought it would hasten the Ayatollah's return, I would be merciless in pursuing you, but it seems to bear little fruit."

Ali Jafari simply shrugged his shoulders. "Then what are we here for?"

"To plan the destruction of Israel . . . starting with Tel Aviv . . . the heart of their military strength."

"Obviously the heat has gotten to you, Hossein. What are we going to attack them with, men on camels?"

"While you have been relaxing in our new home, I've been working. That is the difference between a man of the cloth and a man of the sword."

"And what have you accomplished?" Ali Jafari asked with a smirk.

Taeb turned towards General Saleh and with a nod of his head, signaled him to begin.

Ali Jafari sat straight in his chair, surprised to see his close subordinate working in tandem with Taeb.

"A single silo somehow eluded the attention of the occupying forces. It remains fully functional—capable of firing a missile once manned by a crew of three."

Ali Jafari broke out in a forced laugh, "And what good does a single missile do against a united Sunni Coalition?"

"When it is an ICBM carrying a thermonuclear warhead, it could make a significant difference."

The blood drained from Ali Jafari's face, as his sarcasm turned into open anger. "Why have you not shared this with me before assembling such a meeting?" he demanded of Saleh.

Hossein Taeb interceded. "I gave him little choice. I told him I would consider it an act of treason if he shared our plans with anyone."

"No less an act of treason to plot a military attack without consulting your superior officer!" Ali Jafari snapped in retort.

"Gentlemen, gentlemen, let us not quarrel over rank—not when a great gift has been delivered to us," Rouhani urged. "What prevents us from launching this missile at will?"

"Only one thing—where to target it," Taeb replied.

"What are you suggesting?" Rouhani asked.

"We have one shot at changing the world," Taeb began. "Do we fire it at Tel Aviv, Jerusalem, or Washington? Since time is of the essence, I suggest we resolve this question quickly and move forward."

"Do you have a recommendation, General Saleh?"

"We know that both countries have robust missile defense systems . . . so either one may intercept the missile. My preference would be that we kill the Jews."

"And possibly the Ayatollah in the process?" Hossein asked incredulously.

"We have no idea where he is or if he is still alive. Our decision has to be predicated upon what is in the best interests of our people . . . all Shia." Rouhani said as a pronouncement. "The target is Washington. How quickly can you be prepared to launch?"

"Two days, Mr. President."

"Two days, then."

Three men, carrying falsified temporary ID cards issued by the occupying force, made their way to the outskirts of Chabahar. They knew that there would be multiple check points along the seven-hour drive from Zahedan, and so were unarmed . . . carrying only the codes required for access to the silo. Once they were inside, additional codes would be needed to arm and fuse the missile, then send it careening towards Washington.

The launch site was extraordinarily well camouflaged, having been carved into the hills that surrounded the city's port. The location, a stone's throw from the Gulf of Oman, allowed missile components to be transported from around the world straight to the installation's front door. There had been frequent arrivals from North Korea, and more recently, Ukraine. Such deliveries greatly accelerated the Iranian missile program and benefited all who fought a common enemy.

Outfitted in hiking shorts with backpacks and walking sticks, they approached the site as though they had stumbled upon it. Not a soul was visible. They located one of two concealed access doors, entered a code, and waited for the electronic lock to remove the heavy bolt. Within seconds, they were inside, moving towards the control room.

One man split off from the group and maneuvered towards the launch pad. As expected, an ICBM, topped with a thermonuclear warhead, was ready for launch. He did a quick visual inspection of the fuel hoses, then moved quickly to join his comrades in the launch control room.

As he entered, the control system was lit up like a Christmas tree. His compatriots had successfully entered the initial codes needed to begin the launch sequence. They entered the GPS coordinates.

The intended target: 1600 Pennsylvania Avenue.

A countdown clock on the wall began clicking off the seconds until ignition.

When it reached zero, there was a thundersome noise as the silo filled with flames, and the missile streaked toward the heavens.

Estimated time to impact: forty minutes.

"Sir, we've got a problem," the Secretary of Defense, Mark Oliver, said as he burst unannounced into the Oval Office.

"Our satellites just picked up an infra-red heat signature that looks like a missile launch from the southern coast of Iran. Radar confirmation should follow, as well as a plot of its apparent trajectory."

Within a minute, an entourage had assembled in the Oval Office. The Chairman of the Joint Chiefs reaffirmed Oliver's statement and added that it was an ICBM headed their way. The initial trajectory indicated that Washington was the target.

Fast, pounding footsteps could be heard reverberating in the hallways of the West Wing. A large detail of Secret Service appeared at the door. "We have to leave now, Sir. The threat is imminent."

"We are preparing our interceptors, Mr. President." The nation's highest ranking officer informed him. "Let's pray they are effective."

"If our interceptors fail, how long before impact, General?"

"Thirty-eight minutes, Mr. President."

Conner nodded, then gestured to the Secret Service. There was one last thing he must do before leaving for the bunker.

Conner picked up the phone and dialed Commander Hart. Before it could ring, he shouted an order. "Pick up Commander Hart and Dr. Wilkins—and get them to a bunker, NOW!"

8 SECONDS TO MIDNIGHT

8 Seconds to Midnight takes the reader on a non-stop thrill-ride that begins with the clandestine transfer of nuclear material from a secure Pakistani military installation thirty miles north of Islamabad to a group of radical Islamists bent on the destruction of the West. It culminates in the streets of New York—minutes before the impending detonation of a fifteen-kiloton nuclear bomb.

The city's survival hinges on one man, Commander John Hart, and his ability to ferret out the perpetrators, discern where the weapon is hidden, and disable it before midnight on December 31.

Hart must rely on equal measures of brawn, brain, and prayer to stop the cadre of jihadists whose plan has been in the making for sixteen years. Should he fail, the job of healing America's potentially mortal wound will fall squarely on the shoulders of Dr. Elizabeth Wilkins. It is a job she did not ask for and hopes will never materialize.

TERMINAL

In this chilling prequel to *8 Seconds to Midnight*, the most devastating terrorist attack ever recorded on American soil begins and ends without spilling a single drop of blood. Four jihadists, armed with nothing more than a briefcase and a pen, walk nonchalantly through the country's busiest airports, killing time and killing people. A deadly mist, laden with a universally lethal virus, trails close behind them. Their goal: foment a global pandemic. Their vision: Armageddon, where only the Chosen Ones—those loyal to the United Islamic State—survive.

The job of stopping them falls squarely on the shoulders of one man, Commander John Hart. But will he be in time?

If you've enjoyed this book, please consider writing a review on Amazon.com, B&N.com, Goodreads.com or other platforms.

If you wish to contact John Leifer, you may write to him directly at:

johnleifer@aol.com

To find information on John's other books, visit: *www.johnleifer.com.*